Blood on the Timber Trail

By

JoAnn Conner

Blood on the Timber Trail
Copyright @ 2022 JoAnn Conner

ISBN 9798364388889

Acknowledgements

Special thanks to my friend, Michael Duggan, AKA "Guns," as he was known in his former profession in law enforcement. He has taught me much about guns, an integral part of any Western. He has graciously consented to be our cover on this latest book. The image of him holding a Yellow Boy is too perfect for this story! Credit for the photo goes to his wife, Anne Duggan, a photographer who has the rare ability to capture the spirit of the photo.

I have had the privilege of working on historical reenactment with Michael Duggan, and my friends from Historical Legends of the Old West, Mike Bell, Dennis Dew (RIP), Horse Thief Canyon Desperado, Ross Mortensen, Demetria Lionakis, and Outlaw Dave Borges. They will always be special to me, and are true representatives of the Western Spirit.

The Old West has always been a source of fascination and intrigue in both my personal and professional life. My grandfather, Earl Frank Martin was the first real cowboy in my life, but certainly not the last. He definitely had a profound and lasting positive influence on me and my siblings.

~ ~ ~

It is with extreme gratitude that I give thanks to Andy Michaud, the wizard of the keyboard, who has the amazing ability and patience to develop ideas into incredible covers, and provide formatting options I can only imagine.

This book is dedicated to Earl Frank Martin,
the first real cowboy I ever knew.

JoAnn Conner

Chapter 1

Lucas Randall expertly edged the cattle into the holding pens outside of Virginia City in Nevada. He smiled as his mustang mix, Pepper, nudged the four legged creatures and stopped them at every turn. He barely used the reins or his knees; she knew what to do and did her job very well. No cattle were going to get by her!

The tall, dark-haired owner of the Rocking R Ranch sat his horse and watched the cattle milling about in the large pen. His piercing blue eyes were striking in his tanned face, and his arms bulged with muscle under the dark blue shirt he wore. Nearly twenty-five, he was the youngest rancher in the region.

This was the first herd they were bringing to market, and even though it was small, the cattle were good stock. He reflected on his brother, Thomas, who was still unaccounted for after the War Between the States. He should have arrived at the ranch by now, but Luke had no idea where to begin to look. Luke had been the first one back to the homestead in Ohio after the war, and what he found was enough to make the decision to come west, meet Thomas, and build a ranch together.

His mind drifted back to that day he came around the bend in the road and saw the two graves sitting on the knoll above the farm that had belonged to his family. He had walked up the hill slowly, half holding his breath, dreading what he would see. The crosses bore the names of his mother and father. That left his sister, Anna, there alone. Remorse enveloped him and his eyes misted over as he ran his hands over his weary face. His parents were gone, his brother was still missing, and now he had to go tell his sister the bad news about Thomas. If only he had been able to get home sooner.

"Are you one of the brothers?" The voice was gentle, but it still served to startle him out of his fog.

"I am one of their sons, yes," replied Luke, gesturing to the graves as he turned to face the man who met his eyes at his height. "Who might you be?" He did not recognize the weathered face of the brown eyed, brown haired man that faced him.

"I'm Josh McKenzie," he replied, extending a hand. "I'm sure sorry for all of your loss, mister." He said it with real compassion; a fact not lost on Luke.

"I'm Luke Randall," he said, gripping the man's hand. It was not until that point that he realized two of the man's fingers were missing. "Where is my sister?" He had to know.

"She told us she had two brothers, but she hadn't heard from either one of you in over a year. She thought you were both dead." The farmer looked at him apologetically. "She was pretty worn out herself. Awful thin, and the sadness in her eyes just about made my wife cry."

"Do you know what happened to our parents?" Luke thought it would be easier if he did not have to ask his sister.

"Anna said they died of the fever during the war. She lost them both within a week of each other," he said softly. "It almost broke her to go through that alone."

"We both tried to get back," said Luke sadly, stung by the picture of her facing all this misery alone. "But I lost track of our brother Thomas. I sent word back with the Rogers boy from the next farm over. He was sent back too badly wounded to fight months before the end of the war, and I thought he would tell Anna."

"Are you talking about Robert Rogers?" asked Josh. Behind him at the house, a slender, blond haired woman came out on the porch and shaded her eyes as she watched them.

"Yes! How is he?" A shadow crossed over McKenzie's face and Luke knew the answer before the other man spoke.

"They found him dead on the road, about five miles away from home. The wounds got infected again and he was too far gone to make it all the way home. That was nearly a year ago. Your sister never got that message, Luke." His brows knit in sadness as he chewed on his lip, studying Luke's face.

"Where is Anna, then?" He spoke with a tinge of despair in his voice. His pulse quickened as he waited for the answer.

6

"She sold us the farm and went back East to go to nursing school," he answered.

"What? When did she leave? Why didn't she wait?" Questions mixed with anguish as he felt the pain of missing her. Somehow, he was angry at this stranger.

"She was like a walking shadow when we got here. She was sitting on that very porch the day we drove through on our wagon." He gestured to the place where his wife still stood. "We were afraid she was dead, she sat so still. We couldn't leave her like that, so we stayed to get her back to health. We planned to keep going west ourselves, find a place to farm, and start over again."

"But you're here on our farm now, and she is gone!" he said bitterly.

"That is true," said Josh slowly, "but we didn't steal this land from anyone and we did not push her to sell to us. We talked a lot about farming while she was healing, because we all had that in common. After a couple of weeks, we began to make plans to move on. That's when she asked us if we would consider buying this farm."

"She asked you that?" exclaimed Luke in surprise.

"Yes, she did. Understand, she was a young woman all alone here, with no one to help her keep this place up, no one to talk to, and not enough time or energy to raise enough food to even feed herself properly. After nursing both of your parents, she thought that was something she would rather do. If we bought the farm, she could afford to go to a nursing school."

"I guess I owe you an apology," sighed Luke. "Do you know where she went? What city? I'd sure like to get in touch with her." He rubbed his hands over his face, thinking how hopeless she must have felt.

"Yes, she left us the address in case you came back. And you will probably want to thank her too. That is one smart sister you have!"

"What are you talking about?" asked Luke, puzzled.

"Why, mister, she only took half of the money. We paid a fair price for the land and the house, and she had us put the other half in a draft being held at the bank in town for you and your brother if you ever came back." He grinned. "And if you didn't, she would get the remainder in two years. Smart!" He chuckled, shaking his head.

"Come on, my wife is trying to get me to come in for dinner and you look like you could use a good meal. We can talk out the rest of the details over some food."

Luke had ridden out the next morning a man much more at peace. He picked up the bank draft in town, wired his sister, and then headed west. That was two years ago, and a lot had changed since then. They still had not heard from Thomas, but he and his sister now wrote to each other. Luke had used the half for the brothers to buy an old, run down ranch near Bridgeport, California, and managed to secure a few head of cattle. He had worked hard, picking up a few head here and there, and had grown his herd in the two years since he bought his ranch. Now they had just finished their first drive to market.

"Hiyah!" yelled Cyrus James from the opposite side of the surging mass, pulling Luke back to the present. At thirty-four, the stocky cowboy was the old man on the drive. He swung his long reins in a circle to ward off a cow that was bent on escape. She turned, and protesting loudly, sulked her way back into the line of cattle feeding through the gate. He grinned at Luke as he raised his brown hat off his darker brown hair and swiped a forearm across his forehead to halt the sweat dripping into his cool gray eyes.

Paul Sherwood, his lead range rider, worked them from behind, driving them through the open gate and crowded them within the small fenced area. Cy's Australian Cattle Dog, Jasper, nipped at the heels of a few of the cattle, while artfully dodging the hooves of the horses. Getting the dog along with Cy was a welcome perk.

"Looks like we got our first herd through, boss!" grinned Paul, his hazel eyes twinkling. He loved the work of a cowboy. The young rider had been with Luke since the first year the Rocking R Ranch had been established. Luke had saved his life when Paul rode in, then toppled from his horse in a heap. Paul had been seriously mauled by a mountain lion and barely managed to wrestle his gun from his holster to kill the beast before it made him his evening meal. Luke had treated his wounds and Paul recovered with a few scars to his credit.

The tall, blond drover had regained his strength and proven himself an excellent hand. He was a natural with the cattle and horses and handy with the repairs around the ranch. While Luke came from a farming background, Paul's father had been a carpenter. It was a perfect combination to get the ranch started with both cattle and crops.

When Luke met Ruth, a pretty, willowy blond that had just come to help at the local restaurant, Paul saw the writing on the wall and suggested he and Luke start a new house for the future Mrs. Randall. Her bright smile, laughing green eyes, and indomitable energy quickly captured the heart of the young rancher, and they became inseparable. Together, Paul and his boss built a big house for Luke and Ruth, who were married after a few short months of courtship. It turned out to be a smart move, as Luke and Ruth now had a little tow headed boy to add to their family.

The two men remodeled the original house that was on the property when Luke bought the ranch. By the time they were done, they had turned the older house into a roomy bunkhouse for Paul, Cyrus and another hand, Rusty. Because they left the kitchen area intact, the ranch hands could make coffee and even cook when the weather was too cold to be on the range all day. The range riders at the Rocking R Ranch had never been treated so well in their cowboy lives. Riders generally rode for the brand in the west, but these riders did so gladly.

Luke's eyes traveled over the herd until they fixed on the man who had to be the buyer standing on a platform, surveying the cattle. He took one more look at his two drovers and saw Paul jump out of his saddle to release and pull the gate across the corral opening. Cy watched, rifle ready in case he needed to use a different type of coercion. If any of the cantankerous creatures decided to charge the gate while Paul was off his mount and moving in front of the log gate, Cy was ready. It was a valid concern; from the view of any cowpoke, Paul was doing a dangerous part of the job, and could be trampled to death if the cows charged the man on foot.

Luke smiled, satisfied at the competence of his riders, and gently urged Pepper to the edge of the platform. He dismounted, looped the reins lightly around the post by the bottom of the platform, and took the steps two at a time.

"Mr. Roberts?" asked Luke, even though he was sure of the man before him.

"Luke Randall?" smiled the weathered man who stood equal in height to Luke's six foot two inch frame. The cattle buyer's shrewd, dark blue eyes missed nothing as he surveyed the herd, calculating weights and age of the cattle. His dark hair brushed his collar, but his face was clean shaven.

"Yes sir," nodded the young rancher, extending his hand.

"Call me John," said the buyer, shaking hands firmly. "How many head did you bring in?" He gestured towards the milling stock.

"We brought through fifty cows in good health." He looked at Roberts. "We almost lost one, but my men are determined!"

"I've been watching them," laughed John. "I am amazed that three of you could drive fifty cows by yourselves, and I admit I had my doubts when you told me how you were going to bring the cattle here. But, watching you and your men, it is clear you are experienced and work as a well coordinated team. Having savvy horses and the dog is a bonus!"

The two men stood on the platform and negotiated a fair price for the cattle. It was not a lengthy discussion; cattle were hard to come by in 1869 in Virginia City, and there were a lot of men to feed. After a long day working in the mines, beans and bread did not fill the bellies of the miners for long. They wanted beef, and lots of it. They settled on a price of fifty dollars a head, taking into account that some of the younger steers were only two years old, but at least a third were three years old and had come to Luke as yearlings.

"Any chance you can bring me any more cattle?" asked John as they walked to the bank to get the money for Luke.

"No sir, not until next spring," Luke said with some regret. He wished they had been able to grow the herd faster, but weather had been harsh the past two winters. "We have crops coming in that need to be harvested for the winter, but the cattle we have left are mostly too young to be sold or to travel the distance to market."

"What kind of crops?" asked Roberts, catching Luke off guard.

"We have apples, cherries, beans, carrots, potatoes, and a few smaller crops, but to be honest, there isn't much left over after we set up for the ranch family," explained Luke.

"What about lumber?" asked Roberts suddenly. He stopped and looked seriously at Luke. "You said you came from the far side of Carson City, right? Do you own any land with trees?"

10

"There's lumber; we built a barn, a new house, made a bunkhouse out of the original house, corrals, and some other smaller out buildings," answered Luke, rubbing his chin. "Why do you ask?"

"I need lumber, and I am willing to pay handsomely to get it. You have already proven you are a man of your word and willing to work hard."

"I thought they were logging up at Lake Bigler and shooting the logs down the flume to the railroad for the mining effort?" The young rancher was not sure what Roberts needed.

"They are," clarified Roberts, "but all that lumber is being used in the mines and for the railroad. I need lumber for houses and businesses. Winter is coming and tents are miserable places for a family in the snow."

"How much do you need?" asked Luke. He was doing some fast thinking about the stands of timber on the far side of his ranch. There was plenty there for several weeks of work and the extra money would sure be handy through the winter. If he could get a few more men from town, he could log the timber and bring in the crops too. It would surely make for a more comfortable winter, if it chose to be a hard one.

John Roberts stared up at the mountains for several minutes, then looked slowly around the growing town. Finally, he looked sharply at Luke. "Can you get wagons through the same route you drove the cattle? Is the route the freighters use from Bodie open?" he asked, referring to the mining town at the foot of the Sierra Nevada range.

"The Rocking R is about sixteen miles south of Bridgeport. What are you getting at?"

"Would it be realistic to bring three wagon loads of logs to me here in Virginia City within two months time?"

"Felled trees or logs?" asked Luke carefully. "We do not have a sawmill close, and that would take time and men I don't have."

"Fair question," nodded the buyer. "Logs cut in lengths that can be turned into board feet; four foot minimum length. I would prefer them to be mostly seven feet in length, though." He measured the young rancher with keen eyes.

Luke stood, hands on his hips, chewing on his lip, and staring off into the distance as if he could see his forest of trees from where he stood. Mentally, he was calculating the work that would have to be done. He shifted his gaze and stared at a man slouching on a bench on the walk in front of the general store. He looked, but did not register any particular features of the man, who suddenly rose and walked into the store. He brought his eyes up to meet John's gaze.

"Yes," he said, extending his hand, "we will take the contract. Let's go into the bank," he said, gesturing to the site where the Bank of California resided. "We will settle the bill for the cattle first, and then put the details of the lumber deal in writing so we both know what to expect." While a handshake in the old west was as good as a contract in most cases, Luke had no former dealings with John Roberts. He had learned the hard way that a contract in writing was the best way to conduct business.

The clean shaven bulk of a man who had moved inside to avoid Luke's study stood peering out the window of the general store, standing to the side so he would not be seen. He smiled as he saw the two men shake hands. He turned and started towards the counter. He needed some supplies. He had work to do.

Chapter 2

Cyrus James leaned against the far corner of the building opposite the general store. He kept his hat pulled down low to shadow his face, and with the sun to the west of the building, part of his body was shaded as well. Jasper sat on his hind legs, his eyes fastened on the same thing his master was studying. A low growl emanated from Jasper, coming from deep in his throat. Cy did not move, as he knew movement could draw attention to his presence.

"Easy boy," he whispered and his four legged friend sank down to lay on the ground next to Cyrus. He did not break his concentration, just slowly shifted position. The dog trusted the man beside him, and remained silent.

"Now what is Hal Colter doing in Virgina City?" mused Cy quietly to himself. "And why is he so all fired interested in my boss and Mr. Roberts, huh boy?" Jasper whined softly in answer.

Cyrus had caught sight of Hal down at the pen, seeming to meander casually about, but in reality, edging closer to the two men standing on the platform above him. When the businessmen moved down the street, Cy watched as Hal slunk after them. Clearly, he was following the pair. Keeping his eyes on the man, Cy walked his horse over to where Paul had just slid off his mount.

"Hey Paul," said Cy, dismounting and holding out his reins to Paul, "take my horse for a bit, will ya? There is something I got to do."

"Need any help?" asked the taller cowboy, following the gaze of his friend.

"Not yet," answered Cy, slapping Paul on the arm gently. "You'll be the first I call when I do," he grinned, then set off walking quickly behind the buildings of the town.

He saw Luke and John stop just past the corner of the general store, standing in the street, a few feet from the walk. He also saw Hal pause and try to appear disinterested, pretending to look at something in the store window. Cy walked back and came out at the corner of the building before the general store, on the other side of the street.

He noticed Luke stare at Hal, but he was pretty sure Luke did not know Hal was watching him. He smiled as Hal got uncomfortable and got up and went into the general store. He thought he was clever, hiding to the side of the window like that, but Cy saw his shadow pass the window and the quick glint of the sunlight off the outlaw's belt buckle as he positioned himself.

In his peripheral vision, he saw his boss and the buyer shake hands again, then continue on to the bank. Cy remained in position, waiting. His patience was rewarded. A young boy ran out of the store and to the livery stable, then came back within a few minutes. Cy waited, and once again, his gut feeling was ratified. A few minutes after the boy returned, a rider came from the livery stable, leading a horse behind him. He jumped off his horse and entered the general store.

A short time later, Hal and the rider came out of the store, carrying sacks of goods, which they strapped onto the backs of their horses. Cyrus strained to get a good look at the rider that had joined Hal, but his hat was pulled low over his eyes and he kept his head down, although Cy had the feeling he was surveying the street from under the brim of that hat. They rode down two store fronts and cut through the alley between them towards the back of the stores. *Now why would they do that?*

Cyrus James crossed the street quickly, cutting through one store before the one where they had turned down the alley. He took off his hat and carefully peeked around the corner of the building. They were headed out of town, towards the north. Towards the Rocking R. Cy didn't like it; and he liked it even less when the second rider turned for a few seconds, head up, showing his profile. Cy recognized the hawkish features and wispy gray hair of Colter's companion and swore softly as he stepped back, returned his hat to his head, and walked rapidly back to the corral. He had to find Paul, and the two of them needed to talk to Luke.

Chapter 3

It was well past noon when the details were completed and the contract signed. Luke was feeling elated as he hurried back to the corral to meet his two ranch hands. He had a bank draft to deposit in his bank in Carson City, enough gold to pay his men, and some to take back to the ranch. He was planning to share the details of the new deal over a well earned meal in the Delta Saloon. He was not expecting to find them sitting glumly on the edge of the platform.

"Hey men, let's go get something to eat!" Luke studied them, puzzled as they exchanged a worried glance. Jumping down, both men shifted from one foot to the other, until, hands on his hips, Cy spoke.

"Boss, we might have a problem," began Cyrus.

"Alright," said Luke slowly, "but all of us could use a good meal. We haven't eaten since last night and we can't do anything on an empty stomach. Let's talk about it over a steak and some beans."

The two men walked with him to the Delta Saloon. It was past lunch time, and most of the men in the town were working, mostly at the mines. They quickly found seats at an empty table, against a wall and away from the bar or other ears that might be listening. Luke sensed their conversation should be kept low and private; neither Cyrus nor Paul were easily rattled but clearly, something was bothering his men.

The bartender came around the long counter and walked over to the table. He was used to customers who wanted to eat undisturbed, and was always on the lookout for trouble makers. He packed a small revolver in his waistband, underneath his vest, and

16

while he did not want to start a ruckus, he was prepared to stop rowdy behavior.

"Howdy gents," smiled the man. He was average height and build, but there was a cagey presence about him that clearly said he was nobody's fool. "Can I get you something to eat or drink?"

"What do you have to eat today?" asked Luke.

"Steak, beans, fresh bread and butter, and apple pie, if you are interested." His eyes measured Luke and correctly pegged him as the boss. He looked like he could pay and he did not look like he wanted trouble. "I also have beer or whiskey," he smiled.

"We'll take three plates of food, and," he looked at Paul and Cy, "beer, cold if you got it, all around." His two riders nodded and smiled. They didn't often drink, but it had been a hard drive and the work ahead of them could be tough as well. They waited until the bartender walked away.

"I have a feeling you should talk first," said Luke, turning his eyes to Cyrus. The cow puncher had been with him a year now, and Luke had seen nothing but good instincts, hard work, and honesty in the man. Something big was bothering him, and Luke waited patiently.

"Sure," replied Cy, clearly uncomfortable. "It's just a hunch, boss." He stopped to search Luke's face, scrunching down in his chair like he wished he could be anywhere but here right now.

"Tell him, Cy," said Paul softly. "It sounds like it is at least a solid hunch to me." Paul's face was encouraging, so Cyrus nodded and sat up straight in his chair.

"Boss, have you ever heard of Hal Colter?" Cyrus asked with hesitation.

"No," replied Luke, thinking quickly, "I don't believe I have. Is it important?"

"Could be," Cy nodded. "I was in a posse that chased him back in Kansas after the war. He was a mean son of a gun; killed a family and burned their house." Cy shifted in his chair and cleared his throat."He looted a home with a family. Then he shot the husband and set the house on fire with their kids asleep inside." His voice caught and Luke knew there was more.

"Go on," he said gently. He shot a look at Paul, and to his surprise, the young man had misted eyes.

"This Colter...he...," Cy swallowed hard and rubbed his hands over his face. "Colter had his men hold the woman and made her watch while he did all that. Then...he and his men..." he stopped as the bartender approached. The man set the three mugs of cold beer down in front of them and Cy took a long pull on his, waiting until the bartender walked away before he finished speaking. "When they were all done with her, Colter handed her a gun with one bullet in it. He laughed, and she put the gun to her head and killed herself."

No one spoke. Cy hung his head and rubbed his eyes. Paul looked miserably at his beer. Luke stared at the wall behind the bar, trying to make sense of all this.

"Did you know the family?" asked Randall.

"Yes," he answered simply. "The husband, Alex, was my best friend." He looked bleakly at Luke. "One of the neighbor women was on her way to bring them a quilt she had made for them. She heard shots and pulled up her buggy before the crest of the hill. She got out and stood behind a tree and watched. She was helpless. Her husband came looking for her and found her standing there. Had to have been there for hours, but she couldn't move. Couldn't speak for a couple of days."

"She identified this Colter?"

"Yes," nodded Cy. "The sheriff showed her some posters and she identified Colter and another outlaw. We went after them, but the trail was too cold."

"Why are you telling me this now?" asked Luke, a sense of foreboding wrapping its icy fingers around his neck.

"Because," began Cy miserably, "Hal Colter was in town today." He looked at the rancher with pure anguish on his face. "He was following you. He was listening to you and Mr. Roberts."

"Where..." realization dawned on Luke's face. "He was the man on the porch at the general store!"

"Yes sir. But there is more," sighed James. "He was with someone. A man came up with an extra horse for Hal after you walked into the bank."

"So you followed Colter and were watching him watch me?" Luke was surprised.

"Yes sir, I saw him at the corral and recognized him. When you walked away, he tried to act casual, but it was clear he was following you." He swallowed, looked at Paul, then continued. "It

18

was Sly Booker that met him. He was part of the gang that killed my friends. But he is also wanted in three states for bank robbery and murder."

"You took a chance, following them like that, with no one to have your back," said Luke thoughtfully, "I really appreciate that." Cyrus James had surprised him, in a good way, more than once since he came to work on the ranch. Luke was glad the man was on his side.

"I ride for the brand, Mr. Randall," Cy said, straightening in his chair, "and your safety is part of my responsibility." His jaw set in a firm line as his gray eyes smoldered with memories.

"You are our family," nodded Paul with resolution, looking at Luke. "The Rocking R has become our home too." Both riders exchanged a long glance, then nodded at each other, turning their gazes back to Luke. "We would die for you," Paul finished quietly.

Luke hoped it would not come to that.

Chapter 4

The bartender set heaping plates of steaming food on the table in front of each of them. Luke was still slumped, unmoving in his chair, staring at Cy, trying to make sense of the news he just heard. What did it all mean? He could not shake a nagging feeling that they needed to get back to the ranch, and fast!

While all of them had lost most of their desire to eat, they knew they needed to sustain themselves for the long ride and work ahead. They ate without speaking for several minutes; feeding the hunger and nourishing their bodies for the hard ride home, but the pleasure of the meal and camaraderie was lost.

"Okay, we have to sort some things out while we finish our food," said Luke, finally slowing down his eating. "In addition to the sale of the cattle, Mr. Roberts and I entered into a contract to provide him with some felled trees in the next two months."

"Trees?" asked Paul. "You mean to fell trees up on the north spread, like we did to build the house?"

"Exactly. The Timber Trail is already built, so that will help us."

"I thought timber was coming down from the big lake up in the mountains," he said.

"It is, but it is being used by the railroad and mines. Mr. Roberts wants to build a couple of houses or buildings that could be used for a business and a home before winter."

"Is that what you two were talking about when Colter was pretending not to listen?" asked Cy, suddenly pausing with his fork halfway to his mouth.

"Yes," said Luke slowly. "What are your thoughts about us and Colter, Cy? What do you think he is after?" It would be impossible to talk while they rode, and he had no plans to dally about a campfire any more than absolutely necessary on the way home.

Cy was not done eating, but he set his fork down and rubbed his chin thoughtfully, as if it was too important to think this problem through while he did anything else. Paul and Luke watched him, but kept eating, out of efficiency.

"Mr. Randall," he said finally, meeting Luke's eyes with a steeliness the young rancher had never seen in him. "I'm just gonna lay it all out here and you can tell us what you want to do."

"Fair enough man, go on."

"Colter and Booker are two of the worst snakes I have ever known. I don't think we should rule anything out. So, I think we should expect them to try to ambush us first for whatever money they think we are carrying."

"Between us, it's only a few hundred," said Luke.

"But they can't be sure of that. They know some money exchanged hands, and they may be broke enough to want whatever we have."

"All right; I can see that." Luke was quiet for several heartbeats, then his head came up and he narrowed his eyes as he looked at Cy. "You said first. What else are you thinking?"

"Did you tell Roberts where the ranch sits?"

"Yes, I did," replied Luke, fear running cold fingers down his spine. *Ruth and little Thomas! The only one there with them was Rusty!*

"Colter could be headed there. He does not know who or what is there, but…he knows the three of us live there, and that might be enough for him to pay a visit and see what he can take."

"Get you anything else?" The bartender was at his elbow.

"Coffee, black and strong," answered Luke. "and three big slabs of that apple pie. This might be the last meal we get before we get back to the ranch," he told the two, "so eat your fill now while we plan this out."

"You thinking a straight run back to the ranch, since we don't have cows?" asked Paul.

21

"More or less. It took us eight days to get the cattle here, but we are going to move a lot faster going home," answered Luke.

"Three or four days maybe?" interjected Paul. "Pepper could probably do it in two, but I am not sure my horse could, or Cy's."

"I'd like to shave a day off of the four days, or at least a half day," proposed Luke. "We will need to sleep a little too, but this is going to be a tough ride. We are going to have to watch for those two."

"What do you want us to do, boss?" Cy was finishing his cup of coffee and looked at Luke as the bartender offered a refill. Luke nodded and the man refilled their cups.

"Paul, you and Cy go find us three more good horses, if you can. That way we can trade them out, which will be easier on them." He reached in his pocket and handed his top man five twenty dollar gold pieces. He had already paid them each an extra forty dollars on top of their forty a month wages and found, and he was glad he had kept a little extra out.

"Anything else?" Cy questioned.

"No," said Luke, shaking his head, "I'm going to pick us up some food, more ammunition, and some extra canteens. Meet me back here as soon as you can."

They all stood at the same time and shared a look. They knew they needed to be fast, but careful. They also knew the lives of Ruth and the toddler could depend on how quickly they returned to the ranch.

Chapter 5

Rusty McMath sat his horse in the copse of pines on the top of the hill. He was puzzled as his keen eyes focused on a darker stripe in the sky. The deformed portion of the sky appeared to be at least thirty miles away, on the edge of the Rocking R ranch land. He reached into his saddlebags and pulled out his binoculars, a gift from the general under whom he served in the War Between the States. His eyes were sharper than most men half his age, which is part of what made him such a valuable asset as a crack rifle shot in the military.

The wiry forty-five year old ranch hand lifted the glasses to his eyes and studied the area that caught his interest. Smoke. It was definitely a smoke trail. He lowered the binoculars and pondered the possibilities.

Not Indians; at least not hostile. They were smarter than that; they would not have a fire in broad daylight if they were trying to go unnoticed. Could it be settlers? He rapidly dismissed that idea; it was too far from the trail to town – any town in the area. He didn't like it. He turned his horse down the mountain and rode at a canter back to the ranch.

"Hey Rusty," Ruth called as he rode into the ranch yard an hour later. "Do you want to join Thomas and me for dinner? It's just about ready," she smiled. "Wash up and come on up to the main house." In truth, he had shared every dinner since Luke had gone on the drive with the lady of the ranch and her son, but he always waited for an invitation.

"Thanks, Mrs. Randall," he smiled. He dismounted slowly and stood for a moment before walking with a limp towards the barn to put up his horse. The bullet he had taken in his upper leg affected his ability to move quickly, but his mind and his aim were still as sharp as ever.

Ruth set the table for three and put fresh bread and butter in the middle. She glanced out the window and saw Rusty approaching, with Thomas chattering away like a jaybird from the open door, talking excitedly in jibberish to the old man while he waited for him to come into the house. She liked the older cowboy, and he led the toddler around the ranch with delight. He taught the boy how to feed the chickens with him, holding him in his arms so they could not peck him, but letting him throw the feed to them. She loved hearing them laugh together.

Rusty came in and scooped up the little boy as he pushed the door shut. He deposited the child on a block of wood on a chair, pausing to stare out the window for a few minutes before he turned to the table. He pulled his chair closer to the young boy, so he was between his mother and Rusty, should he start to fall. He sat facing the door, which he did not usually do when Luke was at home.

"Is something wrong?" asked Ruth, surprised that he had closed the door. They usually left it and the windows open on nice days to air out the house. She served him a healthy portion of the stew she had prepared, and waited. He would speak when he had formed his thoughts.

"Stay close to the house today," he said, smiling at Thomas as he buttered a piece of bread and handed it to the boy. "And keep that old Henry loaded and within reach." He looked at her with concern showing through his eyes.

"What is it, Rusty?" She served herself and cut some of the vegetables and meat into small pieces. She placed the little morsels on a small plate in front of her son and smiled as the child picked up a piece of soft carrot, placed it in his mouth, and then made a sound of delight as he chewed. She knew Rusty and all the hands respected her, and did not see her as weak at all.

"I don't rightly know yet, lass," he said, lapsing into the Scottish dialect he sometimes used when things were heavy on his mind. "It's a feelin' more than anything."

"You have good instincts. What worries you?" She took a bite of the stew and waited as he chewed a bite himself.

"Smoke," he shrugged. "It is up by the north section. I couldn't tell if they were on the ranch or just off of your land. But they were not trying to hide their fire."

"They?" she questioned.

"They wouldn't need to have a fire big enough to be seen if there was only one, maybe two people." He buttered a piece of bread for himself, and somehow Thomas found that funny and laughed. Rusty and Ruth chuckled at the youngster. "Something doesn't sit right though, Ma'am, and I would just be grateful if you would be extra careful right now."

"Are you going to ride further out and see if you can find any sign?" Ruth held her breath waiting for his answer.

"No; at least not until the boss gets back with Paul and Cy." His eyes were serious as he met her gaze. "I won't be leaving you and the boy alone. In fact, I'm hoping you won't mind, missus, but I would feel a whole sight better if you would let me lay out my bedroll on the floor here tonight."

"Well," she said, nodding approval, "I think we better get busy after lunch so we can get everything done and get inside before dark then," commented Ruth. Inwardly she breathed easier at his offer to sleep in the house. She had faced outlaws and danger before on her way west, but was glad for the support she would have. Rusty may not be able to move fast, but he was the best shot she had ever seen. "It might be a good idea for you to bring up some extra clothes and such from the bunkhouse. We can move the bed out of Thomas' room into the main room here if you want to be closer to the door, and he can sleep with me. It could be another three or four days before Luke and the boys are back."

That was exactly what Hal Colter and Sly Booker were thinking as they rode hard to meet the rest of their gang.

Chapter 6

It was late afternoon by the time Luke and his riders were ready to leave Virginia City. The three men trotted their horses out of town, then kicked their heels in and sent the horses galloping in a mile eating run. Jasper was across the saddle in a kind of special bed in Cy's lap so he would not tire either. The dog was used to traveling this way when they had long distances to cover; dog and master adapting well to the arrangement.

They led three good mustang horses behind their own trail proven ponies. They knew their horses might be able to run up to forty or fifty miles a day, but they had no intention of risking the death of their horses to get home faster. They were betting on the outlaws being unaware that they had been seen, and therefore, would not be moving as quickly as the Rocking R riders.

What they wanted now was distance between them and the town before it got dark. It was far more dangerous to run your horse after nightfall. They planned to run the horses the first two miles, then slow to a canter for another ten miles. At that point, they would walk the horses for another hour or two, then stop to rest for a couple of hours. With the cattle dog, they could all sleep at the same time. Jasper would warn them of any approaching danger before any of them would see or hear anything.

Cy glanced down at the dog laying across the saddle in his lap and grinned. Cy had made him a special kind of seat sling with a lip, almost like a basket to make sure he did not fall at the high speed they were traveling. Jasper had his head in the wind and his tongue hung out as they ran. The blue heeler was fast, but could only run about twenty-five miles an hour for roughly five miles, and not all of

26

it at that speed. They were pushing the horses at a gait that was bound to cover at least ten to fifteen miles before they stopped. They had nearly a hundred miles to cover to get home, and they were aiming for the ranch in four days tops.

The landscape sped by them, as they kept a keen eye out for any chance of an ambush. They did not think Colter and Booker would try to bushwhack them at night; it would be almost impossible to be successful, and would tip their hand. Moreover, the two did not have any reason to believe Luke and his men would start out that night. They did not realize their actions had been observed.

They rode with care and were alert to avoid stumbling upon the two outlaws who had ridden out ahead of them. The trio of riders branched off and took a little used trail; one that would take them a little longer, but provided less chance of a confrontation. They had ridden another mile when Luke put his hand up and reined in his horse. Jasper had his head up and was looking to the east. Cy and Paul walked their horses forward until they were beside their boss. Silently, he pointed to a spot roughly a mile to their right. A spot of light showed through the trees.

"I'm thinking that may be the two outlaws," said Luke softly, keeping his voice low. Sound could carry miles in the still night air.

"Likely," whispered Cy. "We know they came this way, so what are the odds there would be anyone else in the area?"

"Let's walk our horses, veer off towards the left to put a little more land between us," suggested Luke.

All three men walked their horses and those they trailed behind them off to the left and forward for another mile before they picked up the pace. Luke had planned to stop in another hour, but with the outlaws so close behind them, he did not want to give them a chance to catch up. Five miles later, he pulled up again to take stock.

"What do you two think?" asked Luke. "I was planning on a little sleep by now, but I have to admit I am worried about losing our lead."

"I agree," said Paul, "I am too wound up to sleep right now. I'd like to put a little more distance between us and them."

"I'm thinking we change the horses out and walk at least two miles, then maybe run them all for another mile or two," contributed Cy. "This trail is pretty worn, so we shouldn't have to worry too much about the horses stepping in a hole. That would give us about a ten mile lead. We can grab a couple hours sleep, rest all the horses, and still be up and back on the trail before they get up."

"You think so?" asked Luke.

"Yes sir, I do. When we chased them before, they were not men who got up early."

"I don't think they know we are ahead of them, and even if they see all the tracks, unless they get suspicious and take a close look, they will think there are six of us. They might even hang back a little." Paul rubbed his chin as he spoke.

"Let's get to it, then," said Luke. They dismounted, stripped the saddles off, and brushed the backs and sides of the horses quickly before throwing the blankets and saddles on the fresh mounts.

When they were sure they had at least a ten mile lead, they picked their way carefully up a slope to the root base of a huge fallen tree. They did not plan to have a fire, but it would still give them shelter from anyone passing on the trail below. Three weary men pulled the saddles off the horses, quickly brushed the most recently ridden, then hobbled all the horses. Within minutes, they had their bed rolls laid out, pulled off their boots, and fell into their blankets. They were almost instantly asleep. Jasper settled down next to Cy, his head facing the trail up the hill, on full alert. No interlopers would get past the horses and Jasper without a warning for the sleeping cowboys.

Chapter 7

Hal batted at the fly buzzing around his ear. The unfazed insect simply moved to his nose and crawled around the opening of his nostril. He sat up, waving his arms and hands wildly, angry at being awakened. In his efforts to destroy the offending critter, his hands crossed each other in his half sleep state, striking his own nose, causing him to jerk in pain.

"Damn you!" he snarled. He jumped to his feet and seemed to be dancing to unheard music for a jig, clapping his hands together repeatedly in the empty air in an attempt to smash the pest.

The click of a hammer being drawn back on the pistol in Sly's hand stopped Hal cold. "Just who you cussin' at?" snapped the man still in his bedroll, but propped on one elbow now.

"Now hold on," placated Hal, holding his hands up, palms out. His eyes flicked towards his own gun, lying in its holster next to where his head had been.

"You ain't that fast," laughed Sly, but it was not a pleasant sound. "And I sure as shootin' ain't that slow."

"Aw, it was a dad gum fly! The blasted pest was crawlin' in my ear and nose!"

"You woke me up because of a stupid fly?" Sly grumbled and got to his feet, still holding the gun in his hand. He looked Hal up and down and started to laugh.

"What you laughin' at?" he growled, grabbing his pants off the ground and shaking them out to make sure nothing had crawled or slithered inside. He glared at Sly as he pulled them on and buttoned them. "Put that thing away!" He pointed at the gun, then grabbed his shirt.

29

"Sure," said Sly insolently, letting the hammer down and setting the gun within reach.

"'Bout time you were up anyway," snapped Hal as he stirred the embers of their fire, feeding kindling in until it flared up. "We're burning daylight!" He shot a blistering look at Sly, then added small sticks across the fire, then a couple of larger pieces. Grabbing the extra canteen, he added water to the coffee pot and threw in some more grounds, then set it on the fire.

Both men saddled their horses, then rolled their bedrolls and tied them behind their saddles. Fully dressed now, they squatted by the fire and Hal poured two cups of coffee. He handed one to Sly and they sat, just drinking coffee and not talking for several minutes. Finally Hal exhaled loudly and got to his feet.

He rummaged in his saddle bags and retrieved two chunks of bread wrapped in paper. He handed one to Sly, then sat down. Men like Hal did not apologize and Sly had a hair temper, but they both knew they had to work together. Breaking bread was as good a way as any to relieve the tension.

"You thinkin' we go in and raid the ranch first, or take the timber?" asked Sly, filling his mouth with a chunk of bread. He squinted at Hal as he chewed.

"I don't know yet." Hal ran his hand over his head and resettled his hat firmly, then standing, he kicked dirt over the fire, turned and mounted his horse. "That rancher is still working his way home."

"That might be, but we need to send a man over to read the sign as soon as we get back." Sly studied Hal as he swallowed the last of his coffee and bread. He threw the dregs of the pot into the fire and jammed the pot in his saddle bags. He swung up on his own horse and looked at Hal. "I don't like surprises."

"He only had two men with him on that drive. I don't think he has more than one or two at the ranch," said Hal. "But we do need to know what we are facing," he agreed. "I'll send Snake over when we get back. He will bring us back what we need."

"Then we best be getting' along. Let's ride!" barked Sly, pushing his horse into a gallop. Both men were in a mean, nasty mood, and that would not bode well for anyone that crossed their path.

30

Chapter 8

Ruth scanned the hills surrounding the house, looking for any sign of movement or something unusual. She had spent many an evening in the rocker on the porch next to her husband of just over two years and surveyed their property with him, noting every little detail.

At those times, it was done with a sense of pride and accomplishment. But today, it was to look for danger that could harm her child or ranch. Nothing looked out of the ordinary, so she proceeded to the barn to milk the cow. She carried a bucket in one hand and the Henry rifle, loaded and ready, in her right hand.

She left Rusty inside finishing his breakfast and watching little Thomas. Ruth chuckled and glanced back over her shoulder. Rusty may be chewing on a piece of bacon or biscuit, but she knew he was also at the window, rifle barrel peeking through the opening, and watching for anything or anyone that might try to do her harm.

Ruth stopped and listened at the door to the barn. She was no fool; someone could have slipped inside while they were sleeping and be waiting for her to open the heavy door. She looked at the ground and saw nothing that looked like it had been disturbed. The stick she had laid along the bottom of the door looked like one that had simply blown around the yard and settled against the door. But no one could have opened that door without shoving the stick aside, and it would not have been noticed in the dark.

Satisfied, she opened the door and walked into the darker interior, setting the pail on the ground near the cow, then picking up the small three legged stool that rested on top of a barrel. She sat and milked the animal efficiently, while keeping her ears open for any

31

unusual activity. She started to continue her routine to gather eggs in her apron before she realized she could not carry the pail of milk with one hand, hold her apron up with the eggs inside with the other, and still have a hand for the rifle.

"Good glory," she said, exasperation in her voice. It was already taking longer to get the chores done because they had agreed Thomas would not go outside until Luke came back. That meant one of them had to stay inside with him at all times. "Well, this will have to work!"

Ruth set the pail of milk on the small table by the tack room, and rested the rifle on a bale of hay next to the door into the hen house. She carefully tied the bottom corners of the apron around the waist band, making a soft sack of sorts. Next, she grabbed a handful of straw and stuffed it in the apron, then lay the eggs on top of the straw, shifting it to pad the eggs. When she finished, she stepped to the door of the barn again, then picked up the pail in her left hand and the rifle in her right.

Pleased at her efficiency and cleverness, she walked swiftly to the main house and inside. She glanced at Rusty, and froze. He stood, rifle to his shoulder and eye peering through the sight. He did not move or greet her.

"Rusty? What is it?" Ruth set the pail down and immediately started towards him to look out the window, glancing as she moved to the sleeping form of the child lying on what was now Rusty's bed.

"Shut the door, Ruth!" he commanded sharply.

Startled at the tone of his voice, she both shut and latched the door quickly, swinging the heavy board across the width and into the latch built to secure the wooden barrier. Only when she had completed the task, did Rusty take his eye out of the sight, lower the gun, and step to the side of the glass.

"We will need to stay inside as much as possible until Luke returns." His look was hard and determined. "There was a man sitting his horse on the top of the hill, in those trees, watching the barn and you."

"Oh!" Ruth exclaimed, her hand going to her throat. "I didn't see him! Did he have a gun?" she breathed. She was laying the eggs inside a bowl, automatically and without thinking.

32

"Aye, Missus, he did," Rusty nodded, sharing a glance between her and the opening, "but you would have known if he tried to draw his rifle out of the scabbard."

"How would I have known?" asked Ruth, feeling as if she had missed an important step of some kind.

"Because," he said, sending her a bleak look, "you would have heard the shot when I killed him."

Chapter 9

Luke played his eyes over the hills as he walked Pepper along the trail. They got up before dawn and trotted the horses for several miles this morning and were preparing to pull up to rest them and take a quick break themselves before switching the horses out. He kept an eye out for any place that would be a likely ambush site, but he had no idea where Hal Colter and Sly Booker could be. Paul had been riding ahead, and now Luke watched as he rode back and pulled up beside Pepper.

"Boss, there is a small stream up ahead about half a mile, with a cluster of boulders on a short rise. There are a couple of trees for shade and some good grass too."

"Mebbe we should take it while we can find the water. Even an hour could help save the horses," offered Cyrus.

"I'd sure like to know where those two polecats are right about now," said Luke, turning his head left to right, as if he expected to see them at any minute. He rubbed a hand over his face and considered the situation, then looked at Cy and Paul. "You two go ahead. Pepper is hardly winded yet, so I'm going to back track our trail for a bit and see if I can spot them behind us."

"Do you want one of us to come with you?" asked Paul.

"No. Go ahead and switch out the horses and rest a bit yourselves. Jasper will warn you of anyone coming near," he said, smiling at the dog who stood beside Cy's horse, wagging his tail. "If I get in trouble, you will likely hear the shots, but regardless, if I am not back in an hour and a half, start riding for the ranch and I'll catch up."

34

"Mr. Randall, I would come a runnin' if I thought you was in trouble!" exclaimed Cy.

"And I'd be racing him to see who got to you first," interjected Paul.

"Call me Luke, Cyrus, you've earned it. Respect isn't in a title, and I think of all of us more as brothers." Paul swallowed hard and Cyrus cleared his throat. These were western men, not much given to softness, but family was not always your blood. "I appreciate that you would ride back to help me boys, I truly do," he continued, "but if I don't come back, I need you to get to the ranch and protect my family." The two men exchanged a glance, then caught Luke's eyes for a brief second, nodded, and rode away. Riding for the brand meant you would give your life for the rancher's family too, and no real man of the west would risk the lives of his family for his own.

Luke turned Pepper and rode back nearly a mile, keeping to the side of the trail. His sharp eyes caught a way up the side of a slope, and he took it. Threading his mount through the trees, the young rancher came out on top of a ridge, but still in the tall pines. He could see several miles along his back trail, but he did not discern even a dust cloud.

"Where are you?" he murmured to himself. He did not believe the outlaws had gotten ahead of them since last night. He stayed on the top of the ridge, under the cover of the trees, and kept moving back the way he had come. Suddenly, he stopped and turned his head slowly.   Smoke. He raised his head, closed his eyes, and drew in a deep breath through his nostrils. Wood smoke was coming on the wind from the west. He turned Pepper and descended the hill so he was just below the ridge. He rode with care, knowing the wind could carry an odor miles, but it could also be from something near.

Luke dismounted and ground hitched Pepper. He removed his binoculars from his saddlebags and climbed up on top of a large boulder that was beneath the limbs of a tree. It would give him more cover while he worked at finding out where the outlaws were at this point. The warm sun filtering through the branches felt good on his back, and the rock on which he lay had been the object of enough sun to retain a comfortable temperature. He rested his chin on his leather gloves and held the binoculars in both hands, propping the glasses as close to the rock surface as possible. A small shoot off the tree gave shade in just the right place to avoid a glint off the metal that might give his presence away.

He lay still on the warm rock for a good twenty minutes, studying every crevice, gulley, and tree in view. And then Lucas Randall did the unthinkable. He did one of the most dangerous things he had ever done in his life. He fell asleep right where he lay.

Chapter 10

Hal sat his horse, leaning both arms on the saddle horn as he scanned the first the trail, and then the hills in front of him. He rubbed his chin and swiveled his head slowly. Finally, he dismounted and examined the tracks on the ground in front of him.

"What do ya make of it?" asked Sly, biting off a hunk of tobacco and beginning to work it in his cheeks.

"Six horses came through here less than twenty-four hours ago," said Hal. "The dirt is churned up, so I can't tell if there were riders on all those horses or not." He kicked at a small pile of deer droppings and bent to examine the result. He straightened and shook his head. "A small mob of deer ran over the tracks from the horses," he spat, "and left some pellets besides to mix up the sign!"

A single sharp clink of something that sounded metallic on rock caused Sly to jump and scan the hills around them. "Think it is someone looking to ambush us?" asked Sly, loosening his forty-five revolver in his holster. He sat up straighter in his saddle and did his own viewing of the hills around them.

"Nobody knows we are here yet!" Hal snapped at his riding partner and gave him a withering look.

"Then what was that noise?" demanded Sly. "It sounded like metal on rock!" His eyes worried the boulders on the tops of the hills, but saw nothing more.

"You probably heard the hoof of some animal hitting the rock as it jumped around! I swear, you are skittish as an old woman in a graveyard!"

"I didn't live this long being careless!" Sly snarled, his face scrunched up in an ugly expression.

"There ain't nothin' to worry about yet!" snapped Hal. "Quit barkin' at the knot!" He mounted his horse and turned towards a hill off to the side of the road they had been using. "It's likely just some cowpokes hunting strays and maybe some dinner!" He rode around the side of the hill and into some trees, with Sly following, constantly searching the hills for movement.

"You sure you know where you're going?" Booker said, twisting in his saddle to look behind them again.

"Yep," said Hal, reigning in his horse." His face was hard as he looked at Sly. "You don't have to be here." He said it softly, but there was no give in his manner.

"I came a long way for this!" protested Sly.

"Then you listen, and you listen good! I am the boss on this here job, and I got plenty of men back at my camp that want in. You can come, and I'll keep you as my second in command because I rode on other jobs with you. But I am sick and tired of your quick temper and questioning everything I do. I planned this! I brought men together here in this neck of the woods to find pay dirt! I planned to rob the mines, but this side job fell into our laps, and we are going to do this first!"

"I didn't…" began Sly, flustered as he raised one hand up, palm out.

"In or out?" demanded Hal. "Meet my conditions or ride on out of here, because once you know where we are camped, the only way you will leave is feet first!" The menace in his tone was chilling.

The two men glared at each other in a battle of wills, but it was short lived. Sly broke the stare first, and turning his horse, waved a hand ahead of them.

"Lead the way, boss," Sly said agreeably.

Turning on the charm, huh, thought Hal, not liking the fact that Sly was now at his back. As soon as the trail widened, he would make sure he was behind or beside the other man, and he planned to make that happen sooner rather than later.

Chapter 11

The sound of angry voices woke Luke with a start. The binoculars started to slip out of his hands and he grabbed for them in a frantic effort to prevent them from clattering down the rock. As it was, the metal clinked once on the rock and he held his breath, not daring to move. He held himself still, mentally shaking himself into wakefulness and straining to hear the words being spoken so harshly.

Two men were arguing below him, but he could not make out what they were saying. They stopped talking when the binoculars tapped the rock, and one of them jerked his eyes upward for a few seconds. Luke held his breath, sure the thinner of the two men was staring straight at him. After a few seconds, the arguing continued, but the thin rider kept glancing around.

He took a chance that he was still undiscovered, and carefully eased up a little on the boulder. He brought the binoculars silently to his eyes and turned them until he made out the two shapes below him. He recognized the clothing and vague features of the man Cy had identified as Hal. He did not know the second man, but it had to be Sly Booker. He watched with interest as they appeared to argue. By the way he held his body and placed his hand on his thigh near his gun, Luke deduced that Hal was giving Sly some kind of ultimatum. Sly hesitated, then seemed to defer to Hal and waved him forward.

"Interesting," murmured Luke. "I think, if given the chance, his friend would shoot him in the back," he mused.

He watched with interest as the two outlaws continued around the hill, then wound their way on a course away from the trail that led to his ranch. Surprise kept his eyes glued to the field glasses until he saw them take a path through a wooded area and up the hill on the other side of the one on which he lay.

Luke shimmied down the rock, secured the binoculars back in his saddlebags, and jumped into the saddle. He did not know how long he had slept on the rock, but he knew he had to catch up to Cy and Paul before they started to worry.

He should have been relieved that the men were riding away from his ranch, but he had a nagging feeling this was not the last time he would see them. When he saw them again, he was certain it would be over the barrel of a gun.

Chapter 12

Cy twisted in his saddle and searched their back trail anxiously. It had been almost three hours since Luke had ridden off to check on the whereabouts of the two bad men they believed to be following their trail. Yet, he saw no plume of dust, nor had he heard any shots.

"Do you think we should go back and look for the boss?" The older wrangler reined his horse in and sat across the trail, looking back again, then at his riding partner. Jasper, who had wanted to run for a bit, sat on his haunches a few feet from the horses, lifting his head and sniffing the air for any sign of danger.

"No," sighed Paul. He chewed on his lower lip, staring back down the way they had come before he looked into Cy's face. "The boss has been through some mighty tough times and always came through. And if he doesn't..." he blew out a breath between pursed lips. "Well, he would want us to do our best to protect Ruth and Thomas." Both riders were silent for several minutes, each lost in their own thoughts. "We have our orders," said Paul, nodding hard once, as if to prod himself as well as Cy. Reluctantly, they turned their horses towards the ranch.

"Is this the only road to the ranch?" asked Cy suddenly.

"Truth be told," replied Paul, "I don't know. We haven't come this way more than a few times, and we were always driving a wagon, except this last time, when we herded the cows. What are you thinking?"

"I'm thinking we could cut off some time by going over those hills instead of around them." He pointed off to their left. "The trail leads us close to water and meanders around all those high places,

41

but we don't need as much water or a flat road, like when we were wrangling the cows. It might be faster." He searched the younger man's face, looking for a reaction.

"I kinda hate the idea of getting off the trail where the boss can catch up easier." Paul pondered the idea, lifting his hat off his head and running a hand over his hair. "Then again, Luke knows the way to the ranch and he can read sign. The next stream is about a mile ahead. We'll water all the horses and fill the canteens, then head over the hills."

By the time Luke caught up to them, they had gone off the trail. He studied the tracks, rode ahead a half mile just to make sure they were not deliberately trying to hide their route and double back. He didn't know exactly how long he had been asleep, but judging by the set of the sun in the sky, he had been gone three or four hours. They might be thinking he wasn't coming back and altered the route to throw the outlaws off their trail.

Luke followed their tracks into the trees, then saw where they stopped by a stream. He was puzzled when he saw that they went up over the hills instead of around them, but he followed. After all, he did need to catch up to them.

He had ridden five or more miles when he suddenly reigned Pepper in and sat, stunned by his revelation. Hurriedly, he took stock of his surroundings, then began to push his horse a little faster. He knew she was tired and he hoped he did not have to keep up this pace very long before he could catch his men and change mounts. He would not kill his horse, but he was definitely caught in a quandary.

If Cyrus and Paul kept on the path he suspected they had taken and he could not catch them in time, they would run right into Hal Colter and Sly Booker. They were not expecting the outlaws to be on this side of the hills. His men were riding right into an ambush and he was their only chance.

Chapter 13

"You're going to wear the floor and yourself out now, missus." Rusty flicked a gaze at Ruth as she paced the floor in front of the fireplace. At least he didn't have to warn her to stay away from the windows; she had that much savvy. He had allowed the door to be cracked open for fresh air during the day, for an hour or so.

"She has to be in pain," she lamented, "her mooing is getting more and more aggravated." She wrung her hands together and looked at the sleeping child lying on the bed by the fire. "That cow needs to be milked and Thomas needs some of that milk to drink."

"I know..." Rusty agreed, glancing at the toddler. The boy was a happy child and did not complain much, but he had asked, with pleading eyes, several times for milk. "I just wish Luke would get back." He chewed on his lip, his eyes worried as they scanned the hills.

The lone rider would appear, then jump out of sight quickly, before Rusty could swing the gun in his direction. The intruder would also throw a small object, like a chunk of wood, sending it flying across the old man's line of sight, which was effective in causing his eyes to automatically flit in the direction of the soaring object. It was just for a second or two, but his vision was turned, just the same.

That worried the old veteran even more. The man was arrogant, but wily. He knew Rusty was watching and he knew where the aged former soldier stood. He pondered whether or not the man was acting alone or had back up. Was he trying to create a diversion so someone else could move closer? None of these ideas could be ruled out, and that had the old cow poke on edge.

43

The cow mooed loudly again and Ruth stopped, staring at the wall as if she could see the pained animal through the wood of the house and barn. She turned a forlorn face towards Rusty and swallowed hard.

"We have to do something," she pleaded. "Maybe I can sneak out the back window and into the barn from the back door. Even if I can't bring the whole bucket back, I can at least relieve the pressure she is feeling and bring back a little milk for Thomas." She waited, watching Rusty, knowing he was thinking about their options. Finally, he sighed.

"How are you going to get in and out of that window fast with all those skirts?" he demanded. "The answer is no!"

"I'm your boss!" she snapped.

"Meaning no disrespect ma'am," sighed Rusty patiently, "I will protect you, but I work for your husband. Lucas Randall is my boss." He was treading on dangerous ground right now, and he knew it. But he would do or say almost anything to keep her and the little boy safe. He was praying his bluff would work; banking on her sweet nature to overtake the spirited part of her disposition.

"You! You! Arghh!!" Ruth raised clenched fists in the air, shook them in his direction, and sputtered. Then she strode rapidly into the other room.

McMath remained at the window, rubbing an eye with the palm of one hand. He tried to imagine how close Luke would be, but knew it was a futile endeavor. He was just trying to keep his own spirits up, especially since it was not going so well with Ruth at the moment.

"I'm ready now," pronounced Ruth. She stood with her arms crossed over her chest, feet apart, and a determined look on her face. Her petticoats were gone. She was wearing a pair of Luke's pants, cinched tight around her waist with a piece of cord from the window tie.

"I shoulda known you would think of something like that." Rusty chuckled, quickly taking stock of her outfit. "Even so, how are you planning to get back in that window when you are done? It's one thing to drop out a window, another to climb back in, especially with a pail of milk in your hands." He was not looking at her now; he was scrutinizing the hills for movement. He did not like the idea of her going outside without him, but they could not risk being slow enough to safely carry Thomas. He knew she was not going to listen to him; all he could do was try to minimize the danger. It would be better if he knew when she was going to the barn; he wouldn't put it past her to sneak out.

"Luke put a couple rounds of wood back there before he left, to chop up for firewood," she smiled. "He set one against the house with a wooden box on it for me to start planting seeds under the window. I can step up on it to come back inside." She smiled triumphantly.

"I got a bad feelin' about this, Ruth," grumbled Rusty. "Whoever that man is up there, he is getting bolder every time he moves."

"Thomas needs something to drink besides water. He needs milk, Rusty, and that cow needs to be milked or she will get sick and maybe even die!" She had her hands on her hips now, meeting his eyes without wavering.

Rusty pounded a fist against the window sill, his jaw clenched so hard he thought he might break a tooth. He turned a frustrated stare on Ruth.

"Get yourself ready. When you have everything you need, you will stand by the back window and wait for my call. Next time he moves, I'm going to lay down some fire. You go as fast as you can and pray he is too busy keeping his head down to see you." He turned serious eyes on her, looking for agreement. She nodded and started to move towards the back room.

"I'll hurry," she said, turning away.

"You do that, but you also wait for the next time you hear me firing. Then, no matter what you are doing, you run for that back window and I'll be there to help you through." He looked out the window, then back again. "Do you hear me, Ruth?" His voice was edged with concern and a firmness Ruth had never heard when he addressed her.

She turned back, nodded understanding, then quickly, she picked up the milk pail and walked to the window in the bedroom. She slid the window open and studied the back just to be sure there was no danger to be seen outside the window. Suddenly, rapid fire came from the front of the house, and she slipped down to the stump and ran to the back of the barn. Ducking under the corral logs, she slid into the interior of the darkened barn through the back door.

Swiftly, Ruth milked the cow, filling first the bucket to take with her, then another dish in the barn. The cats could have that milk, she decided, but it would help relieve the cow of the heaviness of the full milk bag. Pleased with herself, she stood at the back door of the barn waiting for the next round of fire.

When it came, she flung the door open and ran. Or rather, tried. She collided straight against the chest and into the arms of a tall, rangy man that stepped from the corner of the barn. She tried to scream, but a dirty hand clamped over her mouth and a strong arm snaked around her waist, pulling her up hard against the wiry form that held her tight. The milk pail clattered to the ground, spilling its contents into the dry soil. Ruth tried to bring her boot up to stomp his instep, but anticipating the move, he spread his legs wider and planted them firmly for balance.

"I've been waiting for you," he whispered in her ear, his breath reeking of unclean teeth, stale coffee, and old smoke. "I've been watching you from the top of the hill. We have plans for you." He chuckled softly and the hair on the back of her neck bristled with fear.

Panic rose in her throat as she registered that he had said "we." How many were there? Ruth struggled, but the man was strong and rough. He dragged her back into the barn and threw her to the floor on her stomach. He straddled her and slipped rope around her wrists, tying them tightly behind her back. Next, he hobbled her ankles together, so she could walk, but not run. She opened her mouth and drew in a breath, but held it when he laughed.

"Go ahead. Scream," he taunted, "I will kill the old man when he comes. And that would leave your little boy alone, now wouldn't it?"

Ruth froze underneath the man, thinking rapidly. He was right; Rusty would likely come running, leaving James sleeping and alone in the house. Even if they didn't hurt her little boy, what would he do, how would he survive until Luke got back if he were left all alone?

"Now, you are coming with me, and you are going to be quiet about it." He yanked her up by her arms, causing shooting pain up to her shoulders. He half dragged her to the door again, then held tightly onto one arm as he peered outside. Satisfied, he shoved her in front of him, backing from the barn, gun in hand.

"Please, let me go," she pleaded. "My little boy is not yet two."

"I don't care about your brat," he sneered. "The boys and I haven't had a woman in a long time. We are going to have some fun with you." Her eyes caught a glint of sunlight on metal near the top of his boot, and she realized he had a knife inside. Did she dare try for the knife?

Moving so the horse was between him and the house, he shoved the gun in his holster to lift her and throw her over the saddle, belly down. He mounted behind her, and was just drawing his gun again went a loud roar sounded and the man jerked in the saddle. She squirmed and he threw her to the ground, out of his way, and got off two quick shots at Rusty as he stepped from the corner of the house.

A red stain blossomed on Rusty's side and he faltered slightly, but he fired again and this time the gunman flew from the saddle with the force of the bullet tearing through his heart.

Ruth uttered a choking scream as Rusty fell, and she frantically pushed her body through her tied arms to bring them in front. She scrambled to the dead gunman and pulled the knife out of his boot, quickly cutting the cords on her hands and feet.

The young mother raced towards Rusty as he sat up, but she ran right by him. Surprise, then fear swept over McMath as he turned his head and saw the reason Ruth had ignored him. He swore, then struggled to his feet, emitting his own cry of terror and anguish.

Little Thomas had tottered out the open front door, curious about all the noise. He was on the edge of the porch when the kidnapper had fired the revolver at Rusty. The young child now lay face down in the dirt, silent and unmoving. There was blood on the ground under him.

Chapter 14

Luke was pushing Pepper too hard. She was tired and the terrain was rough; if he didn't slow down, she could step in a hole or lose her footing and break a leg. He looked across the expanse below him, straining his eyes for any sign of his two ranch hands. He brought his eyes up to scan the hills ahead of him, but still saw nothing.

Luke had no idea how far he was behind Cyrus and Paul. For that matter, he did not know where Booker and Colter had really gone; he was scouring his memory to recall the direction that trail took. He had only been on it once, and that was over three years ago. He had to do something, but what?

If he fired his rifle three times, it would at least make them aware there was a problem and they would be more careful. But it could also alert Hal and Sly. On the off chance that they did not know they were being followed, it might serve to help them set up an ambush. Suddenly, a memory kicked in and he knew what he had to do!

He rode to the top of the nearest hill and dismounted, ground hitching Pepper. Quickly, he gathered small pine branches that would burn quickly. He scooped up handfuls of dry pine needles, avoiding the cones that would pop and snap, sending out embers that could cause a wild fire. Using small broken branches, he created a good sized, triangular stack over the pine needles, then pulled a match out of his small stash and lit the fire.

Black smoke wound its way up high into the sky. He pulled his ground cloth off his horse and unfolded it, then walked back to the fire. He gave it a few minutes to be noticed, hopefully, by his two men. They should be checking their back trail for him, or other danger, as a matter of course. They were experienced and trail wise riders. He expertly flipped the blanket over the fire three times, with a pause in between. Three separated puffs of black smoke rose in the sky. He waited a few minutes, then did the same for two puffs. He hoped Paul remembered the code they had set up last year when they were trailing some wild horses and wanted to communicate without using gun shots, which might scare the horses into scattering. Three consecutive puffs meant danger – be aware and careful. Two meant come towards the smoke. He hoped they would come back towards him, and not ride into the sights of the two outlaws.

He repeated the ritual two more times, then put the fire out and rode away from the area in the direction he thought his men had ridden. He wasn't naïve enough to think the smoke could not be seen, and possibly investigated, by the outlaws. He wasn't wrong.

Up ahead on the mountain, two sets of eyes sat their horses and stared at the smoke. They cut their eyes left, then right, then focused again on the column of black smoke.

"What do ya suppose that's all about?" asked Sly, scratching his stubbled chin.

"Ain't Indians," replied Hal, rubbing his hand absently over his head. "It wouldn't be our boys either. They had orders not to come near town."

"Someone is trying to send a message to someone out here," said Sly, narrowing his eyes, "but who else would be out here?"

"The fact that there could be someone else out here ain't that unusual," growled Hal irritably. "What's got me wonderin' is why they are trying to signal each other."

"I don't like it!" groused Sly. He spit a stream of brown fluid out of his mouth and into a hapless bush beside the trail.

"I didn't invite you in to this job to listen to you whimper like a stuck pig!" snarled Hal.

"Look!" interjected Sly, ignoring Hal. He pointed to a dust cloud down at the end of the little valley they had just come through.

"Who is that?" Hal squinted for several minutes, then looked at Sly and jerked his head. They turned the horses into the trees and dismounted, pulling their rifles out of the scabbards. Hal dug out a pair of binoculars as well. They crept up in a gathering of rocks and sighted down the road, but they could not make out faces or details at that distance. Even the glasses were not strong enough to detail any of their features.

"Why don't we just shoot him anyway?" suggested Sly, grinning. He found killing to be exhilarating.

"Did your mama drop you on your head?" steamed Hal, struggling to hold his temper in check. "We can't just shoot people without someone noticing we are here! We need to stay low until we get the job done!"

Sly grumbled and looked through the sight on his rifle. Paul's face came into focus and he grinned. "It's those two cowboys from that ranch," he gloated.

"Why all the dust if there's only two of them?" Hal glared at Sly. "Do not shoot!" He hunkered down and twisted the focus on the binoculars. "They are pointing at the smoke." He continued to watch and saw them veer off towards the vapor, He could see they were trailing extra horses. He pulled the binoculars away from his eyes.

"Should we shoot them before they get away?" asked Sly eagerly.

"No," replied Hal, chewing on his lip. "My curiosity isn't strong enough to ruin this job." He stared at the receding dust for a few more seconds, then abruptly stood. "Besides, we don't know how many men might be by that fire. Let's ride," he barked. "I need to get some action going." This whole plan was getting far more complicated than he liked, but it was too late to back it all down now.

He did not know Luke was watching them through his own rifle sight on the other side of the little valley.

Chapter 15

Ruth ran up the steps and kicked the door further open, carrying her precious child in her arms. She laid him carefully on the bed and touched his neck softly, praying for a pulse. Her breath caught as she felt his heartbeat through her finger tips.

She stepped to the sink and got a basin, pouring a little cool water into it and grabbing a clean cloth. There was so much blood! *Oh God, please don't let him die!* Ruth quickly checked his clothing, opening his shirt and almost sobbing when she saw his unmarred, pale, little boy skin. The blood that was on his skin had trickled down from the head wound.

Fear gripped her hard as she knelt by the bed and carefully began to bathe the side of his head. Ruth had to know if the bullet was in his head or had creased the side. She stifled a sob as she realized that Thomas was not responding at all. He should be crying, or at least whimpering; the pressure of the damp cloth had to hurt.

"How is he?" asked Rusty. He stood, leaning against the wall by the door, his breathing ragged.

"I don't know, Rusty!" Ruth wailed, then fought to bring her emotions under control. "How bad?" she asked, flitting her eyes from Rusty to Thomas.

"I'll make it," blustered the old man. "You just take care of that sweet little boy." His voice cracked and he let his head fall forward. When he raised his eyes, it was to focus on the chair closest to the bed. Slowly, he inched towards the chair and almost fell into it, leaning heavily on the table.

Ruth looked at Thomas, still lying quiet, but the blood was at least bathed from him. She stood and ran to the sink, where she

51

pulled down more bandages from a shelf and brought them to Rusty. She lifted his arm and guided him to the bed, easing him down next to Thomas.

"Take care of the boy!" He tried to sound assertive, but he grimaced in pain at the movement.

"I can't do anything else for him right now," she said, a catch in her voice. "I cleaned all the blood off and he has a deep crease along the side of his head."

"Where's the bullet?" croaked Rusty, coughing painfully.

"It just passed along the side of his head; it didn't penetrate his...skull." She ended the last word on a breath blown out with a hiccup on the end. She turned Rusty slightly to see the other side of his wound. "Looks like one bullet went through you and sliced through the side of his head. But I am not sure where the second shot went." Her eyes met his with concern. She was very much afraid one of the bullets was still in her friend.

Ruth bathed Rusty's wound, and put comfrey compresses on both of their wounds, binding bandages around Thomas' head and Rusty's ribs. By the time she finished, both of them were asleep. She emptied the blood rich water into the yard, and rinsed the cloths, leaving them to dry, draped over the wash basin in the sun. She knew she might need them when she changed their dressings.

Finally, she looked around the yard, her eyes falling on the body lying by the corral. She started towards the man, but faltered and stopped. She was spent. He wasn't going anywhere, and at this point, she didn't care if the coyotes got him later. He had shot her baby and her friend.

Walking back inside, she secured all the windows and drew the window coverings. Next, she closed and bolted the door. Ruth turned and looked at her two patients. They were both still sleeping. She picked up the Henry and checked to make sure it was loaded, then slumped into the chair Rusty had been in a short time ago. She was bone weary and shaky. She laid the rifle across the table and rested her head on her hand.

"Oh Lucas," she whispered, "where are you? We need you. Please God, please bring him home soon. I'm so tired." She put her head down on her arm and sobbed quietly. She did not realize she drifted off to sleep until a noise fought its way through her consciousness. She jerked her head up and looked quickly around.

Her eyes traveled to the bed, where Thomas still slept. But Rusty's eyes were slitted and he moved a hand in a feeble attempt to motion her over to him.

"What is it, Rusty?" she asked, gliding over to where he lay. "Are you in pain?" A grimace from him answered her question, but he wet his lips and spoke hoarsely.

"You need to go, Ruth," he whispered. His eyes were glazed with pain.

"I'm not leaving you and Thomas!" she said in a harsh whisper.

"No," he said, "take Thomas with you, but you need to go."

"You can't travel right now, Rusty, you have lost too much blood already!"

"I'm not going. Leave me with a rifle and ammunition, and take Thomas and go to Bridgeport. Go to Axel and Adelina at the general store." He knew they were good friends of Lucas and Ruth, and would protect her and the toddler. *Maybe they will even send some men out until Luke gets back.*

"No, we should all stay here! Luke will be back in another day or so, and then we will be fine." Tears misted her eyes as she tried to make sense of what he was saying.

"No," he said with effort. I heard the man talk about his friends when he was putting you on the horse. You have to go! It has already been too long."

"I can't leave you," she said, tears running down her cheeks. She realized she had slept through the night and it was almost dawn. They had all slept for hours!

"They will come looking for that man, and they cannot find you and Thomas here." He was breathing heavily with the suffering. His eyes were bright with concern and agony."You have to go," he said as sternly as he could. "I'm dying anyway," he whispered, drawing his knees up as a surge of discomfort hit him. "You can't do anything more to help me, Ruth," he gasped, beads of sweat coating his face in a sheen of pain induced moisture. "They will come looking for that skunk outside, and they will kill you both. The only thing you can do for me is let me die knowing you got away and are safe."

Chapter 16

"You see anything?" asked Paul. He rode with his rifle across his saddle, as did Cyrus. Both men were watchful and a little jumpy. They couldn't shake the feeling that they were like mice in a maze and being toyed with for the amusement of some unseen evil.

"Nope," Cyrus replied cryptically. "No more smoke, nothing." His eyes moved nonstop over every bit of landscape, searching for any movement or something out of place. "That smoke," he said, "that was some kind of signal you and the boss had from last year?"

"Yes," Paul murmured, scanning everything around him as he rode. *Where are you, Luke?* "I sure would feel better if he would show himself soon, though."

There was a stand of boulders on the side of the hill, and they glanced nervously at each other. Cy looked behind them while Paul was fixed on the rocks. Suddenly, a hat on a stick rose slowly into the air above the highest rock. Staring, Paul broke into laughter when he heard the sound of a squirrel chattering. Cy slanted a look at him, like he was crazy. Then Paul answered with his own squirrel imitation.

"What the heck are you doing?" Cyrus asked, shaking his head in bewilderment. "You talking to animals now? What the...Jasper!" Cyrus watched with amazement as his dog ran to the rock, but did not bark or growl.

At that point, Luke stood on the boulder and waved his hat, then jumped on Pepper's back and rode down to meet them in the road, Jasper trotting contentedly beside him.

"It sure is good to see you, boss!" exclaimed Paul.

"I have to admit, boss, I kinda thought you were...well...dead." Cy kept his eyes trained on Luke, eyebrows raised in question.

"I'm glad I caught up with you," said Luke, "but we need to get off this road. Let's get up in that stand of trees and I'll fill you in." He glanced at the hills in front of them, then back to the cowboys. "Cy, you're the best shot among us, so keep your rifle and your eyes trained on those hills. Paul and I will wrangle the horses, but Paul, don't let that rifle get too comfortable in the scabbard."

"You think we got company?" asked Cy, peering intently at his surroundings.

"I know we do," replied Luke. "Booker and Colter are just ahead of us, and were off to the right last time I saw them."

"You saw those two?" asked Paul in surprise, moving his horse behind the remuda to urge them along, while Luke led them on one side and Cy blocked them on the other.

"I saw them through my binoculars when I was hunting them. They took a short cut and got a little ahead of us, but I am sure they know we are here after my smoke signal."

The three men drove the small group of horses up the hill and behind the nest of boulders where Luke had hidden. When they were safely obscured from at least rifle fire, Luke dismounted and began to slip the saddle off Pepper. He patted her and spoke sweet words of appreciation as he removed the blanket and rubbed her down a little with some soft leaves from the Wyethia plant. Commonly known as mules ears, the plants grew all over the Sierras and were sometimes used in place of paper when a person had to use a bush or tree instead of an outhouse. The gray-green leaves had soft hairs on them, which made them soft and gentle to use.

"She's about done in," he said, patting his trusted steed, "I think we should change horses, ride another several miles towards home, but away from that range," he said, hiking a thumb over his shoulder towards the site he had last seen the outlaws.

"Sounds smart to me," answered Cy, still holding his rifle in ready position and scanning the landscape from his stand between a crack in two big boulders.

The three drovers pushed the horses up and over the next hill, then galloped them over a grassy meadow area to eliminate a dust cloud for another mile to put some distance between them and the outlaws. Luke knew Pepper would be okay for that long since she was not carrying a rider or a saddle. They slowed down to a canter and headed towards a space off to their left, surrounded by Cottonwood trees and a few big rocks for shelter.

"There should be water near those Cottonwoods." Luke pointed to the area, and they turned the horses. They did not need much urging; they were thirsty and could smell the water. All three of them liked the sheltered location, but still surveyed the perimeter for signs of trouble. The fresh horses had only gone a few miles, but Luke took a careful look at Paul and Cy and made a decision.

"Do we have time for coffee, boss?" asked Cy, weariness coming through in his words.

"Yes," nodded Luke. "How about I put some on and you two grab a couple hours of sleep while I stand watch. Then we'll all have some coffee and food before we go on."

"I can take the watch," began Paul.

"I'm not as tired as you two; get some sleep!" The two men shook their heads, but did not have the energy to argue. They pulled their blankets down from behind the saddles and were asleep almost before their eyes closed. Luke was glad they did not ask why he was not more tired; he was still embarrassed that he had fallen asleep.

Three hours later, Luke woke the two and poured hot cups of coffee for all as they stowed their blankets back behind the saddles on the horses. He handed them strips of jerky and cold biscuits, which they ate quickly, then doused the small fire and mounted their steeds.

"Let's put some more distance between them and us," said Luke. "We need to get out of range, but I have a bad feeling I can't shake. Something tells me we need to get back to the ranch as fast as we can."

Chapter 17

Ruth packed the saddle bags with a little food in case they had to stop before they got to Bridgeport. They would not be there before nightfall; another reason to make sure the canteens were full. Rusty watched her as she moved, his eyes lighting on little Thomas, who had only murmured in his sleep. He had not fully wakened, and that had both him and Ruth worried.

"Rusty, I think we should stay right here until Luke gets back," she protested. "He should be here tomorrow or the next day at the latest!"

"Ruth, you don't know that. He could have run into trouble or decided to stay another day and do some shopping or give the boys a break." He coughed carefully, trying not to aggravate his wound. "He has no way of knowing we are in trouble back here."

"Even so," she said, bringing him a canteen, and holding it while he took a sip. "I just can't leave you here alone like this." Tears trickled down her face.

"You know you are the only thing close to a family that I have," he said softly, "but they will come. And they will kill you and this sweet little bairn here, and I cannot let you do that." He winced in pain.

"But you can't defend yourself!"

"Now don't you stoop to insulting me to get your way," he admonished gently. "If Luke does come back as fast as you hope, he can come get you and leave me a man to help. But I need to know you and the little man here are safe." They stared at each other until Ruth broke her eyes away. "Now, hurry up and get ready. I need you

57

to do a few things here so I am set if those coyotes sneak up on me before the hands return."

Ruth quickly finished getting their coats and her rifle ready. When it came time to go to the barn and saddle her horse, bile rose in her throat. She looked at Rusty and he saw the fear in her face. She didn't want to go anywhere near the body, and at the back of her mind, she also feared there could be someone else waiting in the barn by now; maybe more than one!

"Bring me my holster, hanging under my coat over there. He pointed her to the rack on the wall by the door. She retrieved the holster and brought it to him. "You take this here gun and you keep it in your hand or your waistband while you saddle your horse and bring it to the house." He handed her an 1860 Army revolver he pulled from his holster.

Ruth took the gun without comment and brushed a kiss across the forehead of her sleeping son. She stopped at the door and slanted a look back at Rusty, then drew her lips into a straight line, and slipped out the door. She moved quickly, avoiding looking in the direction of the body still laying in the open ground between the barn and the house. Crows flew up from the body as she neared, but she had no time to waste burying him or even moving him. Hand on the gun in her waistband, she opened the barn door and stepped in quickly to the side, allowing her eyes to adjust to the dim light.

Several minutes later, she hurried back through the same door at the house and stopped as she faced Rusty's rifle. He lowered the gun and she came towards the bed, an expression of shock on her face.

"What if that were Luke and you shot him?" she demanded, her lower lip trembling.

"I wouldn't, same as I didn't shoot you. If you were an enemy, you would poke your gun through the door first. I knew it was you; I was just making sure there was not someone behind you with a gun in your back." Silence hung between them as she digested that comment. "Is your horse ready to go?" He spoke gently this time. They both knew it could be the last time they saw each other.

"Yes," she replied, "I put the saddle bags on in the barn. I just need to put the supplies in them."

"Do it," he wheezed. "Then help me set up a few things here before you leave." He grinned in a way that made her feel better about leaving him alone. She was back in minutes.

The bed was already to the side of the room, so someone would have to open the door and look around it to see him. Ruth was strong, and under his direction, she dragged the table to the window at the front of the house. She upended it so it would hamper anyone wanting to climb or shoot through the window. Next, she took a dish towel and secured it with clothes pins to the line holding the curtain. She placed several spoons in the cloth and clipped the sides with clothes pins, letting them gap a bit so that if the cloth was disturbed, the spoons would clatter to the ground. Then she carried a chair to the door between the main room and the bedroom, closed the door, and placed the chair at an angle under the handle, which would make it difficult to enter without being heard.

"That's all good," he smiled in satisfaction. "Just two more things, then I am going to send you on your way. Give me my revolver back and bring me the ammunition for it and the Yellow Boy." Once she had done that, he pointed to his jacket again. "In the inside pocket is a derringer. I want you to keep that handy in your outside pocket at all times. There is extra ammunition in the pocket as well. Put your coat on and fill your pocket with the derringer and shells."

"Okay, but I have the Henry," she began.

"This is if they get close," he said gravely. "Now, fill your other coat pocket with shells for the Henry." When she had completed that task, he gave her one more instruction. "Take that jar of beans and put it by the door. Leave the top open. When you leave, scatter a few on the floor by the door, and reach back inside and slide the jar as close to the door as you can. It will fall over and make a racket if someone opens that door." He watched her with a sadness that hurt more than his wound. This might be the last time he saw this woman and child that felt like family.

"I don't like leaving you," she started again, her voice breaking.

"I know, but this is the only choice. What trail are you taking to Bridgeport?" He listened, nodded, and made a change or two in her route. "Luke will still find you if you make these slight deviations, but it will be harder for the friends of that sidewinder out there to catch you before you can get to safety.

Ruth carefully fumbled Thomas into his coat and eased a knit cap on his head over the bandage. She took a large shawl and tied one end securely, placing one arm through it, turning it into a sling by which she could carry the boy on the horse and keep both hands free to shoot if need be. She placed Thomas in the sling, then stood and walked around the bed to Rusty.

There were no more words to be said. She leaned over and kissed the old man on the cheek. She almost burst into tears when he kissed the sleeping child gently on his cheek.

"Now go, Ruth, ride carefully and with swiftness to the general store in Bridgeport."

She nodded and went out the door, pulling the jar of beans closer, then firmly shutting the door so it would not blow open. Pausing briefly, she pulled the bench in front of the door. It too would make noise if moved.

She slipped the Henry in the scabbard and then turned the horse so she could mount from the porch. It was difficult to swing herself up with the weight of the child in the sling in front of her, but she was bolstered by fear. She quickly settled the boy across the saddle and turned her horse at a canter towards Bridgeport.

Inside the cabin, Rusty listened until he heard the sound of her horse moving quickly away. He knew when she had reached the grass behind the house because he could not hear the hoof beats of the horse any longer.

"Go with God, Ruth and Thomas," he whispered; a prayer he said out loud. Hardly had the words cleared his lips when darkness crossed his eyes and enfolded him as he lay limp upon the bed.

Chapter 18

Hal turned in his saddle, looking behind them. He had not seen any movement or dust in hours, even when they stopped and surveyed their back trail with the binoculars. He didn't like it. He was never happy when things did not go as he planned. Like bringing on Sly Booker. He was already getting on Hal's nerves, like a burr under his saddle blanket!

Sly noticed his saddle partner's interest in their back trail, and turned himself so he could see as well. He scanned the hills, looking for changes in shadows next to trees, watching for the glint of sun light off the metal of a gun barrel, but he saw nothing and turned back to the road before him. Inside, he was seething. If Hal had let him kill those two cowboys, they wouldn't be worried about being followed.

"If I remember right, there is a stream up ahead with some shelter that will make a good rest stop. We can have a hot meal and some coffee," muttered Hal. Sly merely nodded, and Hal searched for the opening he remembered.

Another mile forward and he veered them off the trail to a huge deadfall. Huge trees being uprooted in the Sierra Nevada were not unusual. The wind could reach over a hundred miles per hour, especially over ridges, and if there had been a lot of snow or rain to soften the ground, a tree could topple. The fallen tree roots and brush offered shelter and concealment for both them and their horses. Whether it was the result of man or beast, the branches of the bushes at the base of the trees had been broken to form a sort of cave. They dismounted, took a walk around the perimeter, then satisfied, returned to the horses.

"I'll build a fire and make coffee and something to eat," said Hal. "Why don't you take care of the horses."

"Make that coffee strong, will ya?" grumbled the gun man, leading the horses off to water.

Hal had a dry, small fire and coffee going quickly. He shaved off thick slices of bacon from the hunk in his saddlebags and had it frying nicely by the time Hal was done. He handed him a cup of strong coffee and was surprised when the man actually thanked him!

"That sure smells good!" said Sly, sipping the hot liquid in his cup.

He watched as Hal mixed up flour, a little salt, and some water, then dropped the mixture into the hot bacon grease to cook up into pan biscuits. They ate the hot meal without speaking, both hungry and tired. When everything but the coffee pot and cups were cleaned up and put away, Hal studied Sly for a few minutes as the man had his hands wrapped around his coffee, staring into the fire. *No smart man stares into a fire when there might be enemies about.* He shook his head.

"Let's rest about an hour, then get some more time in tonight on the road."

"But this is a perfect spot to camp tonight," protested Sly, gesturing around them at the secluded, protected area.

"I call the shots here!" reacted Hal vehemently. "I..." he stopped, looked at the landscape, and shook his head. "You know, you're right." He sighed. He could use some sleep too.

"Well..." began Sly, surprise showing on his face.

"No," said Hal, holding up a hand, palm out. "This is a good spot to camp. I think we are both tired and edgy, and we should relax a little and get a good night's sleep, then start fresh in the morning. That timber isn't going anywhere."

The two men spent the next hour sharing coffee and stories, then shucked their boots and settled down in their bed rolls to sleep. They let the fire burn down, not expecting any trouble. They did not know the three cowboys were aware they were in the area. They counted on the horses letting them know if anyone was getting close.

Hal Colter had a point. The timber wasn't going anywhere. But the same could not be said for his top hand back at the camp. Snake Reynolds was antsy. Joe had ridden out two days ago and had not come back. He was supposed to be scouting the area and reporting back any problems he found. Snake suspected Joe had found a problem he couldn't handle, and Snake wanted to know just what had happened. In the morning, he would start gathering a few men together. If Colter was not back by noon, Snake would ride out and find Joe.

Chapter 19

Ruth picked her way along the trail carefully, holding the boy close to her. That made her worry even more, because she could feel any move he would make...but he had not moved. He was breathing normally, and moaned once or twice, but it broke her heart that his eyes did not open. He did not respond at all to her voice.

She stopped more than once, fighting the impulse to return to the ranch and wait with Rusty. Luke would surely be home soon! But each time, she looked at the pale face of her son and urged her mount forward. There was a doctor in Bridgeport, and she desperately wanted his help with Thomas.

She stopped the horse and studied the rocks around her carefully. She knew she was near the short cut over the mountain, the one that would drop her into the small valley of Lee Vining, just before Bridgeport. She might be able to get some help there, at least a wagon to take her and the child on into Bridgeport. She walked her steed up the slope, giving him his head and letting him pick his way on his own.

Ruth was almost to the top of the ridge when the bear rose up in front of them. It had apparently been sleeping just on the other side of a big rock when it heard the horse heaving its way up the slope. The furry beast rose on her hind legs and bellowed, sending the horse lurching away from the huge animal. Ruth fought to bring the horse under control with one hand on the reins and the other holding the toddler close to her chest.

A small bear cub ran out from the cluster of rocks and down the other side of the mountain, with the mother bear hastily behind the baby. Ruth hung on tight, praying she could get the horse to calm down now that the bear was leaving. It was not over.

The mother bear digging into the rocks as she ran away caused a cascade of loose rocks to rain down on the horse and Ruth. Using both hands to shield her son and ducking her head to protect herself, Ruth was pelted on the shoulders with fist sized rocks. She no longer had control of the reins, and the horse reared, throwing her and Thomas off his back. She flew through the air and hit the trunk of a tree hard, somehow managing to keep her arms wrapped around the small child. The world became dark as she fell to the ground, Thomas mostly under her, neither of them moving.

As was common, the rocks tumbling down the hill picked up more of the granite chunks as they slashed downward, beating the horse as he tried to gain his footing. He went to his knees, then listed over on his side and did not get up, his head and shoulders covered with blood.

Night fell in the mountains and the cold descended on the three mounds of warm flesh; leaves skittered and tickled their faces, but nothing moved. The leaves continued to dance against the grouping of bodies, building themselves a bed against and on top of the fallen shapes.

Chapter 20

Snake Reynolds was in a bad mood as he threw his knife into the trunk of a tree. The big Bowie knife sliced through the air as easily as it sliced through flesh, landing with a loud thunk as it imbedded itself into the bark. It was well past morning and he was tired of sitting around the camp. He had grumbled his way through breakfast, abruptly surging to his feet, bumping the man next to him and sending the scalding cup of coffee in the man's hands all over the front of his shirt.

Snake had glared at the smaller man, while his hand hovered dangerously close to the handle of his gun. His big chest heaved with anger, daring the other man to make a move. His yellowish light brown eyes burned into the blue eyes glaring back at him.

Jordy was opening his shirt and ripping it off as his own chest fairly steamed with the heat radiating off of it into the cool morning air. He was cussing and wriggling as he tried to remove the hot shirt. One of the other riders was helping him, but shooting Snake a warning look at the same time. Jordy was one of the fastest guns among them, maybe faster than Snake.

"Back off or I'll douse you both with the wash water!" threatened the cook, standing by a basin of dirty water in which he had been washing the dishes. In his hands, he held a shotgun leveled at both men. "You best be getting' apart and cooling off! You start a fight here and hot lead is gonna fly and the whole operation will be done for!" Every eye in the camp was on them, and they knew what the cook said was true.

"Aw, I didn't mean nothin', Jordy," said Snake without a lot of sincerity. He had a minute to think, and knew even if he survived a shootout with Jordy, the boss would kill him when he got back. He stomped away from the others and proceeded to while the morning away throwing his big knife, then sharpening it, then throwing it again. When the sun was almost straight overhead, he saddled his horse, making sure his rifle was loaded and in the scabbard.

The cook called for the noon meal and Snake walked over to the fire, hitching his thumbs in his belt. The big hulk of a man had made up his mind; he needed to ride, to find some trouble, to find Joe, whatever came of it, he needed some action. He surveyed the group of men in line for grub and spoke to a few of them as they walked by. He handpicked three men besides himself, and when the noon meal was over, they all saddled horses. He went to the cook for some jerky, biscuits, and coffee, in case they had to be gone overnight.

"The boss know about this?" Bean looked Snake in the eye and stood with his hands on his hips. The wiry cook was nobody's fool, and he knew who paid his wages.

"He left me in charge and I need some grub – enough for a few days for five or six men," blustered Snake. He wanted a little extra for the trail, and besides, if Joe was alive, he would need grub as well.

"Uh huh," growled Bean, his eyes narrowing into slits as he made Snake wait for the answer. He took another step towards the big man towering above him. "This will not come back on me," he drawled. "If the boss is unhappy, I will be too, and you will be hunting your grub someplace else." He stared at Snake for another few heartbeats, then turned away and walked back to the chuck wagon.

Skinner fumed inwardly. Nothing was going his way! He dared not cross the cook; Bean got his name standing up to a real hard case on a trail drive. The man had been loud and demanding and when Bean gave him his plate, he complained it wasn't enough. Without a word, the cook took the plate out of his hands and gave it to the next drover in line. The bully's expectant grin turned to shock when Bean handed him a fresh plate with one single bean and a small chunk of bread. The rider opened his mouth to protest, and found a scattergun jammed hard into his stomach.

The story told around cattle drive camp fires was that Bean asked him if he wanted a side of lead to go with his meal. Observers said every man in camp froze, holding their breath at the icy tone when the cook spoke. No one wanted to challenge the death shimmering in the eyes of the crusty old man, and no one ever gave Bean any trouble from that day forward.

Snake waited, shifting from foot to foot, until Bean turned and held out the bag of grub. He quickly scurried over to take it, blubbering his profuse thanks, telling him how much he appreciated the food. Bean never cracked a smile; he just bathed him in a blistering stare. The color mounted up his neck and into his cheeks as the sting of the cook's distain washed over the big man. He strode over to where his men waited. He tossed the bag to one of the cowboys to secure around his saddle, and turned to his own horse.

"Let's ride!" he growled, swinging his heavy frame up onto the hapless horse.

The group of hardened outlaws rode in the direction that Joe had taken almost three days ago. They followed Jed Morgan, their best tracker, looking for sign that would tell them where Joe had gone. Snake knew he went to check out the ranch several miles away, but he didn't know exactly where it was from their camp. The boss had told them to wait at the North end of the land owned by the rancher, and that's where they had set up camp.

But Joe had been into Bridgeport before and knew about the Rocking R Ranch, so he knew where he was going. He also knew there was a pretty woman there, in a land where women were scarce. It would be good to know how many men were at the ranch and what treasures they could take when they raided the ranch after they completed the first mission. The plan was to rob the mines of their payroll, hit the ranch, take what they wanted, then leave the territory. Of course, now the boss had decided to add the timber thievery to their list, and many of the men did not know that was against the law.

Joe had been sent to scout the homestead and report back. He had not returned, and Snake knew the boss would want to know what had happened to the man. If he had been captured, that would not bode well for the secrecy of their venture. Snake was well aware that he would be held responsible for whatever had happened.

"I think it would be best to make camp," said Jed, reining up and looking to Snake. They had been riding for four hours now, and the sun was slowly sinking towards the horizon. His lean form was resting with arms on his saddle horn. The weathered face belied the young age of the man. Jed was only twenty-six years old, but looked at least a decade older. His sandy blond hair had begun to take on a whitish hue already, and his prematurely lined face showed the wear that years of outside work and hard riding had etched on his visage.

Jed came by his tracking ability through necessity. When he returned from the war, he found his family had been killed by marauders during the War Between the States. He took advantage of his family's friendship with a Sioux warrior that lived nearby, and the two of them tracked every one of the murderers down and killed them.

"Do you think we are close?" asked Snake, impatience in his tone.

"Yes," nodded Jed, "but I think it would be best to come up on the ranch in daylight to see what we are facing." He gestured to the horsemen hanging back a bit from the two as they conferred. "They haven't eaten since noon and we are all tired. A cup of hot coffee and something to eat would do us all good." His deep blue eyes did not waiver, a fact that Snake was not sure he liked, but they needed this young tracker, so he let the man tell him what to do.

The group of rough riders pulled up after a couple more miles, into a cluster of boulders and built a fire. The rocks would reflect the heat onto the sleeping men; a welcome benefit as the temperature was dropping in the mountains. They fixed coffee and a simple meal of jerky and biscuits, then rolled up in their blankets and went to sleep, trading shifts on watch every two hours.

Ten miles away, Rusty sat in darkness, cold and too weary to start a fire. He pulled the blankets closer about him, decided most outlaws would not attack an unknown target in the dark, and let his eye lids close again. His cheeks were flushed with fever as the wound in his side festered. He prayed Ruth and Thomas had made it to Bridgeport safely.

Chapter 21

Luke and his riders pushed the horses as hard as they dared. He could not rid himself of the feeling that something was terribly wrong and he had to get home as fast as they could. They stopped only to change the horses; rustling jerky or a biscuit out of their saddlebags to eat as they rode. The men drank from their canteens and answered calls to nature quickly while they traded the saddles. They had been riding since before dawn and were now closing in on darkness. They reigned up as the shadows settled over them.

"What are you thinking, Luke?" asked Paul, his face drawn in the moonlight. He was bone tired, but he would give his life for this man that had saved him nearly three years ago.

"You know we would ride through the gates of hell with you, boss," interjected Cy before Luke could speak. "We ride for the brand, no matter where it takes us, as long as you lead," his gray eyes holding a wealth of respect as he met Luke's eyes. Jasper, who had ridden across the saddle most of the way since he could not run that fast or far, yipped softly in support.

"Thanks, men," said Luke, swallowing hard to clear the huge lump that had appeared in his throat. "As much as I want to get home, I think we should stop for a couple of hours to rest all the horses and take a turn at resting ourselves. Jasper and the horses will warn us if anyone gets near, so we can all sleep for a turn. We'll put coffee on when we roll up, and then have a cup before we hit the trail again."

"You hopin' to hit the ranch by morning?" said Paul, more a statement than a question.

"Yeah. We may have to walk the horses for awhile, but the moonlight will help us see better," replied Luke.

"How about up that rise a bit?" offered Cy, who had been busy surveying the surroundings while they spoke.

"Let's take a look," said Luke.

They walked the horses up the gentle slope and found a perfect spot to stop. There was grass for the horses, and the rocks stacked down a bit over the ridge of the slope, which would make it harder for anyone passing to see their fire. Cy built the fire, first digging a small hole with his buck knife. The earth was soft and it was easy to scrape the dirt out of the indentation.

Luke dug out the coffee pot and filled it with water from one of the extra canteens they carried. He threw some grounds in and set it at the edge of the fire Cy had built. By the time he turned, Paul had unsaddled all the mounts and was brushing his own horse down. Cy and Luke joined him, tended to the horses, giving them water out of their hats, then settled quickly for a short rest.

Cowboys had a unique knack for waking themselves up after a set amount of time had lapsed, and they all woke within minutes of each other, two hours later. They shook their boots out, and poured cups of hot coffee, washing down the dry biscuits they had carried from town. On the trail again, they walked and trotted the horses, whenever they thought it was safe to do so, covering ground as fast as they dared. They hoped to be at the ranch in time for breakfast.

They were unaware of another group of men, camped roughly fifteen miles from the ranch, in the opposite direction, that shared their hope.

Chapter 22

Ruth tried to open her eyes and could not. Something was pasted over the top of them. Panic overcame her as she fought to make her arm move, trying to feel through the darkness for a pulse on Thomas, who was underneath her. Her hand fumbled until she could feel his warm breath against her skin, light, but breathing. She moved her fingers inside his shirt and felt him stir at the coldness of her touch. He had a pulse! He was breathing! Recognition overcame her and she nearly cried out. The fact that he had responded to the coldness of her touch was a good sign, even if he did not wake.

She realized she was cold, and reached the same hand up to her face and felt her eyes. Something was stuck on her eyes. She found a corner and lifted it, and a little light came in. Ruth swiped at her eyes and more of the coverings came off and she could see! Leaves! Leaves had become frosted with the cold and stuck to her face. In fact, she realized she and the boy were lying under a mound of leaves. They also offered some warmth, so she was still for a few minutes trying to remember why they were on the ground in the dark.

It all came rushing back. The bear running away had unleashed a torrent of rocks. She and the toddler had been thrown from the horse and she hit something hard. It hurt to breathe; she feared she may have broken a rib. The horse! Where was he? She had to get up.

Ruth tried to sit up and was met with blinding pain. Lights flashed in front of her eyes and she found she could not use her left arm at all. She had thought it was just asleep, with the bulk of the boy's weight on it for what had to be hours. But now she knew it was broken. She brought her knees up, and twisted her body to get her legs under her, using her one good arm to rise to her knees while letting her back support the weight of the sling holding the boy. She was breathing heavily and felt a little queasy. In the moonlight coming through the trees, she could see the hump that was the fallen horse. She knew he was dead.

"Well, Ruth, this is a fine mess," she said aloud to herself. She ran her good hand over her face and took a moment to think. "We need a fire." She bent forward and slipped the sling off her shoulders, letting Thomas down to the ground. Without his weight holding her down, she managed to get to her feet and look at the area around them. The bear was likely not coming back, so the boulders across from where she stood looked like a good place to make a camp tonight. She picked up the sling with her good arm and toted him to the shelter of the boulders, setting him down carefully, and tucking the shawl around him better for more warmth.

With small steps, she made her way to the horse. She loosened the saddle bags and tried to pull them off the horse, but part of them were under him. Moving around his legs, now stiff with death, she reached the cinch for the saddle and undid the clasp. The saddle shifted enough that she was able to pull the saddle blanket out. She worked at the blanket behind the saddle, and finally got it free. She could not get the saddlebags free, as hard as she tried. She opened the pouch on the free side of the horse and found the matches, a small pan, coffee, and jerky.

Ruth made her way back to the boulders, watching where she stepped, carrying the matches and the saddle blanket. She set them down and clearing a small spot of earth, she groped for a few rocks to frame the fire. She found drier leaves and twigs under the edge of some of the boulders, and scrounged for a few dry sticks. She found one when she stepped on a branch that snapped under her feet. That was a good sign that it was dry wood. She laid the fire well, and prayed as she struck the match. Her first attempt was rewarded as the fire smouldered, then with a small burst, bright flame licked at the sticks.

In the light of the fire, she laid the saddle blanket down and moved Thomas on top of it for warmth from the cold ground. She gathered a few more sticks and put a couple on the fire. Every part of her body seemed to hurt, but she had to make them a decent camp before she sat down. It was going to be cold tonight.

She leaned against the boulder for a minute, trying to catch her breath, but taking a deep breath was impossible; the sharp pain stopped her. She rolled her sleeve up on her left arm and winced at the swollen, red appendage that greeted her eyes. Sighing, she pushed herself away from the rock a walked back to the dead horse. She retrieved the burlap bag containing a pan, coffee pot, coffee, cup, and jerky, then looked about for at least one of the canteens. A glint of metal caught her eye, and she edged around the horse, leaned over, and snagged the strap of the canteen caught in a bush.

She wanted the rifle, but the horse was on top of the scabbard. She still had the small derringer in her pocket, and she had tucked a knife in her boot at Rusty's insistence. That would have to do. She couldn't afford to risk getting hurt in the dark and leaving her son all alone. She shivered as she prayed the coyotes would not come for the horse that night. She would have to keep the fire going to keep the beasts away.

Back at the fire, she put water in the pot to heat and prepared the coffee pot, putting it in the hot coals as well. She forced herself to gather wood, looking for a few good log sized pieces instead of just sticks. She placed the wood within easy reach of her good arm, adding some to the fire. She put some strips of jerky in the pan to make a broth, then reached over and grabbed the edge of the blanket where the child rested, pulling it towards her until his head was beside her leg. Ruth stroked her son's cheek gently, closing her eyes against the pain.

She jerked awake at the sound of a twig snapping. Her eyes searched the woods around her, lighting on a raccoon shuffling through the woods over by the tree she had hit when she was thrown from the horse. It stopped, glared at her, then scuttled around the tree. She looked at Thomas, who was still and pale.

Leaning forward, she dipped the cup into the broth and set it beside her. Lifting the boy's shoulders, she set his head up on her leg. Blowing on the broth to cool it, she sipped to make sure it was not too hot. Carefully, she drew her knife out of her boot, then lifted her skirt to find a clean piece of her petticoat. She cut a strip with her knife, then replaced the knife in its sheath and folded the rectangle of cloth in half. She eased open the mouth of the child. Holding the cup in her lap close to his head, she dipped the cloth into it, then placed the wet strip at the corner of the boys mouth. The tepid broth dripped into his mouth. She was relieved when he swallowed, something she was not sure he would do with his head injury. She repeated the process until she had nearly a cup of the nourishing liquid in the boy, then scooted herself over to let the boy lay down again, bunching up her skirt to provide a little pillow.

Leaning forward, she took the pan from the fire and set it beside her to cool. She managed to bring the coffee pot to her as well, without disturbing the child who now lay beside her. She drank the remainder of the broth straight from the pan, then drank the small amount of coffee she made from the cup. She set the pans aside and placed more wood on the fire. Covering herself and Thomas as best she could with the bedroll blanket, she finally felt exhaustion overcome her. "Luke, please find us," she whispered as her eyes closed. Too tired to even be kept awake by the pain, she slept. From the woods, eyes watched her and the boy sleep, waiting for their chance.

Chapter 23

Rusty opened his eyes slowly. What sound had caused him to wake? He strained his ears to hear any sound, unusual or normal, outside the walls of the house. He moved his head to check all the safeguards he could see from his bed. Nothing seemed to have changed, but something had roused his subconscious.

He tried to move, to swing his legs over the side of the bed, but the wound in his side angrily protested, and sent him quickly back to his original position. He was breathing heavily with the pain. He moved his shirt aside and lifted the bandage, at least as far as he could. He could see swollen, infected flesh beneath the bandage, which was partially stuck to the wound.

Yet, he knew he must somehow gather the strength to move. He had defied death so far, but that meant he had to eat, drink, and find a way to relieve himself. He would only get more weak if he stayed in the bed. Using his arms to half lift himself, he inched his hips towards the edge of the bed. He brought the rifle around and poked it under the bed, managing to get it behind the chamber pot and pull it forward.

When he was done and had pushed the ceramic pot back under the bed, he leaned sideways against the wall. He desperately wanted to sleep again, but did not want to waste the progress he had made. The cow interrupted his thoughts with loud mooing. At the same time, he heard the horses restlessly nickering. Something was definitely outside.

He reached over and took a long drink of the whiskey Ruth had left, then, using the rifle as a cane, pushed himself off the bed. He had to lean against the wall, giving his legs a chance to get used to his standing again. He shuffled to the side of the window with the table against it and peeked through the side of the curtain. Nothing moved in the yard in front of the house.

He shifted to look the other direction and saw a coyote slink to the front of the barn and begin to paw at the door. When it lifted his head to sniff the wind, Rusty's stomach clenched. The snout of the beast was bloody. Disgust and anger overtook him, and he raised the rifle to his shoulder, took aim, and fired. The wretched animal dropped dead where it stood.

Unfortunately, Rusty paid his own price. The force of the rifle firing knocked him off balance in his weakened state, and he too fell rapidly and did not get up. Fresh blood oozed out onto the floor under his unconscious body.

Chapter 24

"Do you think we will get there this morning?" asked Snake, bringing his coffee cup to his lips and taking a gulp of the hot liquid. He looked at the younger man over the rim of the cup.

"That is likely," replied Jed, suppressing a shiver. Snake's eyes were a golden yellowish brown with black pupils more silted than round. It gave his eyes a snake-like appearance, and his form had been described as fairly slithering from rock to rock in a fight, in spite of his size. Jed did not break his stare back at the older man, but inside, his distaste grew. There was nothing about this man that Jed found to like or respect.

Snake cut his eyes to the others, lounging on rocks or fallen logs, finishing coffee or caring for their horses. They were ready for some action, and so was he. He threw the dregs of his coffee into the fire, then stood and kicked dirt over the embers.

Jed walked to his horse, stowed his cup, and mounted up. He walked his horse out from the others and sat, deciding the course they should take. He heard the others moving up behind him, and started to move without speaking just as Snake came abreast. Maybe he would take it as a snub. Jed didn't care. They rode at a trot for an hour, then pulled up at Jed's signal.

"Hang back here," he instructed, "I'm going to go check something out and then I'll be back." He glanced at the other men to make sure they had heard.

"You giving the orders now?" snapped Snake. Silence hung in the air for several minutes.

"Nope." Jed sat his horse easily, his face showing no emotion. "Go ahead," he said, gesturing forward with a seemingly innocent smile. He watched as Snake struggled with a desire to be tough and mean, while knowing he could ill afford to alienate Jed.

"Go check it out and report back, and make it quick!" he growled. He watched Jed ride away, tamping down his anger. There were too many men here that wanted to challenge him, and he was ready to kill someone, just to show them who was boss. He just had to be careful he could justify it to Colter.

The men dismounted, walked around, and stood watching the spot where Jed was last seen. Nearly an hour passed when one of the men pointed off to the hills far to the right of where Jed had ridden. The scout was riding in from that direction. They all mounted the horses and waited.

"The ranch is actually off that way," Jed said, pointing to his right.

"How can you be so sure?" growled Snake.

"I found Joe's horse and backtracked him far enough to know the direction."

"His horse? Where's Joe?" demanded Snake.

"I don't know that," replied Jed, "but there is blood on the saddle."

"Then let's ride!" shouted Snake. "Lead the way!" They were still riding the small hills and valleys when they heard a rifle shot. It stopped them all in their tracks. Snake exchanged a look with Jed. "That could be Joe! We need to hurry!" He started to turn in the saddle to signal the other men, but Jed spoke.

"I don't think so," said Jed calmly.

"Why not?" snarled Snake.

"Because the blood on the saddle was dry, so he was probably hurt or shot more than a day ago." His easy, cool eyes held Snake's, and he was not intimidated by the fury in the other man's face. "Besides, there was only one shot." All the men were listening and Jed was right; there had not been another shot fired.

"Just git us there quick so I can see for myself," he demanded. Snake did not like this at all. He did not feel like he was in control, and that caused the bile to rise in his throat.

The men rode for another twenty minutes before Jed reigned up and dismounted his horse, ground hitching the animal, and signaling for the others to wait. The young scout crouched low as he mounted the rise and lay on his stomach, peering over the edge. As he expected, Snake slithered up beside him almost immediately. Jed took binoculars out of his pocket and carefully began to scan the buildings below. Suddenly, he stopped and swung the glasses back, holding them steady for several long seconds.

"What do you see?" barked the big man beside him.

"I think I see Joe," said Jed, his eyes grave as he held the glasses.

"What do you mean you think? Your eyes gone blind even with those glasses," he snapped derisively.

"Between the back of the barn and the house," said Jed simply, handing Snake the glasses.

"All I see is a bunch of what looks like bloody clothes, I don't see..." Snake stopped talking, his mouth gaping, before lowering the binoculars to stare at Jed. The color had left his face and his hands were shaking a little. "Are you saying you think..." he stopped, unable to finish the sentence.

"I think that's Joe...or what's left of him," replied Jed. The young man did not flinch. "I think the coyotes got to him. Look in front of the barn door."

"It's a dead coyote. Good!" exclaimed Snake.

"I also think that is the rifle shot we heard." The lean cowboy sent his eyes skittering over the ranch again.

"I don't see any people, but I bet they are all hiding in those buildings! How else would they have got Joe?"

"Mebbe," sighed Jed. "Do you hear that sound?" He wondered how Snake had ever come to be in charge. He was hot headed and had no skills at reading sign at all. He watched the other man squint at the ranch, then shake his head. "It's a cow mooing," said Jed, filling in the blank in the mind of the man beside him.

"What the hell do I care about some damned cow mooing? I want to go down and kill the yellow bellied coward that killed Joe and left him to lay out for the coyotes to pick apart!"

"It means," said Jed, rubbing his hands over his face and wondering how this man even could get himself up in the morning, "the cow has not been milked in some time." He pointed to the buildings below them. "Do you see anyone out and about down there? No one is milking the cow. No one moved Joe's body, which most western people would do out of decency. No one is tending to any chores in the middle of the morning and there is no smoke from the chimney." He waited, clamping his jaw tight to keep disgust from showing on his face.

"So there is no one there now!" exclaimed Snake. "We can go take what we want!"

"No, it does not mean that at all," snapped Jed, turning his head before he told Snake what he really thought. "Someone shot that coyote recently; probably this morning."

"How in tarnation do you know that?"

"If it was shot last night or yesterday, the coyotes would have been at it too," he explained with great control. "They will eat any dead carcass, even their own."

Snake studied Jed, an ugly scowl on his face. "Okay, sauce box, what's your take on all this?"

"I think Joe got caught in the barnyard and he got himself shot. Maybe he shot someone too, I won't know until we get closer, but that looks to be blood on the edge of the stoop there. I also think there is at least one person inside that house with a rifle, and they are good with it – they got that coyote with one bullet."

"That's all you know," taunted Snake.

"Yep. You got any ideas?" Jed's eyes were bright with anger, and Snake cleared his throat, looking away from the young man's piercing look. Neither spoke for several minutes as they stared at the house and out buildings.

"So, what do you think we should do?" Snake asked finally, not looking at Jed. He spoke quietly, obviously hoping no one else would hear.

"Well, we could creep down and around the house and wait, or…we could send one man in who would call out to the house, like he was just a cowboy ridin' through."

"Now that there is one smart idea!" Snake was grinning. "You go on in and see if you can find out who is there and how well armed they are." This could accomplish two good things for Snake. Whoever was inside might just kill this smug kid and Snake could not be blamed. Or, they would get the information they needed and recover Joe's body for a decent burial. Either way, he would come out looking good.

Jed stood without speaking, glanced once at Snake, then walked back to his horse. In truth, he was glad he was the one to go down to the ranch. Robbing a payroll was different than raiding a ranch and killing innocent people. He had heard one of the men talking about how Joe wanted to go see if there was a woman at the ranch. He had cringed at the talk, then grew angry. He didn't hold with hurting women at all. Jed deliberately slipped his binoculars back inside his saddlebags. The view of the house would be difficult to see without the looking glasses, and he decided he liked that idea. If Snake wanted to put a bullet in his back, he wasn't going to make it easy for him to see his chance.

Jed rode carefully down the hill on the far side so he would come into the yard from the west. He rode slowly, with his hands in plain sight, but one resting on his thigh, not far from his gun. Most people would talk first, especially if you came in hailing the house, but he was no fool; dead men were men who trusted too easily.

It was too quiet. He felt the hair at the back of his neck prickling as he looked for any movement – a curtain, a shadow, even a small animal scurrying away. He walked the horse slowly into the area in front of the house. He could see what was left of the body of Joe, as he looked past the corner of the house. He could only guess that the outlaw had been shot, but the coyotes had certainly been at him for at least a day and a night. He noted drops of dried blood on the porch leading up to and disappearing inside the door.

"Hallo the house!" he called. No response. "Is it okay to get a drink of water from the well? My canteen is empty." He dismounted and walked up on the porch. He heard the click of the hammer being pulled back just before the bullet whistled by his head.

Chapter 25

Luke and his two saddle partners heard both rifle shots, with the gap in between. They rode hard now, dropping the leads on the remuda behind them. They were on Rocking R range, and the extra horses could be gathered later. Now, they raced their horses as fast as they could towards the main area of the ranch.

They reigned up for seconds on top of the wooded rise a half mile from the house. Luke was thinking fast, and signaled Cy to go north and Paul to go south, while he rode straight in. None of them knew what they were facing, but they all knew it could not be good. No one would fire a rifle unless it was to defend themselves from man or beast. The young rancher knew his men were savvy riders and fighters and would approach with caution, but quickly.

Luke rode between bushes and trees to give himself some cover. Cy and Paul had the rocks and trees for shelter, but he knew they could see him as he rode since they were above him. He came up behind the barn and dismounted. Immediately, he smelled the body and drew his rifle. One look at the figure sprawled on the dirt at the corner of the barn told him the man had been shot and in the sun for more than a day. *Why didn't they pull him inside the barn?* More and more uneasy, he slipped inside the big structure. He noted the heaviness of the udders on the cow, which obviously had not been milked recently and was mooing mournfully. Her noise hid any sound he might make. Peering through the slats in the door, he saw a young man in the yard, just getting to his feet.

"Hold it right there!" he commanded, the sound of the rifle being cocked loud in the quiet air. He had his sights right on the man's chest.

"I just wanted some water, mister," answered Jed, lifting his hands high and away from his guns.

"I heard two rifle shots. Who is doing the shooting?" shouted Luke. He noted the young man wore two holsters, tied down and low. Most cowboys and range hands only wore one gun, but even so, this man, if he had a rifle, was not holding any long gun.

"I rightly don't know," he said honestly, shaking his head. "I heard the first shot and was headed this way looking for water, so I came on in. There didn't seem to be anyone here, but when I stepped up on the porch, asking if it was alright for me to get some water, someone inside liked to have blown my head off."

"The shots came from inside the house?" asked Luke, uneasy that no one was calling out at the sound of his voice.

"The last one did. I think the first one killed that coyote right by the door there." He pointed without lowering his hands and Luke looked down.

He saw grayish brown fur near the bottom of the door, off to the right. He hadn't been looking for it before, but he did see fresh blood on the fur. He stood, thinking. *Where was everyone? Why wasn't anyone calling his name or coming out of the house?*

"Paul?" yelled Luke. "You got this man covered?" He deliberately did not call to Cy; it was better not to show his whole hand until he knew what was going on.

"Got him dead to rights," answered the blond foreman from behind a cluster of boulders a little way up the hillside. "Just stay where you are and don't move, young feller."

Luke smiled at that; this cowboy was probably the same age as Paul. He went back out the rear door of the barn and slipped up to the side of the porch, glancing briefly at the man in the yard, then scanning the hills facing the house. There was dried blood on the edge of the porch, and drops all the way to the door. A chill ran down his spine. Someone he loved was hurt! He saw nothing, so he edged to the window. The curtains were not moving and the window was shut tight. Through the bottom of the window covering, Luke could see wood up against the window frame.

"Ruth! Rusty!" he called. Complete silence met his ears. He didn't like this at all. "It's Luke! Don't shoot, I'm coming in!" He ducked under the window and proceeded to the door. He reached across quickly and pulled the handle down, then pushed the door inward. A crash ensued, and then the sound of something like pebbles scattering. He also heard the racking of the lever of a gun and a moan. "It's Luke! Don't shoot!" he shouted. Then, his own rifle ready, he pushed the door further open and entered cautiously.

Rusty lay on the floor, eyes slitted in pain and struggling to stay open. He was breathing heavily and the rifle he held was pointed at the door. Luke's image and voice finally registered, and he let go of the gun, sighed Luke's name, and passed out cold. The ominous silence descended like a blanket of ice over Luke as he realized neither Ruth nor Thomas were in the house. Quickly, he threw back the curtain to the other room to confirm his fear, then Luke stepped to the door.

"Paul! Cyrus! Come on in, and bring our friend with you!" He turned back and knelt over Rusty, speaking softly, cajoling the old man to awaken and answer questions. Paul came through the door and immediately set his rifle down and came to the two men on the floor. "Help me get him on the bed."

They carried him carefully and laid him gently on top of the blanket. Luke went to work opening his shirt, trying to be careful with the bandage that was stuck to his skin. Paul knew what to do and went to stoke the stove and boil some water. Cy came through the door with the young man at gunpoint in front of him. He kicked aside the beans on the floor so no one would slip.

"Sit," said Cy, motioning to a chair. He had the man's gun belts in his hand, and after the man seated himself at the table, Cy jerked his coat off his shoulders and buttoned two of the coats buttons behind the man's back. It wasn't the same as tying him, but it was quicker and would hamper any movement the man might make. Jasper followed Cy in and sat, baring his teeth and emitting a low growl at the man confined to the chair, letting him know he was watching and the man better not try anything funny. Cy patted the dog on the head, then set his rifle down against the wall well behind Jed and filled a small pan with water for the dog.

"Rusty! Can you hear me?" asked Luke. "Where are Ruth and Thomas?"

"Here's the water," said Paul, setting it on the small stool beside the bed. "There's more heating."

"Get me some bandages too, and some of those comfrey leaves from the can to the right of the stove, on the top shelf."

"Is he going to be alright?" asked Cyrus.

"I don't know yet. I need to find out if the bullet went through or is still in there," said a worried Luke. "If I thought we could move him, I'd get him to doc over in Bridgeport. I'm afraid we don't have time to send someone in and bring him back. I did some medical help in the war, but I am not a doctor," Luke lamented.

"We'll have to do what we can," said Paul. "I agree, I don't think we can wait."

Cyrus looked at Luke significantly. "He is our only clue as to where Ruth and little Thomas could be, isn't he." It was a statement.

"Yes." The young father and husband did not say more; there was no need, they all knew that the lives of Ruth and Thomas could depend on saving Rusty's life as well.

"Maybe we should put him up on the table," offered Cy. "It would be easier to work on him then on the side of the bed."

At Luke's nod, Paul and Cyrus pulled the table back from the window and settled it on all four legs. Paul rushed to the sink and returned with a clean, wet cloth and wiped the dust off the table. The three men carefully moved the wounded man to the table. Luke ran a hand over his face, and looked at his two men.

"Help me turn him," said Luke. He studied the older man's back and shook his head. "It looks like a through an through, but I can't be sure. In any case, it needs to be cleaned out. Rinse this," he said, handing Paul a small hunting knife he pulled from a sheath on his belt. "I sure hope this works." He took the wet knife from Paul and had it poised above the old man, who lay bare chested on the table, when another voice broke the silence.

"I can help," the voice said quietly. As one, they turned to face the man bound to the chair.

"We can handle this," snapped Paul.

"I'm a doctor," he said, his gray eyes meeting Luke's with a sadness the young rancher had only seen one other place in his life: the medical tents on the battlefields of the War Between the States.

"You know what to do?" asked Luke, stepping forward, scrutinizing the man's face. He wanted to believe him, but he did not know this rider.

"It's been a long time..." Jed replied, looking sadly at Rusty. When he brought his eyes back up to Luke's, they were still melancholy, but there was something else. There was a determination Randall had seen in the faces of the doctors who got tired of losing men on the tables. "Yes," he said resolutely. "I know what to do."

"If you are playing us," started Cy, "you're a dead man."

"Even that relief would not tempt me to let this man die." Jed stared at Cyrus until the man tore his eyes away and stared at the floor. The heavy silence in the room reflected the deep sorrow in Jed's comment.

"Free him," directed Luke. "It's the only real chance we have." He and Jed held each others eyes in silent communication until Jed was freed.

Jed stood, removed his coat and rolled up his sleeves. He rubbed his wrists, scrubbed his hands over his face, then stared up at the ceiling, as if in mournful prayer. He looked at his hands and shook his head. Walking to the sink area, he pumped water and washed his hands thoroughly. As he did so, he gave commands.

"I will need that," he said, pointing to Ruth's apron that hung on a nail near the stove. Paul scurried to bring it to him, slipping the top strand of cloth over his neck as Jed bent his head to receive the loop. Next, Jed looked at the pot of hot water. "Bring that knife over here and throw it in this pot of water for a minute or two," he said. Luke looked at him in surprise.

"Why?" The young rancher asked the question in puzzlement.

"I believe the Scottish surgeon, Joseph Lister, had the right idea when he proposed sterilizing instruments before surgery." Jed smiled slightly. "It is sound practice."

"I heard about that a couple of years ago," said Luke. "I think Doc in Bridgeport mentioned it. He said it only made sense that you should make sure your hands were clean before you put them inside someone's body, especially for surgery."

"Yes," he nodded. "Maybe it would have saved a few lives in the war too." Jed held his hands out in front of him and looked at the pot. "Would you take that big spoon and fork and lift that knife out for me please?" He looked at Cy as he said it. "But don't touch it with your hands; I'll take it from you as soon as I can stand the heat."

Cy took the two utensils off a hook by the sink and dipped them into the near boiling water. He followed Jed to the table where Rusty lay, holding the knife carefully. He waited expectantly as Jed surveyed Rusty.

"I'm going to need more hot water and maybe more clean bandages." Paul moved to the stove. "Take a metal cup and throw it in that water as well." He looked at Cy and took the knife from him. Paul put another pan of water on the stove, moved a chair next to Jed, and placed the hot pot of water next to him. With a nod of his head, Jed signaled Cy to withdraw the cup. He looked at Luke. "There is a woman that lives here, correct?"

"How did you know that?" asked Luke, suspicion mounting.

"Does she have a sewing basket?" asked Jed pointedly ignoring Luke's question. "We are going to need a good needle and some strong thread. Go get it." Luke left and returned quickly, carrying the basket, which he set on the end of the bed, and retrieved a sail needle and some strong thread.

"Will this do?" he asked.

"Yes. Now, do you have any whiskey here in case he starts to wake up?"

When everything was in place, Jed directed Luke to stand beside him and help hold the wound open as he probed with the knife. Paul stood on the other side of the table, bracing against Rusty in case he tried to move suddenly. Cy stood at his feet, holding his legs. Jed told Luke to carefully pour some cooler, but still warm water over the wound area.

For the better part of an hour, the wound was cleaned with bandages and warm water, then probed, until at last, Jed removed the bullet. His mouth set in a grim line as he did so; it was the same caliber as the gun Joe had carried. Finally, he heated the knife in the stove, cauterized the wound to stop the bleeding, and stitched the opening carefully. Clean bandages were wrapped around Rusty's waist and Jed stepped back, looking at Luke. Sweat beaded on his forehead.

"Will he live?" asked Luke.

"I think so, but I can't promise," answered Jed, gazing at the man. "Do you have clean sheets for the bed?" He nodded at the dried blood on the sheets where Rusty had apparently lain before getting up to try to defend the house.

"I'll get them," said Paul, moving into the other room while Cy started to strip the bed. They carefully moved Rusty onto the clean bed and Jed staggered backwards and sat hard in the chair, hanging his head and resting his forehead on his wrists.

"Whiskey?" offered Luke, holding the bottle out to the man.

"Thanks," he replied simply, taking the bottle and taking a good swallow of the burning liquid. His eyes were heavy lidded, as if he had just done a full day of hard work.

"Do you think he will come to so I can talk to him anytime soon?" Luke was chewing on his lip as he stood, hands on his hips. "I need to ask him about my wife Ruth, and my son Thomas. They should be here. They would not leave him like this without good reason."

"I don't know. He seems really strong," said Jed thoughtfully, "but he has been seriously wounded and without care for at least a day and night." He met Luke's eyes. "Could they have gone somewhere for help?"

Jasper growled and sat up on his haunches, looking in the direction of the door. All eyes turned to him. Cyrus picked up his rifle and stepped to the window, peering outside.

"Boss, we got company," he said.

"How many?" asked Luke, whirling to the sound of hooves clomping into the yard.

"Three men on horseback, armed to the teeth," replied Paul, who had edged a look through the cracked door.

"Let me ask them what they want," said Luke, stepping towards the door. He was stopped by a firm hand on his arm, and he whirled, ready to draw.

"They want me," said Jed dolefully. "I was sent in to scout the ranch and see who was here."

"You low down buzz worm!" snapped Paul, turning his rifle towards the doctor.

"Let me talk to them," said Jed, raising both arms chest high, palms out.

"Why should we trust you!" growled Cy.

"You probably shouldn't," admitted Jed, "but I might be able to get them to go away."

"Why would you do that?" demanded Luke. Jed just stared at him for several heartbeats.

"I've seen enough death to last two life times," Jed whispered, just loud enough for Luke to hear. Suddenly his face looked years older than his age.

Then Jasper did the most amazing thing. He walked over to Jed and rubbed against his leg, looked at the young doctor, then walked back and sat next to Cyrus.

"Well, I'll be jiggered," whispered Cyrus, opened mouthed. "He's never done anything like that before!"

The silence in the room was broken by a shout from outside the house.

"Hallo the house!" yelled Snake. "We are looking for one of our men! Have you seen anyone about?"

Jed walked towards the door and no one stopped him. He opened the door and stepped out, on the small porch, hands hooked in his belt. He realized too late he still had blood on his hands and the apron he still wore. He also suddenly became aware that he did not have his guns.

Chapter 26

Ruth woke with a start. The sky in the east was tinged with a faint pink glow, and the fire had died down. She touched Thomas, needing to know he was still alive, and sighed at the pulse she felt with her fingertips. She leaned forward to throw another stick on the fire, and caught her breath at the sharp pain in her side. Her arm was numb, which she knew was not a good sign. She did not look at either her arm or her side; there was nothing more she could do until she got to Bridgeport.

Movement in her peripheral vision caught her attention and turning her head, she looked, full into the eyes of a coyote. Ruth's pulse quickened. She had to get to her feet! Coyotes would not usually attack full grown adults that appeared strong , but if they are hungry enough and you look weak enough, they will. She rolled to one side and rose to her knees, then getting her feet under her, she stood, leaning back against the rock to still the dizziness.

It was then that she realized she and little Thomas were not the object of the coyotes attention. The scavenger beasts were intent upon eating her dead horse. Relief flooded over her, with a twinge of sadness at the fate of one of her favorite horses. He was still serving her, she thought, as the coyotes would be more interested in a carcass that offered no resistance than a live woman and boy. She built the fire up, gathering a few more pieces of wood as long as she was still within a few steps of the child.

The warmth felt good as she put more water and coffee grounds in the pot, then took a few pieces of jerky and placed them in the pan with water again, pushing them a little into the edge of the fire to heat. She sank to the ground again and rested, glancing from time to time at the industrious coyotes. She repeated the process of last night, drinking coffee for herself, then dribbling the broth in the toddler's mouth, then finishing the broth and jerky herself.

The sun was higher in the sky now, and the spot where she sat was bathed in light. The horse was in the sunlight, and the coyotes slowly slunk away. Ruth waited several minutes after the last one crept away to be sure they were gone, then struggled to her feet again. Slowly, she walked to the horse and gazed at the ravaged body. It was not morbid curiosity; it was practicality. The scabbard now hung more loosely and the flank of the dead creature had been gnawed to the point the saddlebags looked as if they might come free. First, she worked at the scabbard, wiggling the rifle with her one good hand, until it finally came out, the sudden lack of resistance nearly causing her to fall to the ground. As it was she cried out in pain at the exertion and the jerking of her body as the rifle came free.

It took the young wife several minutes to recover, as she knelt, breathing heavily, leaning slightly forward. Her forehead was beaded with sweat as she opened her eyes and focused with determination on the saddlebags. The extra ammunition for the Henry was in those bags and she might need it. There were some extra biscuits in there as well, which they might need. The other canteen had been looped around the saddle horn, and although it was covered with blood, she was frontier woman enough to know you never left water behind. There was no telling how long it would take her to get to Bridgeport on foot, carrying her son. She looped the canteen over her head and good arm, shifting it so it hung down her back. Slowly, she moved to the saddlebags, using the rifle as a sort of cane to help.

The saddlebags were slick with blood, which made them slide more easily. When she had them free, she pawed through and removed the ammunition for the rifle, stuffing it into her hanging pocket under the hem of her blouse. She removed the biscuit packet and opened it, then stared. The paper had leaked and the fall of the horse had crushed the biscuits into crumbs, which were now blood soaked. Ruth dropped the putrid packet to the ground and stood.

Fifteen minutes later, Ruth had kicked dirt over the fire, slung the other canteen over her shoulder, shoved the pouch with the remaining jerky in her hanging pocket, and had pulled Thomas over her shoulder in the sling. She painfully lifted her wounded arm with her good arm and placed the injured appendage in the sling, resting against the limp body. Jaw set in stubborn resolve, she climbed slowly, one small step at a time, to the top of the ridge.

She stopped at the top, breathing heavily as she stared at the slope to the bottom. She could not fall. A stumble would send her and her child rolling down over rocks and brush to almost certain death.

Chapter 27

"Lookin' for me, Snake? I'm touched," drawled Jed sarcastically. He stepped to the left of the door as he said the words, standing wide legged on the porch.

"Where the hell you been?" growled Snake, his beady eyes flicking over the house, then back over Jed. "What happened to you?" He leaned forward in his saddle, looking at the blood on Jed's hands and clothing.

"I was doing what you sent me to do," replied Jed with a calmness that irritated Snake.

"I told you...!" snapped Snake, then stopped himself as he cast a wary eye on the house. He did not know who was inside, but he knew the blood on Jed's shirt was not there when he left their camp. He could not yet be certain it was not Jed's blood, although the young doctor did not appear to be injured in any way. "What happened to you?" He tried to infuse compassion into his rough tone, but he did not fool anyone, including those watching from the house.

"Someone needed my help," replied Jed simply, almost daring Snake to challenge him. He was not disappointed.

"I don't pay you to be helping other people!" growled Snake. "You have a job to do with us, and you better not forget it!" He was all the more unsettled by the bravado Jed exhibited, especially considering he was not wearing his guns.

"You don't pay me at all, remember?" Jed's eyes narrowed to slits and his voice dropped dangerously low.

"I am the top dog for..." he caught himself just before he said Colter's name. Suddenly, he knew that was what Jed was hoping; that he would give the name to whomever was inside. His hand

94

inched towards his holster. He wanted to draw and shoot this insolent pup into the grave, but he was not certain about who was on the other side of those walls. The latter question was answered for him, at least in part, when Luke came through the door, cheerfully calling out.

"Hello there!" Luke smiled big, but it did not reach his eyes; a feature that was not lost on Snake. "I'm real sorry about detaining your man here," he said, gesturing towards Jed with his left hand. His holster hung on his right hip, which Snake also noted. "One of my men got shot and Jed here was real helpful in getting the bullet out and patching him up." He stood, legs wide apart, hands at his side, and looked the big man straight in the eye. "You wouldn't know anything about that, would you?" The smile never left his lips, but clearly, his hand was ready.

Snake was seething. All eyes were on him, including the men with him who were taking their cue from his actions and words. They sat their horses ready, but not moving. The big ram rod could feel the color creeping up his face, and he toyed with the idea of a shoot out. There might not be anyone else inside, and even so, there were still three of them.

The decision was made for him again, as two rifle barrels eased through the window, pointed towards them. The two men on the porch could likely dive back in the door under the cover of that fire, while he and his men would be left sitting ducks on horses in the yard. A couple of his men realized what was happening, and tried to appear casual as they edged their horses further apart, trying to break up the tight cluster that would make easier targets.

"I'm real sorry if I caused you any loss, Mister..?" Luke let the words hang. He knew it would make Snake squirm, not wanting to give his name. "If you would just give me your boss' name, I would be sure to get in touch with him and offer to pay him for the time his man has spent helping us."

Luke's smile was easy and bright, which only added to the red rage beginning to turn in the stomach of the man who sat his saddle with arrogance in the yard. Luke had taken his measure and thought him wanting in courage and good sense. His eyes held those of the would be big man, unflinching, until the angry eyes cut to the side and focused on Jed's face.

"We gotta ride," snarled Snake, "we got work to do. You comin"?" He issued the challenge to Jed, who met it with an iron stare.

"I think I'll stay awhile longer," he said, "I need to clean up and make sure the man inside is doing okay before I leave."

Snake would have killed Jed at that moment, if he thought there was a chance he would live afterwards. Angrily, he whirled his horse around, and digging his spurs into the sides of the unlucky horse, he charged out of the yard with the others trailing in rapid succession. Luke and Jed watched until they were a considerable distance away, then the young rancher turned to the young doctor.

"I think you have made an enemy," he said softly, watching Jed's reaction.

"I think I did that long ago," replied Jed, a twitch at the corner of his mouth. "He just didn't know I knew until now." He turned and walked back into the darker interior of the house.

Inside, Luke went to Rusty and studied the man as he lay on the bed. He touched his forehead and found it cooler than it had been before the surgery. He sighed as Jed walked up and stood beside him.

"How long do you think it will be before he wakes up?" Luke chewed on his lower lip as he gazed at his friend lying so pale and still.

"You need him to wake up and tell you where your wife went." Jed turned his eyes from Rusty to Luke.

"Yes. My wife and son should be here. I have no idea why they aren't, or where they are. But I know they would not have left if everything was alright."

"It could be another couple of hours before he wakes up." He studied Luke's face.

"I know she's in trouble," said Luke, "I can feel it." He ran his hands over his face. "I have to go look for her; there has to be some kind of trail," he said bleakly. "Cy, you and Jasper come help me find sign first, then we'll know what to do."

He grabbed a rifle and headed out the door, trailed by the man and his dog. Things had happened so fast when they got to the ranch, they had not unsaddled the horses yet. He jumped in the saddle and began riding in a circle, with Cy and Jasper going the opposite direction. Jasper knew and liked Ruth and Thomas, and

Luke was hoping the dog would pick up their trail. Jasper was true to his breed, and soon started whining and barking, trotting out from the ranch and towards the wooded slope, looking back to see if the men were still following.

"Call him back, Cy," said Luke, "we have the direction now. Let's grab a few supplies, tend to the horses, and get on that trail." They hurried back to the front of the house, and leapt up the steps.

"Did you find her tracks?" asked Paul as soon as they came through the door.

"Yeah," answered Cy, "Jasper picked them right up. I'm going to get the horses ready," he said, hooking a thumb over his shoulder towards the yard.

"Can you put together some supplies for us Paul? Cy and I are going to need food and some bandages, just in case..." He stopped and cleared his throat.

"There was blood on the porch as well as in the yard, close to the other body." Jed let the thought hang in the air, his visage a mask of stone. "It would be good to be prepared. Maybe take along some whiskey too."

"If either one of them are hurt, I might need Cy to help me get them back here or to the doctor in Bridgeport," explained Luke, blowing out a breath. He looked at Rusty, then back at Paul. "I hate to leave you here alone, especially with Rusty needing care, but I don't think I could handle both of them if they are wounded."

"I'll be fine," said Paul, with a stubbornness Luke knew well.

"Thanks, Paul, I just wish..."

"He won't be here alone," said Jed, interrupting.

Luke stared hard at him, feeling a chill at what he saw in the eyes of the other man. But he also felt an unexpected sense of trust.

"You should be getting on her trail," said Jed quietly. "It's going to be cold tonight. We'll be fine here."

Chapter 28

Snake rode hard back to camp, his men strung out behind him to keep from eating all his dust. They knew his bad temper had been triggered; he had been challenged by Luke, rebuked by Jed, and had nothing to show for all the trouble he had gone to in an effort to scope out the ranch and make points with the boss. He reined his horse in hard, pulling the animals forelegs off the ground for an instant as he reached the camp. The big man literally jumped off his horse, nearly tumbling a man simply standing with a mug of coffee in his hand.

"Get out of my way!" he bellowed at the hapless cowpoke, who turned and walked away from the angry leader of their little band.

"What do we do now, Snake?" The man had just dismounted and was standing next to his horse, as were the others who had come into camp behind him.

"We get the rest of these no good, lazy dogs off their butts and into saddles and we go back and take that ranch apart!" He shouted the words, fists balled up by his sides, his face contorted into an ugly, red and purple blotched visage. "Even if the woman isn't there, I want Jed dead! No one challenges me like that! He's a filthy traitor and I'm going to kill him!"

"No, you are not."

The voice rang in the still air as Snake stopped raging. The whole camp had stilled to watch the man many detested as he lost control and ranted, streaming profanities about the character of Jed's mother and the destruction he planned to reign on the Rocking R Ranch. Snake whirled, hand on his gun, itching to shoot someone in

98

his fury. The color drained out of his face as he realized he was standing in front of Hal Colter and Sly Booker, who had his gun drawn and pointed at Snake.

"Mr. Colter! I didn't hear you come up!" faltered Snake.

"It's no wonder. You were screaming loud enough to be heard clear to town. There isn't a creature within two miles that doesn't know we are here now." Colter's voice was icy and his disgust showed as he glared at Snake.

"No need to have that gun on me!" protested Snake as it registered that Booker had not holstered his gun, but kept it leveled on him.

Booker did not lower the gun, nor did he take his eyes off Snake. In fact, he neither blinked nor appeared to breathe. The effect was eerie and unsettling, as evidenced by Snake's growing agitation. The gunman did not smile, but his eyes danced a little, enjoying the fact that the other man was uncertain and at least a little afraid.

"Put it away, Booker," said Hal without inflection. It irritated Snake that Booker smiled slightly at him as he slid the gun back into his holster. "You men stand down. Get something to eat or a cup of coffee and tend to your gear and horses, then rest up. We will have work to do soon."

The men seemed glad to have the direction, and drifted away from the confrontation to find a rock to plop on and drink coffee while they talked. A few settled down for a nap, with heads on their saddles and hats pulled over their eyes. The group that had ridden with Snake led their horses away to be tended to, then walked towards the chuck wagon for food.

"I'll see you over by my quarters in ten minutes," Colter said to Snake, low and tight lipped. Booker smiled at Snake and turned his horse towards the tent as well.

Dismounting, Colter and Booker handed the reins of their horses to another man, who took them to be unsaddled, brushed, and fed. The two outlaws entered the spacious tent, Colter sitting in a chair behind a table and Booker plopping onto an upturned stump by the door of the tent. The cook entered almost immediately with a coffee pot and two mugs.

"Want food?" asked Bean, who had an uncanny ability to make common campfire beans taste like a feast. He poured the coffee, handed a cup first to Colter, then to Booker, and set the pot on another stump in the tent.

"In about a half hour," replied Hal, "but we'll come to you. The cook nodded and left without saying another word. "We have a problem," said Hal to Sly.

They had just finished their conversation when Snake approached the tent, deliberately making noise so they did not think he was someone sneaking up on them. He cleared his throat outside the flap before speaking, obviously being cautious.

"Mr.Colter?" he inquired tentatively.

"Come in," he replied evenly.

Carefully, Snake moved the flap aside and stepped inside. He did not like it; having to stoop to enter, and going from the bright sunlight outside into the darker interior. He knew that put him at a disadvantage, and even though he thought the boss would not shoot, he was not so sure of Booker. He stood just inside the tent, and became aware that Booker sat to his right, an even more dangerous position.

"Sure glad to have you back, boss," he began in an attempt to smooth over the situation. He knew Hal was upset with him.

"Sounds like I got back just in time," said Hal slowly. "What the hell is going on?" He scowled at the standing figure before him. "Where's Joe? Where is Jed?"

"That's what I was so fired up about, boss!" Snake was regaining his confidence. "I sent Joe to scout that ranch and see what was there for the taking! We heard there was a woman there too, but we wanted to know how many men were there before we moved in on that ranch." He was feeling smug now.

"Where is Joe?" repeated Hal softly.

"Well, that's the thing. He didn't come back, so I sent Jed out to track him."

"What did Jed find?" Hal gave no indication that he was angry, so Snake continued.

"He found Joe's horse with blood on the saddle, so I took some men and we went to find out what happened!" He was pleased at his story and since the boss just sat looking at him, he kept talking. "That's when we saw Joe's body! It was just laying there in the yard at that ranch, and the coyotes had been at it! Jed went in to see if anybody was alive so we could kill them!"

"Where's Jed?" asked Hal, taking out the makings and rolling up a cigarette. He struck a match and shook it out, before throwing it at Snake's feet.

"That lowdown cuss! First he gets himself captured when those three men came back to the ranch, then when we went in to find out why he didn't come out, we found out he done throwed in with them and helped them save the fella Joe must have shot! That's why I was gonna take some men back and kill them all, especially Jed!"

Hal Colter rose slowly to his feet and walked around the table to face Snake. He blew smoke in his face, then reached out and grabbed his shirt front, dropping his lighted cigarette inside the clothing of the big man in front of him. Sly stepped up quickly behind Snake and pinned his arms behind him.

"Ahhh! Boss, please!" cried Snake, twisting and turning, trying to get free to stop the cigarette from burning his bare skin.

"You cost me two good men with your stupidity!" hissed Colter. "Now you listen, and you listen good. We are here to take the timber first, do you understand me! The ranch is not the job, you stupid crow bait!"

"I'm sorry, boss," whimpered Snake as the cloth on his shirt began to smoke. "Please!"

"Sly is replacing you as my new foreman. Now get out of my sight before I change my mind and decide to shoot you after all!"

He nodded to Sly, who threw Snake out of the tent, laughing as he hit the ground on his face, then rolled frantically, slapping at his chest and ripping open his shirt to rid himself of the burning tobacco.

Open red sores were on his chest and stomach as Snake got to his feet. He shot Sly a murderous look and edged his hand towards his holster, but stopped cold when Sly almost carelessly drew his gun and, still grinning, taunted him.

"You got your own red targets there, Snake," he jeered. "You ain't thinkin' of giving me a reason to try to hit a couple of them, are you?" He lost the grin and with a wolfish look in his eye, stared down the bigger man. "I'd be happy to oblige," he hissed.

Snake turned away and walked back towards the rest of the camp. But he did not stay on course. He veered off and went down to the stream, where he bathed his burns with cool water while he plotted a murder in his head.

Chapter 29

Ruth used sheer will to put one foot in front of the other, slowly switch backing down the side of the hill, refusing to look back. She knew her progress was dangerously slow. Both she and little Thomas needed medical care, and the longer he remained unconscious and unable to really take sustenance, the more she worried. If they had been on horseback, this was the better course to take; a cross country short cut to Bridgeport. But on foot, it was a more rugged path than the road to the little town nestled in the Sierra Nevada Mountains. She had no choice but to keep going and hope she could at least make it to the bottom of the hill before night fell over them.

The sun beat down on her, more exposed on the brushy slope than in the wooded hills. She used the rifle from time to time as a sort of crutch. She was tempted to sit and fire off three shots, but she was too far from any homestead to be heard. She dared not just waste the ammunition. She shuddered at the thought that the coyotes might decide they were easy prey.

Ruth clenched her jaw. The young rancher's wife pushed a shock of loose blond hair out of her face as she sat on a rock and took a drink from one of the canteens. She tried to dribble some into Thomas's mouth, and he did move his mouth as if in response, but she was still concerned. He looked so pale.

She would not give up! Her eyes scanned the landscape, searching for shelter, or Cottonwoods that would indicate water nearby. It might take her two days to walk to Bridgeport and there was nothing left in the first canteen. She slipped the strap over her head and set it down on the rock as she stood. Maybe it would at least serve as a clue for Luket, who might be tracking her.

It was nearly full on dark by the time she reached the bottom, shuffling her feet, too weary to lift them any longer. She trudged towards a small gathering of boulders she had used as a point of reference earlier, before the sun had sunk below the horizon. Through bleary eyes, she scanned the area for any signs of danger, at least what she could see in the fading light. Carefully, she placed the shawl with the child inside on the ground and dragged a few small pieces of wood and kindling toward a sunken spot in the ground. She had not been able to carry their blankets, but she did have a match, which she used to light the fire. Before settling down, she brought more wood closer. They were at a lower elevation now than they had been last night, but she knew it would still be cold and they would need a good fire to stay warm.

She took the pan from the sling over her back and added a little water, then put it on the edge of the fire. Adding a piece of jerky to make a broth for both of them, she settled down on the ground, drawing him closer, and chewing on another piece of jerky. She was almost too tired to chew, but she had to keep up her strength.

Ruth stroked the cheek of her son until the broth was ready. She used the same method as the night before, using another piece of the cleanest cloth from her petticoat to dribble the nourishing fluid into the corner of her son's mouth, again gratified as he swallowed. Finally, she drank the rest of the broth herself and with her son in her lap and her rifle resting at her knee, she threw another few small logs on the fire and fell asleep, leaning against a large rock.

Two hours later, she did not hear the man as he walked up to the fire and stared at her and the toddler. His eyes quickly assessed the situation. He leaned down and stroked her cheek, but her exhaustion was so great, she did not awaken or respond.

"Well, now, what's a pretty little thing like you doing out here all alone? And with a babe, too," he said softly. He moved her rifle to the side, and stooping, eased the sling over her head and laid the boy on the ground next to her. He knelt slightly, effortlessly picked her up, and carried the unconscious woman into the darkness.

Chapter 30

The next morning the camp buzzed with activity just as the sun was rising. Bean was already cleaning up breakfast dishes and men were saddling horses as Hal Colter climbed up on the chuck wagon and stood above them. Sly banged on a tin plate with a serving ladle and all eyes turned towards the noise. Men stopped what they were doing and drifted towards the wagon.

"It's time to get started on the job at hand," said Colter. "We are here to take all the timber we can off the north end of this range before anyone even knows we are here. We found it first, and I want to keep it that way!" He had no intention of telling them it was part of a legally claimed ranch; some of his hands might have scruples about stealing. "It will be long days – sun up to sun down, with no stops in between. Fill your canteens and grab a few strips of jerky from Bean on your way out of camp. Take everything you want to keep, we are breaking camp and reestablishing closer to the timber. Bean will follow us, but he will need time to set up, so we won't be returning until dark for any dinner. We are going to get in and get out with all the timber we can haul."

"Are we dragging it out by horse, boss?" asked one of the men.

"No. Wagons should already be close to our destination, with saws and real loggers to start logging immediately, then start taking out what we cut this morning. They will be going back and forth delivering the cut trees. You will be helping with the logging and standing guard. We don't expect anyone to interfere, but keep your guns close. Anyone who doesn't ride for the brand better leave now." His eyes ran over the crowd and saw one or two men that might not stand, but he would try to get some work out of them before he had to kill them. "Take your orders from me or Sly here," he said.

He fixed his eyes on Snake at the back of the group, but no one else looked at the former ram rod and Snake showed surprise for a moment, then lowered his head and did not meet his eyes. Hal nodded at Sly and jumped down from the wagon.

"We ride in fifteen minutes!" Sly commanded, and smiled in satisfaction as the men scattered. Maybe he could work with Hal after all.

The group moved quickly to get bedrolls behind saddles and dismantle the few shelters about the camp, packing tarps that had been used as protection against the weather or privacy of sorts, and packing saddlebags with jerky, and small personal items. They were moving across the open grassland towards the acres of timber before the sun topped the mountains. Colter and Sly rode at the lead, the men keeping a tight knit grouping as they cantered the horses.

An hour later, they came in sight of the timber and rode to the far end of the forest. There were six wagons lined up along the road. Several lumberjacks were already using the two man saws to cut down some of the trees.

"You four," yelled Colter, pointing to the cowhands in the lead, "secure your mounts and get axes to clean the trees of any branches." The riders responded and hitched their horses at the edge of a clearing. They shed their dusters and walked towards the loggers, who pointed to a pile of axes on the ground. They picked them up and got to work on the downed trees.

"Who do you want on guard?" asked Sly.

"You men there," directed Hal, pointing at another group of four, "get up on those ridges and watch for trouble. Sly, give them the flags." Sly pulled four white squares of cloth out of his saddlebags and passed them to the cowboys. "They are bigger than a neck scarf, so they should be easy to see," Colter continued. "If you see anything, step down from the ridge a bit and wave these flags back and forth over your heads."

"What if no one sees them?" asked one man.

"Why, that will be Snake's job," grinned Sly, directing the jibe at the big man who had not been assigned a duty yet.

"Snake will be stationed in the meadow," said Colter, meeting the man's eyes with a coolness that made the former ram rod

106

uncomfortable. "It will be his job to watch for the flags, take care of the horses, and help Bean."

It was a demotion and a cut to his ego, and everyone knew it. Snake wished he could just ride away, but he wanted to follow through with his plan first. He would get his revenge before he left, and then see who was laughing!

Chapter 31

Luke and Cy followed Jasper, who was better at tracking Ruth and the boy than just about any human they knew. The breed of the dog was known for its herding and tracking ability and Jasper did not disappoint. Luke had worried the dog would not move fast enough, but that was quickly dispelled when the medium sized dog ran ahead and turned to bark at them as if to prod them into coming along faster.

"She sure chose some rough country," commented Cy, as his horse picked the way gingerly through the thick brush and up slopes covered with shale.

"My wife is a good rider and knows this country well. What worries me is that she felt the need to try to take a short cut," said Randall, meeting Cy's gaze. "She wouldn't do that unless she felt it was unsafe to be on the main road, or..." he stopped, swallowed hard, and Cy finished the thought for him.

"Or unless she or your son were hurt and she was trying to get help fast."

"Yeah," the younger man nodded, "she would not have left Rusty like that unless she was afraid for our boy. If she was just going for the doc, she would have stayed on the main road."

Both men turned their attention to Jasper as he stood in a cluster of trees near the top of the ridge and barked furiously at the two. He ran to the cover of the trees and back again repeatedly while they made their way up, anguish permeating his animal sounds. As soon as Cy and Luke reached him, he ran forward again and they followed as quickly as was prudent.

He stood, barking loudly near a mound of something dark brown. As they approached, they could smell the death. Dismounting, the men walked forward until they stood in stunned silence at what clearly were the bloody remains of a horse. Luke recognized the saddle as one that belonged to the ranch; he knew the horse was one of his as well.

"Coyotes been at it, but they didn't bring it down," said Cy, slowly walking around the horse. "See the rocks? Something caused a rock slide and must have knocked the horse to the ground."

"She camped here," said Luke, stooping to pick up a piece of light brown material. He quickly recognized it as a piece of cloth from a petticoat that had been soaked in a beef broth. He fingered the cloth as he stood, reading the sign. "Coyotes came close, but the horse was easy prey."

"Coffee pot is still here, but the fire is cold," Cy filled in as he squatted to hold a hand over the coals. They were completely devoid of heat. "She couldn't carry it."

"She left the blankets too," said Luke, kicking at leaves that had blown over the blankets on the ground. "She's in trouble, Cy." He suddenly bent and picked up a blanket, smelling a brown spot on the cloth. "Blood." He didn't need to say more. At least one of them was wounded.

His face a mixture of fear and sadness, Luke turned to the sound of Jasper barking again. The dog stood on the top of the ridge, urging them to follow. The riders did not need any more encouragement; they were in their saddles in seconds and following the herder over the top.

Jasper bounded down the slope, but wisely, the range wise men gave their horses their heads and let them pick their own path down the shale laden hill side. Brush and shrubs grew among the loose rock, which helped keep it from just giving way and sending them all tumbling to the bottom, but still, it would do no good to have horse or man break a leg.

It took them the better part of three hours to wind their way down the side of the mountain until it became little more than a slope. It was pitch black, with no moon where they stopped. Luke strained his eyes, thinking he saw a small, bright spot in the distance, but it disappeared and he could not be certain. The ground was unpredictable here.

"What do you think, Luke?" asked Cy. Jasper had settled down to rest a few feet from the hooves of the horse.

"I think we should stop before we kill one of our horses," sighed Luke. "I really want to go on; I think we are close, but we can't see anything." There was no moon and clouds shrouded the stars, leaving them in near pitch black darkness.

Cy immediately built a small fire. They unsaddled and rubbed their horses down, giving them water out of their hats. When they were done, they sat at the fire, chewing on some jerky while they waited for the coffee to be ready.

"If she is somewhere she can see this fire, even if it is a couple of miles off, it could give her hope. It might make her believe she only has to hang on a little longer," spoke Cyrus gently.

"You're right," said Luke in resignation.

They bedded down, planning to start before dawn. They did not know, at this very moment, that a wagon carrying Luke's unconscious family, was moving away from them in the night.

Chapter 32

Bean had arrived, and with the grumbling help of Snake, had managed to set up the chuck wagon and roll out biscuits and bacon, with lots of fresh hot coffee, for dinner the night before. He found he barely had enough plates and cups for all the men, and he did not like that one bit. He worried about running out of food, which is something a cook never wants to face.

Snake was relegated to collecting wood for the fire, which caused his temper to smolder as he caught the looks of the men he used to command. Once the top dog under Hal Colter, he now found himself a laughing stock, at best pitied, and it fed the anger in the pit of his stomach. He spent every spare minute plotting revenge; sometimes chuckling at the cruel things he wished on his enemies.

The sentries had come down from the mountain tops in shifts to eat, and with the additional six lumberjacks, the cook was busy and cranky. Things came to a head when a big lumberjack wanted a third helping of bacon and biscuits.

"You've already had six biscuits and four big slices of bacon!" snapped the harried cook.

"I'm a big man and I work hard all day!" growled the timber cutter, who towered over the cook. The lumberjack stood six feet four inches tall, with massive shoulders and upper arms; the result of years of hard work. He was double the weight of the slender, five foot six inch tall cook, but Bean operated on the premise that the man might be bigger, but he was meaner! He reached over and picked up a huge meat cleaver and brandished it with menace.

"You reach for another biscuit and it'll be the last thing you reach for with that hand!"

The lines were being drawn with the cowboys lining up beside Bean and the lumberjacks bracing their own, when the snap of a shotgun being racked and the sharp voice of Hal Colter split the air.

"That will be enough! You all work for me, and there will be no fighting among you as long as you are on my payroll!" Colter strode into the firelight and glared at the men. "Bean, what is this about," he asked, showing deference to the only man in camp at least as important as himself.

"This big galoot has already had seconds and he wants thirds! There ain't gonna be enough for the men on the mountain tops to eat if he keeps it up!"

"Are we running low on food?" asked Hal in surprise.

"Well, yeah, the boys ate as much when they were not working as they do now, probably because there was nothing else to do. Now we added six more men that eat more than our cowboys and we ain't restocked! I can only stretch the food so far!" The cook was clearly upset that he did not have the supplies to do his job.

"What do you have for breakfast?" asked Hal.

"I got a few eggs, some bacon, coffee, and more biscuits, but I am running low on flour too. I got bread and beans for the nooning and a little beef for a stew tomorrow night, but then we got nothing unless you send someone out to hunt."

"Alright, you men all settle down. What's your name?" he asked the big logger.

"Sean," he answered.

"Well, Sean, we got to have something to feed everyone tonight, so no more for anyone beyond seconds, got it?" A few grumbled, but most nodded, realizing the fairness of the statement. "Tomorrow I'll send one of the men into Bridgeport to buy some supplies and tomorrow night, there will be plenty of food." He stared Sean down until the huge lumberjack turned and walked away.

"I'll make a list," said Bean.

"Sounds good!" replied Colter. "Everyone get some sleep!" The men were only two happy to comply, rolling up in their blankets and dozing off.

One of the men from the mountain walked in, looking beat. Colter eyed him sharply. He looked around the camp, then called Sly over to him. He motioned to the cowboy half asleep as he ate, then swept an arm around the camp.

"We need to rotate the men on the mountain. Put them on four hour shifts and notify their replacements. We need everyone to be sharp and rested in case of trouble."

"Just our cowboys?" asked Sly.

"Yes, the lumber jacks are much better at their job and I want them efficiently cutting all day." He thought for a moment. "Send Snake up for duty too, but don't sleep where he can see you." Sly understood and nodded.

"Good advice," he said. "You too, boss." Both men knew Snake could no longer be trusted, but they needed every man they had right now.

"I want you to be the one to go into town for the supplies tomorrow. No one knows you, so you can tell them a story about needing some supplies to grubstake a friend in Carson City. Take an extra horse and load up. I'll give you the money in the morning. Eat first and leave right after breakfast."

Colter stood off away from the fire watching the men as Sly went to a few who were not in bedrolls yet and sent them up the mountain, telling them who to wake to relieve them. Hal did not miss the belligerent look Snake cast at Sly as he was told to take a watch on the mountain. He also saw the murderous look on his face as he stalked away. He would need to keep a close eye on the man. This would not end without someone dead, and he didn't plan to be the one put six feet under.

Chapter 33

Ruth had a sense of being moved. Someone was carrying her! Luke! She opened her eyes briefly, but all she saw was the underside of a big, bushy, dark beard. Panic coursed through her. Where was her baby? Where was she? Who was this man? He bent slightly to enter a dark room that felt like a cave. She was aware of another voice, but she could not keep her eyes open. She felt her son placed next to her and she breathed a sigh of relief. Eyes too heavy to open, she felt for his small hand. It was so cold! She struggled to come awake; she had to warm her son!

Ruth heard soft voices and hands reached between her and her son. She struggled to come to consciousness, but they took him away. She tried so hard to fight, to stop them, whoever they were, but her left arm would not move at all and her right arm felt so very heavy. Her eyes would not stay open. Someone was unbuttoning her blouse and she could do nothing to stop them. They took her pocket purse off her waist and she felt a sharp stab of pain as it pulled underneath her. She could hear the voices, but she could not respond.

"What have you done? Why did you bring them here!" It was a woman's voice, and it was tinged with fear.

"I had to bring them here! Look at them!" said a man's voice. "I found them in the desert with no protection, a dying fire, and they are in bad shape."

"It's too dangerous! You should have taken them to the doctor in Bridgeport!" The woman was close to Ruth and it seemed as if she was cutting the sleeve of her blouse.

"Look at them, woman!" The man repeated himself, an edge to his voice. "I don't think they could make it to Bridgeport. They

114

likely would have died on the way! They are barely alive and we have to help them."

"And what if they die here? You know what they will do to us." The woman sounded as if she were fighting back tears.

Silence followed for what seemed several minutes, as they continued to undress Ruth, examining her arm and her ribs, and speaking a language Ruth did not understand or recognize. She was using every ounce of her will to stay conscious enough to listen, even if she could not move. But she faded out, her ears ringing and bright light flashing in her head as the pain hit her again. She fought her way back through a gray fog to listen again. There seemed to be another person there, a woman or girl, and it sounded like she was undressing the small boy, washing him and examining his wound. She heard the woman cluck her tongue.

"I am sad for them, especially this little one, but it has brought much danger on us. If they die here…" Her voice trailed off.

"Then we will bury them in the desert and have a big brush fire over their graves and no one will ever find them." The man spoke quietly, matter-of-fact, and as if he had already made up his mind.

No! Luke will never find us! My baby! He cannot die! Oh God, please help us! Ruth   felt a scream welling up inside her: she wanted to scream, but her body would not obey her. She could not move, she could not speak, and suddenly, there was a jolt of pain that was excruciating. She felt herself falling, weightless, down into a darkness that wrapped itself around her and refused to let her go.

Chapter 34

Lucas Randall was up before the sky even began to turn gray around the edges. He had the horses saddled and coffee made by the time the smell of the dark brown liquid reached Cy's nostrils and stirred him to a wakeful state. The cowboy sat up, looked at his boss, rubbed his hands over his face, and reached for his boots, tapping them out to make sure nothing had crawled inside them while he slept. He pulled them on and, having slept in the rest of his clothes, he stood, then leaned over and picked up his gun belt and strapped it around his slim hips.

"Thanks," he grinned as Luke handed him a hot cup of coffee. He took a few swallows, then accepted a biscuit, which he ate hurriedly. Luke drew a softer piece of jerky out and gave it to Jasper, with a small pan of water. Cy knew and understood the rancher's need to get going as soon as they could see.

The sun was not yet over the ridge fifteen minutes later when they walked the horses slowly forward, each man searching carefully for sign, and letting Jasper go ahead, sniffing and weaving back and forth. Suddenly, the dog yapped a couple of times, pointed his nose towards some rocks, and began running.

The two were in their saddles in seconds, and cantering after the dog, trusting their horses and hoping the mounts would be able to see any holes in the ground and avoid them. The land was still mostly in shadow, but the rising sun sent light forward to announce its coming and it was easier to see what lay before them.

A half mile from the base of the mountain, Jasper stopped and barked loudly, running back and forth and whimpering. The two men urged their horses on until they came up to the dog, then they

116

slid off and let the reins drop as their momentum carried them forward.

A fire smoldered near the base of a rock, untended, and obviously hours old. No new wood had been added recently. A pan sat at the edge of the fire, all the liquid gone now, the bottom blackened. There were indentations in the sand at the base of a rock, where someone had rested. The near empty canteen lay in the dirt on its side, accompanied by a small bag that held a few pieces of jerky and some coffee. There were tracks that led up to the rock and then away again.

"Those are a man's boot prints," said Luke, pointing to the impressions in the sand.

"He just walked on in here. It doesn't look like she tried to stop him." Cy looked at his friend. They both knew that likely meant she was unconscious. Even asleep, she would have awakened and fought him, or stood on her own.

"The prints are deeper walking away, so he must have carried her." Luke was kneeling, examining the prints.

"Seems he took her this way," said Cy, following the tracks. "There was a wagon here." He pointed forward.

"The man came back a second time for the boy," said Randall. "I'd like to think that makes him a good man, but who is he? Why was he out here? And where did he take my family?"

"Let's see if we can track the wagon," suggested Cy, watching Jasper trying to pick up the scent. "He is having more trouble because he can't get anything off the ground or a bush," said the older rider, rubbing his chin. They followed for a mile, until they came to hardened granite slabs. They circled and crossed back and forth, but could not find a trail. Jasper nosed back and forth, whimpering in concern and frustration.

"One thing is for sure," said Luke, "the wagon was not headed to Bridgeport."

"What do you want to do, Luke?" asked Cy softly, switching to the familiar use of his boss' name. He waited patiently, feeling the anguish of any decision.

"Let's keep circling," said Randall. "I have to." He looked at Cy, seeking his reaction.

"I was hoping you would say that," replied the cowboy. He read the relief on Luke's face and was very glad he did not have the burden on his shoulders that was bearing down on his boss. Still, this was the only family he had, and he would do anything to help.

They circled, letting Jasper have the run of the land, until noon, stopped briefly, then continued until they could no longer see. The tracking was painstakingly slow with the drifting sand and no scent on the ground for Jasper. It was a silent campfire that night. It was as if Ruth and the child had just disappeared into thin air.

Luke slept restlessly, which caused Jasper to stir and Cy to wake frequently. By pre-dawn the next day, they were all bleary eyed, sitting around the campfire, drinking strong coffee, and waiting for enough light to keep going. Jasper chewed on his jerky strip, but even he seemed to be sad.

"What do you want to do this morning, boss?" asked Cy, scratching Jasper behind his ears with one hand as he drank the strong brew.

"I think we head to Bridgeport and ask for help looking for them," sighed the rancher. "Maybe get someone to go to the ranch and help out, in case that salty crew comes back before we do."

"Yeah, I think medically speaking, Rusty is in good hands, but they might need another gun if trouble rides in." Cy looked at the sky and rose to his feet. "I'll get the fire if you want to get the horses," he said.

Minutes later, they were in their saddles and riding. But they did not move too fast; they were still looking for any tracks or sign that would lead them to the missing woman and child. They rode into Bridegport, a sorry duo, a couple of hours after sunrise.

"Lucas! It is good to see you!" Axel had looked up from sweeping the walkway in front of his general store at the sound of hoof beats. His face lit up as he saw his friend, and he leaned the broom against the wall, calling into the interior for his wife to come and greet their visitor.

Two very weary men slid from their saddles, tied the reins loosely around the hitching rail, and stepped up on the boardwalk just as Hannah and Adele bubbled out of the store front, laughing and hugging him.

"Where are Ruth and Thomas?" smiled Hannah, but her smile faltered at the pained look on the face of her friend.

118

"What has happened, Luke?" Axel spoke gently. "Come inside," he motioned to the two men and shot a glance to his wife, who nodded and took Adele's hand, leading her back inside.

In the kitchen, the three men sat, while Hannah set four mugs in front of them. The young girl carried a plate of cookies to the table, looked up at Luke, and hugged him fiercely around his waist. She didn't know what was wrong, but she knew he was sad. They waited until Hannah poured coffee for all, then sat, with Adele curled in her lap, munching on a cookie.

"Last I heard, you were taking your cattle to market in Virginia City," opened Axel, "what has happened, Luke?"

The young husband and father sighed and rubbed his hands over his face, looked into the eyes of his friends and told the story. No one spoke until he was done. Luke stared at his coffee, both hands wrapped around the mug. Axel looked from Luke to Cy, waiting; he knew there was more.

"We need help to find them," said Cy, guessing his boss had a lump in his throat. Luke looked at his ranch hand with gratitude.

"Stay here," said Axel, standing and striding out of the room.

As if on cue, Hannah stood, deposited Adele in her now vacated chair, and began to prepare lunch for all. She fried up some strips of beef, warmed some beans, and sliced some bread. She refilled the coffee cups of the two men who sat silently at her table. The store keepers wife put down a dish of water for Jasper, and a small plate of meat scraps. Placing fresh butter on the table, she set plates in front of all, and by the time Axel returned, had served up big portions of hot food.

"Eat," she said," I know you haven't had a good meal in days, and you will need your strength," she commanded.

"I talked to Mark at the hotel," interjected Axel between bites of the delicious food,
"and he is getting a few men together. They will be here in a few minutes, so clean your plates." Just as they finished the last of their coffee, Mark walked through the store and into the kitchen.

"I've got eight men outside, Luke, and we are all ready to stay on the trail until we find them," he said, his mouth set in a grim line.

"Take these," said Hannah, who had busied herself at the sink while the men finished their coffee and then planned their search."

She handed Axel, Luke, and Cy each a cloth bag. "It will get you through at least a few days if need be." She handed Cyrus a smaller package, wrapped in a waxed brown paper. "For Jasper," she smiled.

Jasper rubbed against her legs as if to say thank you, looked up at Hannah, then walked to the door and sat on his haunches. He knew something was about to happen and he had no intention of being left out. He followed the four men as they walked through the store and out to the porch.

Luke recognized all but one or two of the men, and he stood on the porch, telling them what he knew. They exchanged looks with each other; this family was well known and liked in the town.

"I hope we find something today," said Luke, not wanting to voice his fear, "but if not, we could be out a couple of days." His eyes searched the faces of each man in the group, and were reassured by what he saw.

"We're in it until we find them," said Kaleb, owner of the livery stable. He quickly surveyed the knot of men and saw the nods he expected. "You would do the same for any man of us who was searching for their family." Rumblings of assent passed through the crowd.

"We brought your horse up, Axel," said Jim, one of the new comers to town. The tall, lanky man was clad in buckskins and a hat fashioned from the pelt of a raccoon. His voice was steady, and his eyes held steel in them; a look of determination and capability that gave Luke hope.

Axel stowed his rifle and filled his saddlebags with extra ammunition and the food Hannah had packed for him. He went back inside and got his canteen and a few extras.

"Anyone need more ammo or any supplies? This is my best friend, and I will give ammo, water, or food to any man who is helping."

"I could use a few more rounds of ammo, just in case we run into real trouble," said a man Luke did not know. "But I can and will pay for it," he said stubbornly. Everyone understood; pride was big in the west.

"Go get what you need, Clay," said Axel. "New family in town," said the store keeper to Lucas. "Clay Matthews is the kind we hope sticks around." The other young rancher quickly dismounted and just as quickly returned, stuffing a few boxes of rifle rounds into his saddlebags.

They rode out of town at a gallop, anxious to get to where they lost the wagon tracks and fan out from there. The day was already half gone and every hour counted. Jasper lay across the saddle on Cy's lap to save his energy for the real hunt.

Six miles out of town, they came to the spot where they had lost the tracks. Jim, looking even taller in his buckskins was off his horse and walking, studying the tracks, before all the men had caught up. When he came to the end of the granite field, he knelt and sifted the dirt, looking to the east. He stood and walked back to Luke.

"I think we need to go that way," he said, pointing to the east and then turning his piercing dark brown eyes back to Luke.

"We didn't find any tracks that way before," protested Randall, "what makes you think they went in that direction?"

"They covered their tracks well, using soil, but it is not the right soil for this land."

"I don't understand," said Cy.

"It is soil that comes from another area, likely this dirt came from a plant box, something they would use to transport seedlings."

Luke dismounted and walked with Jim to the place where he knelt again and picked up a handful of dirt. He opened his palm to Luke and the young rancher cursed.

"I should have seen that; I come from a farming background! Luke shook his head.

"Hard to tell the difference until it is in full sunlight," replied Jim.

"Okay, we look east!" said Randall, standing. "Thanks," he said to Jim.

They searched another mile before Cy rode up to his boss and pointed to the northeast.

"Wagon," said Cy, pointing. In the distance, a wagon was raising a little dust as it headed diagonally across their back trail towards town. Luke, Cy, Jim, and Axel galloped in that direction, coming up on the wagon and its occupants.

A man and a woman sat on the seat of the wagon, which had a low cover over the top. The bed of the wagon was deep and wooden with only a few feet of canvas stretching over the top. It was a shorter than usual wagon and looked custom made.

"Ho the wagon!" shouted Luke, but it continued on as if they had not heard. The man and woman on the wagon seat sat rigid, staring straight ahead. They were trotting the horses and moving at a good clip. The four men looked at each other, then shucked their rifles. Cy rode to the far side of the wagon, Axel was near the front closest to Luke, Jim covered the rear, and Luke galloped up in front, then swung Pepper around and faced the oncoming team of horses. He brought his rifle up, aimed straight at the chest of the man driving and shouted again. "Stop the wagon now!" He fired a warning shot over the top of the wagon and then brought the gun to bear on the shirt front of the driver again.

The man pulled hard on the reins of the horses and brought the wagon to a stop. He was a big man and was obviously nervous, shifting his eyes back and forth to the sides of the wagon, then to Luke. The woman was frightened half to death, her black dress and bonnet only serving to accentuate the stark white, bloodless pale of her face. She was clenching her hands in her lap so hard her knuckles were white.

"Why didn't you stop?" demanded Luke. "What are you hiding in that wagon?"

"Hiding?" stammered the man. His black, flat crowned hat was pulled low, obscuring a clear view of his eyes. "My wife is in the back. She is ill and we are hurrying to get her to the doctor. We heard there was one in Bridgeport."

"Jeremiah..." began the woman next to him, tears starting down her face. She clutched his hands with her own now.

"It will be alright, Susan," he assured her.

"She looks awfully pale," said Cy, who had come closer to the wagon and was searching the face of the woman on the wagon seat. "Is she sick?"

"No, my wife is just frightened."

"I thought you said your wife was in the back of the wagon and she was the one that was sick," said Luke, a prickly feeling climbing his spine.

Suddenly Jasper jumped off the saddle and ran to the back of the wagon, barking furiously and running back and forth.

"Come out of the wagon with your hands up!" shouted Jim from the back. By now the other riders had reached them and surrounded the wagon.

A younger woman with blond hair, dressed completely in black like the woman in the wagon seat, stood up slowly in the back of the wagon, holding her hands up. Mark and Kaleb dismounted and moved to the sides of the wagon, dropping the gate. Mark reached up and handed the woman down to the ground.

Luke and Axel walked the couple from the wagon seat to the back, where the women immediately flew into each others arms and stood crying. Jasper was leaping at the gate of the wagon, trying to get into the back, alternately barking and whimpering.

"What is it, boy?" asked Cy, dismounting and joining his dog. He looked into the back of the wagon and froze. "Luke." He tilted his head in silence and the young rancher handed his rifle to Axel, then walked to look into the back of the wagon.

What he saw made him feel sick. Two lumps lay under blankets in the back. Lumps that were the size of Ruth and Thomas.

"Ruth!" he started to leap into the back, but Jeremiah grabbed his arm and pulled him back. Luke's face contorted into pure fury as he shook the man's hand off his arm and grabbed the front of his shirt with both hands. "If that is my wife and son in the back of this wagon, I will kill you with my bare hands!" he roared.

"They are very sick! You must not move them!" sputtered Jeremiah.

Luke jumped into the back of the wagon and carefully pulled the blanket back, holding his breath, afraid of what he would see. He sucked in his breath as he saw the pale faces lying beneath the blanket. His hand shook as he reached his fingers out to touch their necks, first Thomas, then Ruth, feeling for a pulse. The breath whooshed out of his lungs and he bent forward, eyes closed. They were alive!

"What happened to my wife and child?" demanded Lucas, jumping out of the wagon.

"I found them and we tried to care for them until they could be moved," said Jeremiah softly. "They were badly hurt when I found them. They were both unconscious." His hazel eyes stared bleakly into eyes filled with fear and anger at the same time.

"Where did you find them? When?"

"We can talk later. Right now, we need to get them to the doctor," said Jeremiah.

"Get back on the bench," said Lucas, realizing he was right. "The two women can ride back here with me and Axel will ride with you."

"It is not proper!" The younger blond woman was disconcerted.

"It will be alright, Faith, you and Susan will be together. He helped them into the back and Luke climbed in after them.

Luke sat on one side of the wagon and the women sat on the other as the wagon started to move rapidly towards town. He held Ruth's hand and moved his son to his lap, stroking the young boy's cheek. Suddenly, Thomas opened his eyes and looked into the face of his father!

"Oh, sweet God!" said Faith, looking at Susan. The two women stared into Luke's eyes, their mouths agape.

"He has not opened his eyes or really moved the whole time he has been with us," said the older of the two women.

She spoke softly, and Luke pulled his eyes from Thomas to study her face for a moment. He saw nothing malignant there, and shifted his eyes back to the boy. Anguish twisted in his stomach as he realized the small boy had closed his eyes again. Ruth had not moved, nor did she give any indication that she knew he was there with them. What did all this mean?

Chapter 35

Sly Booker rode with a wary eye on the hills around him. He never rode anywhere without watching for trouble. He did that once, and it almost got him killed. Now, he trailed a horse behind him with a sawbuck saddle sitting atop the mount to carry supplies on the trip home. It added to his image as a simple cowpoke going into town for supplies, but it irritated him to be assigned what he considered errand boy duties.

"Snake should be running around fetching all this stuff," he grumbled. "If he weren't such a foozler, he would be doing this rat bag work instead of me!"

It was a beautiful, mild day, but Sly rode with a dark cloud of unhappiness over him, and he noticed none of the bright blue skies, deep green pines, or the turning leaves of the aspens. He was a few miles from town when his attention was drawn to a dust cloud rapidly approaching the town from the north east. He reined his horse in and sat watching the brown air for several minutes, scratching his chin. If there was some kind of raiding party headed towards the town, he sure didn't want to meet it on the way in, or be trapped in the town for a fight.

"Naw," he muttered out loud, "we are the only outlaws around with any size group, and there hasn't been any trouble with the Piute or Shoshone in years." They were easy to get along with as long as they were left alone. His curiosity got the better of him, and he kicked his horse into a trot and entered town, watching carefully.

There was a commotion near the general store and a gathering in front of the doctor's office. Sly turned off the main street and rode between the buildings to near the back of what he pegged as the general store. He dismounted, slipping the reins of the horses over the handles of a wheelbarrow then walked back to the front of the building and blended into the crowd.

The wagon was in front of the doctor's office, so he moved there first, standing at the corner of the alleyway, partially hidden in shadow. He watched as a young cowboy came to the back of the wagon and handed an unconscious woman down to a big man who had come from the front of the wagon. Another cowboy had dismounted and climbed into the back of the wagon. Mark reappeared, carrying a silent child in his arms as he squatted, sat, then eased to the ground so he would not jar the boy.

The two men carried their unconscious patients into the doctor's office as the crowd talked in hushed tones. Sly was about to leave when he noted another big man dressed in black with a white shirt come to the back of the wagon and help two women dressed completely in black down to the ground.

One of the townspeople broke from the crowd and walked rapidly to the general store, talking excitedly to those that were gathered at a respectful distance. It was then that Sly noticed Cyrus coming out of the store with another woman. He spoke sternly to the people and they parted to let the two through.

What is Cyrus James doing here? Sly stepped a little further back into the shadows of the alley. If Cy saw him, it would arouse suspicion. Especially if he saw the supplies on the horse as he rode out of town. The supplies! He slipped down the alley and came up on the opposite side of the general store. Across the street, Cy was intent on speaking to a tall, slender woman he was guiding through the door of the doctor's office.

Sly considered his options. He did not want to step up on the porch and risk being seen, but he needed to get the grub and get out of town. The door. There had been a door in the back of the general store. It likely led into the living quarters for the owners, but if he was lucky, everyone in town was gathered around the doctor's office. It was worth a try. Maybe he could get in and out without being seen. He grinned. He might get away with stealing the supplies and keep the money Colter had given him.

"Go in and help with Ruth and Thomas," said Cy, reassuring Hannah. "I'll handle the crowd at your store."

"What's going on?" Axel asked, looking at the people milling in front of the store as he came out of the doctor's office. Hannah exchanged a meaningful look with her husband, then disappeared inside.

"One of the drovers over there is firing up the crowd, accusing the three from the wagon of being Latter Day Saints." Cy motioned to the three people in black, standing uncertainly beside the window of the doctor's office. "That idiot is saying this man tried to kidnap Ruth and make him another one of his wives!" He gestured to a scruffy looking tall, skinny man he did not recognize.

"Tell me what happened," said the big German shop keeper, as he stepped up to the man in black. His voice was level, but he conveyed that he would brook no lies.

"I found them in the desert, unconscious," answered Jeremiah, his voice trembling slightly, his arms around the two women.

"Where?" asked Axel, noting the two ladies looked at him in fear.

"About a mile from the base of the mountain, there," said the man in black, pointing to the range that sat between The Rocking R and Bridgeport.

"What was she doing there with the child?" puzzled the merchant.

"Sir, I do not know. I was out looking to fill our water barrels and try to find the trail to meet our people. I saw a fire, and found them unconscious. I could not leave them there." His steady eyes met Axel's without flinching.

"We only tried to help," said Susan earnestly.

"We were afraid our husband would bring trouble to us by bringing them home. That seems to be true," said Faith, looking fearfully across the street at the small crowd at the general store. The voices were louder and sounded more angry.

"Your husband...," started Axel. He stopped, as he remembered it was part of their belief that a man could have more than one wife at a time.

"But he was right," said Susan, "they needed some care before they could survive the trip into town. We cleaned them both and set her arm and wrapped her ribs as best we could."

"And the poor babe," said Faith, shaking her head. "We put a poultice on his head, but both of them were severely in need of water and nourishment."

"Axel," said Cy, a tone to his spoken word that made the man turn quickly. Several men that had recently been hired to work a cattle drive at one of the new ranches were striding across the street, anger written on their faces.

"What's going on here?" Axel turned to face the men, putting himself between the advancing mob and the three people behind him.

"We don't want their kind here!" snarled the leader, a big, burly man with a dirty shirt and down at the heel boots.

"Their kind?" asked Axel. The man did not know the big storekeeper or he would have backed away once he saw the set of his jaw and his thinned lips.

"Filthy adulterers! It is sinful to have two wives!" The skinny drover shouted the words with an ugly tone.

"He kidnapped that woman and her child so he could force her to be his third wife!" shouted another man. "They have no shame!"

"No!" exclaimed Jeremiah, taking a step forward. "That is not true!"

"Liar! We're gonna make you wish you never came near this town or touched that woman!" The big man with the dirty shirt reached behind his back and pulled a large knife. "I'm gonna make sure you never touch another decent woman again!" He fixed his eyes on Jeremiah and started forward.

The big German assumed a fighting stance, and Cy put his hand on the butt of his revolver, but before he could draw his gun, a shot rang through the air and the dirt at the foot of the knife wielding man spat upward. All eyes turned to the man on the horse holding the rifle to his shoulder.

"That'll be enough," said Jim. The buckskin clad newcomer to their town had hard eyes and a ready trigger on his Winchester. "I may be new here, but I ain't new to these kinds of vigilante shenanigans. As long as I'm holdin' this rifle, you are going to sheath that knife and wait for the law to sort this out."

"There's only one of you, and six of us," sneered the man wielding the knife. "You can't get all of us before we get you." His eyes flitted to his compadres, some of which were watching the man on the horse, with their hands on the butts of their guns.

"You better count again," said Luke. He had come from the interior of the office when he heard the rifle shot. The man with the knife turned and went pale as he saw Axel, Cyrus, and Luke all standing with guns drawn. As if on cue, Jim racked his rifle.

The silence was broken by the stomp of boots on the boardwalk, and Luke, knowing the others would keep their eyes on the mob, turned to see Clay walking towards them. He stopped next to Randall, and hands on his hips, glared at the group of men in the street, then turned to Luke.

"What's this about?" Clay demanded.

"These men were about to attack these three people behind me," answered Luke, throwing a thumb over his shoulder with his free hand.

"Why?" asked Clay in surprise.

"They kidnapped that woman and child inside!" The man with the dirty shirt puffed up his chest in righteous indignation. "He is one of them unholy bastards that take more than one woman in a land where women are scarce!"

The two women behind Axel gasped and covered their faces, pressing into the chest of Jeremiah, who stood like a rock, his face turning red with anger.

"Watch your mouth!" growled Clay. "There are ladies present!"

"Them ain't ladies, they ain't no better'n whores..." began the scruffy man.

Clay stepped off the porch so fast no one had time to respond. The young family man swung a powerful fist full into the mouth of the man with the grease spotted shirt, sending him sprawling into the dirt, causing his friends to step back.

"I told you to watch your filthy mouth!" barked Clay, standing over the man, his fists still clenched.

"Come on, boss..." began one of the other men.

"I'm not your boss anymore!" He whirled on the speaker, but his eyes burned into every one of them. "No man who acts like this will work for me, now get out!" He reached into his vest pocket and removed three twenty dollar gold pieces, which he tossed into the dirt. "That's more than enough to pay all of you for the work you did," he seethed. "Now it would be best if you got out of my sight, and take this piece of trash with you!"

Clay reached down and yanked the man on the ground up by his shirt, and threw him at the group of men. Two of the discharged cowboys grabbed his arms before he landed face first in the street, and dragged him off towards the saloon. Another man stooped and picked up the gold pieces, then followed the others.

"Those are your men?" asked Luke, appraising the young rancher.

"Not anymore," said Clay, lifting his hat and running his fingers through his hair. "I hired them over in Carson City to help me get my cattle branded and my ranch fixed up before winter, but I won't have men like that working for me. I don't want them around my family either!" He stepped towards Susan and Faith, hat in hand. "I'm sure sorry for all that, ladies, they had no call to say those things or use that language around you."

"We didn't hurt that woman and child," said Jeremiah earnestly. "We would not do such a thing. We were trying to help."

"I know that, Jeremiah," said Luke, thrusting his hand out to the big man in black. "I owe you an apology as well. The doc says if it weren't for you and these two ladies, my wife and child might not be alive."

"They will be okay then?" interjected Susan.

"Yes. In fact, Ma'am, the doc and Hannah sent me out to ask if you would be so kind as to go in and help. They could use the extra hands."

"Go," nodded Jeremiah as his wives looked to him with entreaty. "Help them in whatever way you can." Jeremiah nodded at the women and Susan and Faith slipped quickly inside, followed by Luke.

"We are not like those men," said Axel, his heavy German accent showing more than usual. "There are many people here of different beliefs. You helped our good friend and his family. You are welcome to stay here if you wish."

"Thank you. But we wish to join a group of our own people outside of Carson City. We got separated when the yoke on our wagon cracked and we fell behind. I was out looking for a trail and filling our water barrel when I came upon the woman and child in the desert."

"I'd be happy to guide you to their settlement," said Jim. All eyes swung to the man on horseback. They had almost forgotten he was there.

"We would be so grateful," said Jeremiah in surprise, turning his eyes to the man who had first stepped in to defend them.

"If you need a little more help with that wagon and a day to rest up, we have room at my ranch," offered Clay. "It's only a couple miles outside of town." He stood, surveying the wagon tongue, noticing it was coated with a tar like substance and bound in cloth. "We can cut some wood to replace this wagon tongue if you have the time," he said, meeting the eyes of the big man in black. "It looks like you patched it up as best you could, but it still might not make it to Carson City."

"That's very generous of you!" Jeremiah looked uncertain for a moment. "You are right, we had some pine tar in the wagon and coated the tongue, but we did not have any leather to bind around it. We cut up one of our canvas patches for the wagon cover, but I admit, I am worried it may not hold for any distance." Jeremiah looked relieved for the first time since he had encountered the group of townsmen.

"It's the least I can do. I was desperate and hired those men. They mistreated you and your family," said the young rancher. "My wife would love to have the company of a couple of women. Not many come all the way out to the ranch."

"Well," said Jeremiah with slight hesitation. He studied Clay and looked at Jim, then nodded decisively. "We will come. Thank you; it will be a good test for the wagon tongue and I know Faith and Susan would enjoy the company of another woman."

"I'll ride out tomorrow morning and see how it is coming along," said Jim. "I can be ready to go whenever you are ready."

"Actually," said Clay, rubbing his chin. "If you want, I have a near empty bunkhouse now, if you want to sleep at the ranch tonight." Clay grinned at Jim. "We hired a top notch cook, and his food is so good my hands have been known to lick their plates. Grub comes with the bunk."

"Sounds better than that tree I was going to throw my blankets under," smiled Jim, "and a hot meal beats jerky any day. I'll follow you when you're ready."

131

"I'd like to stay in town long enough to see what the doctor says about the woman and child," said Jeremiah, a question in his eyes as he split a look between Jim and Clay.

"Sure," replied Clay, "I need to pick up a few things at the store anyway." He turned and walked across the street towards the store.

He entered through the open front door just as he heard the back door close. Curious, he walked through, passing the room where Adele napped peacefully. He knew Axel was across the street, and he was sure Hannah was in helping with Luke's wife and child. He looked out the window in the back and saw a man riding rapidly away with a packhorse loaded with goods. Clay ran back out the front door and up to Axel.

"Axel, I think you may have been robbed while we were standing here!" said Clay.

"Adele..." started Axel, jumping off the porch in a leap, worry etching his features.

"She is fine," clarified Clay, holding up a hand. "I checked as I walked to the back where I heard the noise. She is still sleeping."

"Let's go check it out," said Cy, stepping off the porch with Jasper at his heels. The three men strode across the street and up the steps, hands on the butts of their guns. They stepped quietly through the store, looking behind counters and into the room where the little girl slept, then continued into the kitchen.

"That dirt was not on the floor when we ate lunch in here," said Cy, indicating small smudges of mud that looked like they may have been where someone walked. Jasper began to growl softly and sniffed at the back door.

"I am missing bags of flour, sugar, coffee, and some cans of peaches," said Axel, an edge to his voice. "I would need to look more closely to see what else is missing, but he certainly took enough to feed a small army!" His mouth was set in a grim line.

Cy drew his gun and stood to the side of the back door, motioning for the other men to step to the side. He carefully opened the door a crack, but Jasper shot through the opening, barking and growling. Seeing Jim outside, kneeling on the ground, Cy holstered his weapon.

"These tracks are fresh," said Jim, standing and pointing to the disturbed dirt. "Two horses, but I think only one held a man. They are minutes old."

"What is it, boy?" said Cy to his dog. Jasper was running back and forth, barking and whining, entreating Cy to follow him.

"He recognizes a scent," offered Jim.

"Yeah," agreed Cyrus, "he sure does." He looked at Jim. "You up for a little tracking?"

"I'll get my horse," grinned Jim.

"I will get mine back from the livery," began Axel.

"No, I think you should stay here with Adele and be here for Luke in case there is anything you can do for him. Your family might need you, and the two of us can handle one man." Cy looked at Clay. "Do you think you could stick around a bit in case they need more help or that crowd comes back?"

"Absolutely!" nodded Clay. "I would be glad to help with anything you need," he said, looking at the shop keeper. "I can even watch the store while you check on your wife."

"Then let's go catch us a thief!" said Cyrus, meeting Jim's gaze. His eyes were dark and dangerous. He had a hunch that Jasper had caught the scent of an old enemy.

Chapter 36

Sly Booker rode as fast as he could while leading the pack horse. If he went too fast, the sacks of flour might break open or the canned goods could bounce up and down in their burlap bag and irritate the horse to the point he would try to buck them off. He took as much bacon, flour, coffee, beans, sugar, and peaches as he dared take time to load. He laughed as he thought of the handful of cookies he had grabbed off the plate on the table in the kitchen. Stuffed in his pocket, they would make a tasty treat later.

But the outlaw had not taken the time to tie the sacks down properly; he wanted to get away before he was caught. Sly had ridden away from the back of the store, past several backs of buildings, then ducked down an alley and came up two buildings before the end of town. Seeing no one on the street, he walked the horses to the end of the street, trying his best to be nonchalant to avoid attention.

Then he heard the dog. Sweat broke out on his brow and his stomach twisted. He just knew it was that cursed dog that belonged to Cyrus James. *I should have killed that mutt when I had the chance.* The barking subsided as he rode further out from the town and he breathed easier, sure he had escaped.

His lips curled back as he thought back to the day he had first stumbled over the flea bitten cur. He had been drinking, but so what? It gave him the courage to stop Janet Kirby on the walk in front of the hotel and block her path. He backed her up to the wall, his arms on either side of her, pinning her against the wooden wall with his body. He was angling for a kiss even as she pushed against him, her hands flat on his chest, trying to turn her head away and down to avoid his sloppy lips.

"Let me go!" she had said, looking from side to side to determine if there was anyone around who would help her. She fumbled a handkerchief out of her sleeve and held it over her mouth with one hand, against his drunken breath and advancing mouth.

"Aw, just give me a little kiss! You know you been teasing me for awhile now," he leered, sniffing her hair.

"Leave me alone!" she cried, managing to free one leg enough to draw a pointed toed boot back and kick him in the shins.

"Damn you!" he screeched, jumping back and rubbing his shin. "I'll teach you your place!" He drew his arm back, intending to backhand the pretty young woman as he grabbed her arm with one hand and prepared to strike with the other.

Suddenly there was a blur of brown, black, and white fur and a dog that had appeared out of nowhere clasped Sly's wrist in his jaws, growling as he did so. Sly swung his arm out and slammed the back of the dog into a porch post, causing the animal to release the man's wrist. Janet screamed and Sly kicked the dog while he lay temporarily dazed. Sly glared at the shaken animal as it lay sprawled in the dirt beside the walk.

"I'm gonna kill you, you rotten cur!" Sly ripped the hanky out of Janet's hand and wrapped it around his bleeding right wrist, tucking it in the cuff of his shirt. He reached for his gun in the holster on his hip.

"I wouldn't do that," said a quiet, but firm voice.

Sly turned his head and looked into steel gray eyes that had no give to them. The man stood facing him, and wore two guns tied down like they knew what they were doing.

"This ain't none of your business!" Booker snarled. Janet stood frozen in fear while the dog lay shaking his head, trying to clear his vision. "Move on before I make this your last day on earth!" This cowboy might have sand to stand up against him, but Sly knew he was fast. He had killed too many men to doubt himself.

"I'm makin' it my business," said the man. His eyes did not move off Booker's face. "The lady and the dog don't seem to want your company."

Sly grinned, an evil action, and turning his body to face the stranger, he started to draw. He would take care of this intruder, shoot the dog, and then drag Janet into the trees behind the town buildings and teach her a lesson. Only he found himself suddenly

135

facing two guns pointed at him before he could even clear leather. He fumed as he let his gun drop back in the holster.

"They ain't worth it," said Sly with false bravado. "Take both the bitches! I got better things to do!"

With one fluid motion, the cowboy dropped both guns back in his holster, took two steps forward, and smashed a fist into Sly's mouth, sending him sprawling in the street.

"Take your dirty mouth away from the lady before I decide to teach you some more manners!"

"Who do you think you are?" Sly was livid, but had just enough sense to know danger too. "If that mangy excuse for a dog hadn't bit my wrist, I woulda killed you!"

The cowboy stepped into the street and grabbed Sly by his shirt front, hauling him to his feet. His face was inches from the alcohol sodden head of Booker, and his eyes burned with fury.

"Any time you want to try that, ask for Cyrus James," he hissed. "But fair warning. If I ever see you abuse either a lady or a dog like that again, I might just kill you on the spot. Now get out of my sight." He pushed him away and Sly staggered across the street. With some difficulty, he mounted his horse, rode down the alley, and out of town.

Sly had hated Cyrus from that day on, and he detested the dog. He had run into them one other time and discovered the dog was a male and had been adopted by Cyrus. He and some bad characters had tried to steal some horses from a ranch where Cy was working. They had watched the ranch for a day before they hit it,watching the dog barking and herding the horses.

They thought they had waited for the men to ride out, but Cyrus and another man had ridden back on an errand for the boss. When the outlaws swooped in, they met Cy and the other hand coming back up the trail. Cy recognized him as they rode in, and fired the first shot, grazing his shoulder. The cook grabbed a shotgun, and the rancher's wife did the same. The outlaws were lucky to get away with only a few wounds. Sly did not know the cook identified him by name to Cyrus.

All these memories washed back over Sly as he rode rapidly away from the town. One of these days, he was going to kill Cyrus James, and then he was going to kill that dog.

Chapter 37

Jed fidgeted at the window in the small room, resting the barrel of the Henry on the window sill while he waited for Paul to come back from the barn. He studied the hills surrounding the ranch and chewed on his lip. It was quiet. Too quiet. Why hadn't Snake come back with more men and tried to ambush them or burn them out? Even if he knew the woman was not here, there were other things of value on the ranch. Snake was just mean enough to come back and try to kill them all just to prove he could. He was a cruel, petty man, and that made him dangerous. Most men would not kill unless they were defending themselves, but men like Snake killed because they liked it; it gave them a dark rush of satisfaction.

"Don't move, mister!" The voice may have been weak, but there was no mistaking the cocking sound of the hammer being drawn back on a six gun. "Take your trigger hand and move it up to the barrel of that rifle, then raise the other hand in the air."

"You must be feeling better, Rusty," said Jed, hoping to calm the man who had come into consciousness by using his name. He did as the old cowboy had instructed, then turned slowly around, the rifle barrel gripped in his non dominant hand. There was no point in testing the old man's reflexes; they were on the same side.

"I don't know you, so don't try anything funny," snapped Rusty. His hands were shaking with the exertion, and that concerned Jed as much as anything. A twitch of the finger and the gun could fire.

Catching movement in his peripheral vision, Jed turned his head slightly and shifted his eyes to glance out the window. Moving his gaze back to Rusty, he found the old man was scowling at him.

Weak he may be, but he wasn't missing a thing! The cowboy on the bed was flicking his eyes to the door and then back to Jed quickly.

"I can get both of you, so don't try anything funny! I was a sharp shooter in the army, and I know my way around a gun!"

"No need, Sir," replied Jed softly, deliberately giving deference to the man's military experience. "That is Paul coming back from the barn, so please hold your fire. If you will allow me, I will call out to him so he comes slowly."

"Go ahead," replied Rusty, looking a bit uncertain, but not wanting to risk killing a friend either.

"Paul!" yelled Jed, raising his voice to carry. "Come in slowly; Rusty is awake and has a gun on the door."

"That old sidewinder better not shoot me!" The words carried a tinge of humor and were loud enough to be heard inside. Paul stepped up on the porch and called out before he opened the door. "Rusty! It's Paul! I've got some fresh milk for your coffee!"

"Then git in here with it! I'm wantin' some coffee awful bad!" Rusty's bravado was laced with relief as he lowered the gun, easing the hammer down, and placed it beside him on the bed. He was smiling, but obviously grateful to be able to lean back against the wall.

Paul came through the door and looked first at Rusty, then at Jed. He set the milk pail on the table and walked over to his friend, his brows knitted. He gently clapped the old man on the shoulder, taking note that he was pale, his brow was sweaty, and he was breathing a bit harder than he should.

"Doc..." Paul started, but the doctor was beside him before he could finish. He thrust the rifle at Paul and bent to look at the wound.

"I have an uneasy feeling, so keep an eye out the window while I take a look at these bandages," he said, already peeling away the cloth covering the wound. Paul stepped back to the window and peered out at the surroundings while Jed began to evaluate Rusty's condition. He worked quickly and probed gently as he examined the incision.

"He called you Doc," said Rusty, scrutinizing the serious face of the stranger bending over him. "You ain't the doctor from Bridgeport."

"No, I'm not," answered Jed, without further elaboration. His eyes were focused on the wound before him, as he gently probed and prodded around the edges.

"Then what are you pokin' at me for?" demanded Rusty.

"I'm not the doctor from Bridgeport, as you observed," said Jed, a twinkle in his eyes now as he looked up at the face of the feisty old soldier. "I am a doctor though," he continued. "I did a lot of my training in the war." He focused on the wound and cleaning the dried blood away, his gaze sharp as he looked at the decreasing infection.

"Which side were you on?" asked Rusty, while suspicion tinged his voice.

"Does it matter anymore?" Jed met Rusty's eyes with a bleak frankness that caused the other man to turn his eyes away quickly for a moment.

"No," said Rusty with a new softness in his gaze, "I reckon it don't make a bit of difference now."

"I think the doc here saved your life, you crusty old soul," interjected Paul, setting down three cups of hot coffee on the upended wooden box he had placed by the bed. One of them was lighter in color, the milk turning it a tan concoction that made the old man's mouth water.

"That smells so good I could drink the whole pot!" Rusty looked with longing at the steaming cups sitting just within reach. He turned his face to Jed, a question in his eyes.

"You're all patched up for now," he said, appreciating the deference his patient had given him by tacitly asking for approval to drink the coffee. He picked up the soiled bandages and basin of water from the bed and stood. "I don't think a whole pot is a good idea, but a cup or two might help." He smiled and Paul handed the eager patient his cup.

Jed put the basin on the sink and walked back to stand at the foot of the bed. Paul picked up one of the cups from the box and offered it to the doctor, who accepted with a nod. The three men silently sipped their coffee for a few treasured moments until Jed walked to the window. He sipped the dark brown brew with appreciation, but his eyes could not stop scanning the hills.

"What's chewin' at you, young fella," asked McMath. He studied Jed's profile and knitted his brows together as he held his stare on the former stranger, over the top of his cup.

"You don't miss much," Jed grinned, slanting his head in the direction of the bed. He looked out the window, took another swallow of his coffee, and then leaned against the wall by the window. "I rode with the men who did this to you for a couple months." He let it hang for a few minutes in the still air.

"What?" Rusty froze, the coffee halfway to his lips. Too late, he realized both of his hands were nestled around the warm cup. His eyes slanted quickly to the gun beside him, as if he was gauging his chances. Then he shot a look at Paul, who was standing to the side, smiling like he was the cat that just ate the canary, one hand casually on his hip, and other holding his own cup of coffee.

"It's okay, my friend," laughed Paul. "Jed already confronted the gang when they came for him. He chose to stay here and work on you."

"How can you be sure we can trust him?" snapped Rusty. "He could be the inside man for that group of yellow bellied skunks! That one in the yard grabbed Ruth and would have taken her if I hadn't shot him!" He was angry now and the other two men stopped smiling.

"You remember what happened?" asked Jed, stepping closer and fixing him with an intent stare.

"Of course I remember, I ain't addle-brained!" The old rider had set his cup down and rested his hand nearer to his gun."

"I'm not saying that at all," soothed the doctor, "but sometimes when people get shot or suffer something bad, they forget for awhile."

"Tell us what you know, man! Luke and Cy are out there looking for Ruth!" Paul's face was serious now.

"Mr. Randall was here?" Rusty looked surprised, then thoughtful for a moment. "So he met the doc?" He appraised Jed again in a manner that declared he was not yet fully sold on the stranger's loyalty.

"Yeah," affirmed Paul. "He trusted him to stay here with you and me." Paul was antsy. "Now, tell us the story!" He flushed as he realized he had snapped at his friend. "I'm sorry; I'm just worried about the whole Randall family." He shifted his feet as he looked at his friend.

"I don't blame you none," smiled Rusty. He told his story then, looking back and forth between the men as he spoke. He noticed Jed split his attention between the window and the bed, and he had picked up the rifle again as he watched. When he finished, both he and Paul centered their attention on the new man. Silence hung in the air as they waited.

"I don't know why they haven't attacked us," Jed said finally. "They have enough men and they have to know there are only two of us that are really battle ready." He cut a look between McMath and Paul. "No offense, Sir."

"None taken, doc," replied Rusty. He was struggling to stay awake, in spite of the coffee.

"What do you make of it?" Paul stood expectantly.

"They were after more than the ranch," the doctor said. "I just don't know what else they are gearing up for; they did not tell us everything yet."

"They tried to take Ruth," spat Rusty, his blood rising at the thought. "No good western man would do that!"

"These are not good men," verified Jed. "But the ranch was supposed to be the secondary job...along with Ruth." He chewed on his lip as the three men mulled over what he had said. "I think we should start sleeping in shifts, limit our time outside, and prepare for an attack," he stated. "I don't trust Snake, and I think we should be prepared and stay low until Luke and Cy get back.

"What do you want me to do?" asked Rusty. "I could load guns from here."

"That would be good," smiled Jed, "but right now, put your gun on the table next to you and get some sleep."

"I'm alright," protested McMath, trying to raise up to a sitting position and wincing as he did so.

"Not yet you aren't," Jed answered with authority. "You're still too weak. Sleep is the best thing you can do to get your strength back so you are ready to fight when they hit us." He walked over and gently took the handgun and set it on the makeshift table, which he moved a little closer to the bed. "Please," he said, softening the blow to Rusty's pride. "We are all going to take turns sleeping. You go first." He barely had the words out when the old man's eyes closed and he fell into an exhausted sleep.

"I'll get some stew and biscuits going and make plenty of coffee," started Paul. "We can eat off that for a couple days if we have to, and we have enough wood inside for several days. Luke built a wood box outside against the house that opens from inside too."

"Your boss is a clever man! What about water and ammunition?" asked Jed, still at the window.

"Luke built the kitchen here because an underground stream runs just outside that corner. When you pump the handle, you are pumping right out of the stream," Paul beamed. He walked over to a curtain that seemed to hang over a closet. He pulled it aside to reveal several shelves with boxes of ammunition. "Mr. Randall may be young, but he is one to ride the river with. He likes to be prepared. He says the war taught him that," said Paul, giving Jed a significant look.

Jed nodded. So Luke and the old man were soldiers too. If they had seen even half of what he had, they were no strangers to the nightmares of an attack.

Chapter 38

Luke sat by the bed where Ruth lay, and ran his eyes over her face. She looked so pale and small with her eyes closed, and her arm in a sling. Her lips were dry and cracked from exposure, and the salve the doctor had put on them gave them almost a grotesque, shiny sheen. She moved slightly and groaned from the pain in her cracked ribs.

"Luke!" she cried out, " save him, Luke! Save our son!" Her free hand thrashed on the bed beside her. Luke took her hand and spoke softly to her, even as his eyes caught movement to his left.

"I'm here, Ruth," he said, hoping his voice would penetrate the dark fog that kept her away from him. Thomas squirmed again in the cradle beside him, and Luke, continuing to hold the hand of his wife, turned his full attention to the boy. The small child whimpered in his sleep and Luke thought his heart would stop beating. He lay so small, looking pale, but he was moving his arms! Flailing slightly beside his body, the toddler turned his head back and forth.

"He's moving!" said the doctor, who had come back into the room with coffee for the young rancher. He set the cup down and touched the boys head, gently looking at the wound. At his touch, the child opened his eyes.

"Thomas!" exclaimed Luke, letting go of Ruth's hand. He shot a question with his eyes to the doc, and received an affirmative nod. Luke reached down and gently took the boy into his arms, cradling him, and staring into the eyes of his son. For several moments, the two just sat, and then, Thomas smiled at his father. "Does this mean he's alright?" Luke laughed out of pure joy.

The doctor moved to the front of the two and took one of the toddler's small hands. The boy turned his head and smiled at the doctor, then turned back to Luke.

"Da!" said the little voice, reaching a hand up to touch the face of his father.

"This is a very good sign that he will be okay," answered the doctor. The toddler turned his head towards the doctor when he spoke, and played his little eyes over the man's face, then smiled.

"Do you know who he is, son?" asked Luke, and when his son swiveled his head and grinned at him, thought his heart would burst. Laughter filled the room as Luke pulled his son up against his chest and cried while he laughed. He closed his eyes and rocked back and forth. His son had come back.

"Luke?" The voice was scratchy and barely above a whisper.

"Ruth!" Luke opened his eyes and saw his wife staring at him.

"Is Thomas..." she began, then seemed to almost choke on her words. The doctor moved quickly to offer her a few sips of water.

"He's right here, and he seems to be fine!" Luke glanced down at the child, who suddenly seemed limp in his arms. He felt panic welling up inside, and turned his eyes to the doctor.

"He's fallen back asleep," said the doctor, answering the question that was never spoken. "I think he is going to be fine, but he is probably exhausted from his ordeal."

"Luke," began his wife, reaching out an arm towards the sleeping child. "I need..." but she did not have to finish. Luke half stood and, leaning over, placed the sleeping boy beside his wife in the bed. She grimaced as she shifted to kiss his head and place her hand on the child's back.

"Ruth, be careful about moving," cautioned the doctor, "you have a broken arm, some bruised ribs, and if I am not mistaken, one of those ribs might be cracked."

"You two gave me quite a scare," interjected Luke, bending to kiss his wife's cheek. He moved the chair a little closer and sat at the edge of the bed where he could look at his family. "Oh God, thank you, thank you!" He whispered the words in a near silent prayer as he watched them both sleep again.

He knew he could not push Ruth yet, but he also had a very uneasy feeling that he needed to get back to the ranch soon. He needed her to tell him what had happened first, and he hoped she could do that soon.

Chapter 39

Cy studied the tracks as he squatted on his haunches. There was nothing special about the
boot prints in the soft dirt. A big man had dismounted from the lead horse and walked back to the horse he was trailing. The second horse was carrying a heavy load too, but it was not human. This was the man who had robbed the general store, and clearly had been hasty in securing the canvas bags of stolen goods. He shifted the sacks of flour, apparently to keep them from leaking any more of the white powdered food. There were traces of flour on the grass under where the horse had stood.

Cyrus had no proof for what he felt, but in his gut, he knew this was Sly Booker. He had felt it the moment he saw the rapidly retreating back riding away from the rear of the general store. Nothing good would come of the outlaw being in the Bridgeport area.

"Find anything else?" asked Jim, walking back out of the trees.

"No," answered Cy, looking towards the land ahead of them. "I just..." He stopped, standing still, not meeting Jim's eyes, staring down the path ahead.

"What is it, Cyrus?" Jim prodded gently, eyes narrowing as he studied the other man.

"I just can't shake this feeling that I know who we are following." Cy met Jim's eyes and was surprised at the glint of humor he saw. "Go ahead and laugh," he snapped, feeling a flush rise up his neck.

"I'm not laughing at you, partner," said Jim softly, his face turning serious. "I am alive today because I listened to my gut feelings."

"You don't think I'm crazy?" asked Cy with surprise.

"Man, I spent a lot of time with the Lakota Sioux. I also had many a day out in the wilderness, all alone, and listening to the mountains and the wind tell me their stories made me pay attention to what my own senses tell me. If you think you know who we are following, I believe you."

Cy saw only sincerity in the eyes of the mountain man, and a fresh respect for this new friend settled over his shoulders. He nodded his head and the two men conferred for a few minutes, deciding to circle around from two sides and close in on the rider ahead. Cy filled Jim in on the bad man they were pursuing, and watched Jim's mouth set in a grim line. They could travel faster as they had no baggage holding them back, and the element of surprise would be wise, and more likely to get Axel's' stolen property back untainted.

"Where is he headed with all those provisions?" asked Jim thoughtfully. "From the depth of those hoof imprints, he is carrying far more food than one man could eat."

"That's what I was starting to wonder," answered Cy, rubbing his chin. "The Rocking R is the only ranch out this way, and he sure isn't headed there, so who or what is he headed towards? There is nothing out here!"

"Maybe we just don't know who or what is out there yet," said Jim grimly. "I think we better ride carefully and make sure we don't go charging into an encampment of some kind."

"Yeah," said Cy, shaking his head. "From what I know of this buzz worm, he is probably up to no good. I have a bad feeling about this." Both men slipped their rifles back into their scabbards and mounted their horses.

"How far is the Rocking R range?" asked Jim.

"The main ranch buildings are about ten miles that way," said James, pointing to the left, "over those hills."

"Are there any buildings or cattle in that direction?" asked Jim, pointing after the trail Booker took.

"No, that's Randall's land too, but it is just forest land. We just sold most of the cattle from the ranch, and the few left are on the other side of the ranch."

"Let's ride," said Jim, "but watch your back." The two men spurred their mounts off the trail, closing Booker in between them. Jasper, loving the chance to run, kept pace with the horses, tongue hanging out of his mouth. Cy looked over once, and could swear the dog was smiling.

Chapter 40

Hal Colter sat his horse, watching the activity below. With satisfaction, he noted six wagons loaded with logs and ready to begin the drive to Virginia City in the morning. A handful of loggers were still applying two man saws to a stand of trees, and his cowboys were hacking off the branches with axes. It had gone smoothly; brutal hours of work, and pushing the men hard.

The boss man swung his eyes over the ridges, noting the sentries, standing or sitting, and facing away from the camp. Suddenly, his eyes stopped and hardened. He fumed as he watched Snake lounging against a rock, his rifle propped beside him, his back to his post. He was casually smoking a cigarette, oblivious to the fact he was being watched. Colter clenched his jaw. *You're a dead man, Snake, and you don't even know it!* He forced himself to rip his attention away from the source of the acid rising in his stomach. He could do nothing about Snake right now; to shout an oath or fire a shot at him might bring attention to their operation. There could be someone passing through the area that might become curious or suspicious and report the shouts or shots to the law. *That's all I need, a law dog sniffing around here!*

Disgusted, he turned to the right and saw a man on horseback approaching the camp. He watched the man as he was stopped by a guard, who then pointed in Hal's direction. The man squinted at Hal, then slowly started picking his way up the slope towards the other man astride his horse on the top of the hill. Colter played the plan through his mind while he waited.

Booker should be back any time, and Bean had orders to fix a big meal for the whole crew, loggers and cowboys alike. When their bellies were full, he would drop the news that more wagons would

149

arrive at first light, and they would all work from sun barely lighting the sky to the stars coming out at night. The cowboys would work the logging effort too; relieved of their sentry duty by the riflemen coming in with the wagons. They would work harder and longer for the promise of more pay.

Movement caught his eye and he turned his head. He watched the man wind his way up the hillside to meet him at the crest. They nodded at each other, then sat silently surveying the scene for several minutes.

"You think they can clear cut this whole mountain in a week?" asked the newcomer.

"Yep," said Colter,"or die trying." He laughed and the other man looked at him.

"I don't understand." He sat stoically, eyes fixed on Colter.

"I'm bringing in some riflemen tomorrow with the extra wagons. The men will stay on and work hard, or else!" His smile sent a shiver through the other man.

"I did not hire you to commit murder!" he snapped back, suddenly understanding what Colter meant.

"No," said Colter slowly, his eyes narrowing into icy pools of black staring at the man beside him. "You hired me to steal the lumber off the land of an upstanding citizen. We discussed terms, agreed on a price for the merchandise, and decided on delivery. We never talked about my methods of getting the job done."

"I just can't let you..." protested the tall man.

"Can't let me?" hissed Hal. "You are in this over your head now. You contracted with a known outlaw to steal property worth a lot of money. That makes you guilty of a crime." He let his words hang in the air and enjoyed watching the other man squirm in his saddle.

"Well, I don't like it!" the other man protested, wetting his lips with his tongue. "I don't like it one bit!" he blustered.

"You don't have to like it," replied Colter, in a voice dripping with menace. "But get this straight! You will not tell anyone about this deal, and you better have the money ready when we get the lumber to that sawmill outside Virginia City."

"I'm sorry I ever entered into this deal with you, Colter!"

"You can be sorry all you want," spat Hal, "just don't even think about double crossing me, or it will be your last thought."

"Are you threatening me?" Indignation rose in his voice as he drew himself to his full height in the saddle.

"No, sir." Colter leaned forward in his saddle until he was a mere foot from the other man's face. "I'm making you a promise, Mr. Roberts, and you best not forget it."

John Roberts wilted under Colter's glare, and turned his horse, riding away. He was cursing himself for being greedy and ever entering into a deal with the outlaw. He wished he had never heard of the Chinese operated small sawmill between Virginia City and Carson City. It had seemed too good to be true, and now he knew it was. It was the devil's own business he had entered into and he already regretted his choice. He hoped he would live long enough to at least enjoy some of the profit, but at this moment, he had his doubts.

Chapter 41

Luke hated to leave his family, but he knew they were in good hands with Axel and Hannah. He felt an overwhelming sense of foreboding he just could not shake. To make matters worse, Cy had ridden off with Jim yesterday afternoon and had not returned. The two men took off to chase the thief from the general store, but both Axel and Luke thought they would have returned by now. Something was going on that felt sinister, and leaving his family in the care of the shop keepers, he was driven to get out to the ranch. He was just swinging into his saddle when Clay and Jeremiah rode up and reigned in beside him.

"Morning, Luke!" Clay smiled at his new friend, and Jeremiah, nodded at the rancher as well.

"Good morning, Clay...Jeremiah," returned Randall. "What brings you two into town so early?" He looked down the trail out of town quickly. He didn't want to be rude, but he needed to get to the point.

"We came in to see if Jim stayed in town last night after all," said Clay. "We expected him last night, but when he still had not come in by breakfast, we decided to ride in and see if we could find him."

"Jim and Cy went after the man who robbed the general store yesterday afternoon," said Luke. "They did not come back last night. As a matter of fact, I was headed out the direction they rode right now, to try to find them and check on my ranch."

"Want some company?" offered Clay, his eyes steady as they met the gaze of a fellow rancher. "There could be trouble, and if so, I'd be right proud to be at your side."

152

"I can't ask you to do that," began Luke, "you have a family."

"So do you," grinned Clay, "and if we don't stick together to fight trouble, it will come to our families, one at a time."

"You've got sand, I'll say that for you!" Luke Randall smiled, and motioned towards Jeremiah. "I'm sure you could stay with Axel until he could take you back out to Clay's ranch."

"He's a sharp man," stated Clay, looking at the man beside him. "I am sure he can find his way back, right Jeremiah?"

"Yes, I could, but it won't be necessary right now," said the big man in black.

"Do you want me to go inside with you to get you settled with Axel?" asked Luke. He really wanted to ride, but he thought the Latter Day Saint might still be uncomfortable with being new in the town, and he had to admit, the big German could be intimidating until you got to know the man.

"No, thank you, Luke. I think you misunderstand," said Jeremiah. "If you think you are riding into trouble, I will come along." He pulled his rifle from the scabbard, checked the load, patted his pockets, clearly packed with bullets, and set his jaw as he slipped the rifle back into it's leather sheath.

"That's real kind of you, Jeremiah, but you don't even live here, and you aren't planning to stay," said Luke, shaking his head. Yesterday, he thought this man had harmed his family and was ready to kill him with his bare hands if that had been true. Today, Jeremiah was volunteering to put his own life in danger to help him!

"It is our country too. We will be living only a day's ride away, so in a sense, we will be frontier neighbors. We must all stand together against bad men or none of us will have peace for our families." Pulling his hat down tighter on his head, he said firmly, "I will go with you!"

Jeremiah's stare did not falter. Luke and Clay exchanged a look, shrugged their shoulders, and turned to the road out of town. The three men pressed their horses into a canter until they were beyond the buildings, then touched the spurs to their mounts and galloped towards the Rocking R.

Chapter 42

Cy James sat on the ground in the trees close to the top of the ridge overlooking the huge logging operation. His horse was hobbled behind and below him, under the shade of a stand of aspens, giving the animal shelter not only from the high mountain sun, but from any eyes that might happen to stray up the hill. He sat behind a Manzanita bush, Jasper beside him, and peered through the glasses, thrust partially through the low branches, to keep the sun from bouncing a glint of light into the line of sight for the men below. Especially the men with rifles. He counted twenty men working the lumber under close scrutiny of eight hard cases with rifles that never waivered.

He and Jim had shadowed Sly Booker until Cy was sure he was headed for the outer, forested edge of the ranch. They closed the gap between themselves and let Booker go on ahead. Jim grabbed Cy's arm and pointed skyward. Squinting, Cyrus James followed Jim's finger as he pointed to the sky and a faint smoke trail.

"That's a camp, and likely a big one," said Jim.

"What makes you think so?" asked Cy, inclined to believe the mountain man, but still wanting to hear the reasoning.

"No traveler in the wild sticks around a fire all day, and no man alone advertises his presence to anybody who may be happening by with ill intentions," explained Jim. "That's a camp, with coffee hot all day and chow being prepared with the supplies we saw Booker bring in. He took enough to load a packhorse."

"It was enough to feed an army," agreed Cyrus. He chewed on his lower lip, staring at the column of smoke. He turned his head to find Jim watching him.

154

"It's your friend's ranch," Jim shrugged. "What's your call?" The trail wise tracker sat silently, knowing Cyrus was mulling over the options and thinking each one through. He respected that Cy James was not one to charge in blind, especially when he had the ability to sit back a moment or two and think. Several minutes passed before the cowboy nodded his head decisively and faced Jim.

"I know Luke will already be worried that we haven't returned." Cy pondered the thought for a moment more. "So the question is…will he trail us or go check on the situation at the ranch first?" He looked at Jim, who said nothing, waiting patiently. "He will go to the ranch first," said Cy decisively. He knows Rusty is wounded and he will want to make sure all is well there. He also will figure if we ran into trouble, we would head for the ranch."

"So, we should go to the ranch?" asked Jim.

"No," said the other rider, shaking his head. "We should go scout out that camp and see what Luke might ride into, or even worse, what might be heading for the ranch. Then we go back and tell the boss everything we see here."

Jim split to the right and Cy took the left, agreeing to meet back at this spot in one hour. Cy watched from his vantage point for nearly another hour, then crept backward and took the hobbles off his horse. He was just about to step into the saddle when he heard Jasper growl low. The cocking of a hammer behind him made him freeze, one foot in the stirrup, and clearly at a disadvantage with his back to whoever was holding that pistol, likely pointed at his back. He gave a silent signal to Jasper to stay. He did not want the dog to get shot defending him.

"Gotcha," chuckled an evil voice. "Turn around real slow. I want to see your face when I give it to you in the gut."

Cy stayed still, his mind frantically racing. Maybe he could swing the horse between him and the gunman. Maybe he could fall to the ground and draw as he fell. Rapidly, scenarios flashed through his mind, and he discounted them just as fast.

"Move!" snarled the man behind him. "I will blow out your kneecap from behind and then kill you even slower! Now move! And don't try anything funny with your horse either!"

Cy slowly removed his foot and then turned carefully, his hands in the air.

"Sly Booker," he spat! "I shoulda killed you the first time we met."

"Well, you didn't, and now I am going to really enjoy this! Unbuckle that gun belt with your left hand and let it fall to the ground, nice and easy." He was grinning from ear to ear, standing legs wide apart, the gun leveled at Cy's stomach. "Gut shots take longer to die, and they hurt. A lot." He chuckled again. "I've watched a few die that way, begging me to finish 'em off and stop the pain. You...I'm gonna watch you die slow. Maybe even carve you up a bit while you are grabbin' your gut."

Cy watched his eyes. They were dancing with delight at the idea of making Cy suffer. He was preparing to launch himself sideways, hoping to make it into the brush, when Booker, suddenly lowered the gun, aiming it at his knee.

Everything happened fast then. Cy kicked to the side, and Booker fired, hitting the back of Cy's calf. He scrambled as fast as he could, trying to get into the brush for cover before the next shots came.

But nothing happened. Cy stopped moving and listened. Jasper slipped through the brush to his side and they both listened. There was no crunch of a boot on the sand. No other shots fired. In fact, it was so quiet, it was eerie. He turned slowly, and rising to a crouch, he saw Booker staring straight at him! He jumped a little, then realized the eyes were not moving, not blinking, and Booker was lying on the ground.

Jim walked out of the brush from behind Cy's horse. He bent over Booker's body and pulled the big Bowie knife out of the center of his chest, wiped the blood on the dead man's clothes, then plunged the knife into the sand before returning it to the sheath on his leg.

"Ready to ride?" asked Jim. He reached down and rubbed Jasper behind the ears as the dog ran to thank him for saving his master.

Cy nodded, stepping out of the brush, while Jim led his mount out of the trees on the other side of the small clearing. Once again, Cy put his boot toe in the stirrup, but completed the rise to his saddle this time.

"That need tending?" asked Jim, pointing to the blood on the lower leg of Cy's jeans.

"Not now," answered Cy. "Let's get moving before someone comes looking for him." They turned their horses towards the Rocking R, riding carefully until they got off the small mountain, then urging their battle wise horses, they galloped towards the ranch.

Chapter 43

Hal Colter watched as his logging foreman approached. The
big man strode towards him with a determined look on his face. He
was at least six foot four inches in height, and Hal guessed his
weight at two-hundred and forty pounds of lean, bulging muscle.
The man's coal black hair was cut short to stay out of the way of a
saw or hatchet in close work. His hands were huge, and Hal
wondered if he could even get those fingers inside the trigger guard
of a pistol.

"Is that the last load?" asked Hal as the man named Mickey
stopped in front of him.

"Yes, it sure is, boss." Mickey threw a thumb back over his
shoulder. "Unless you want us to clear cut the little mountain over
there." He half turned now and pointed to timber that was not on
Randall's land.

"That's tempting," replied Colter, "but fighting with a little
rancher and starting a war with the government are two different
things."

"We will fight where you want us to, as long as the money
keeps coming," smiled Mickey, but there was no warmth in the
smile. "What do you want us to do now?"

Hal considered this. He was planning on sending the wagons
ahead with Sly Booker, half his cowboys, and the loggers. He would
lead the other half of his range riders and his riflemen to the Rocking
R Ranch, kill everyone on the place, take what they wanted,
including his remaining cattle, and burn the ranch so there was no
evidence to connect him to the crime. Then he and his thugs would
catch up with the wagons to get his payday from John Roberts in

Virginia City. But he had not seen Booker since he came back with the supplies.

"First, spread out and find Sly Booker. He is probably drunk somewhere after his trip to town, but haul him back in here to me!" Mickey nodded and Hal turned on his heel, fuming all the way to his tent. Maybe he should just kill Snake and Booker at the ranch, and leave their bodies in the burning rubble. He grinned. He was a genius! Then he could be rid of both of the thorns in his side! He was sure he could handle the riflemen and loggers, and as soon as he paid them, he would light out for somewhere no one knew him, and live high.

Suddenly, he had a thought that made him feel absolutely giddy! Maybe he wouldn't even pay the men! If he could find a way to get the money, then disappear on some pretense of taking care of a final detail, he just might be able to ride away with all the money! Lost in reverie about all the wealth he would have to himself, he did not hear the man approach his tent an hour later. He jumped when Mickey spoke from outside the temporary canvas home.

"Boss?" Colter had not given the men his name. He didn't want any more ties to his misdeeds; all but a few of the men had been instructed to just call him "boss."

"What is it, Mickey?" He recognized the voice even before he drew back the flap of the tent, standing side ways, with one hand on the butt of his gun. He stood so the logger could not see his hand on his weapon, using caution to guide his moves.

"We haven't found Booker yet, but we found Snake, drunker than a hoot owl, sleeping at his post. What do you want us to do with him?"

"Tie him up!" snapped Colter. Drag him over by the corral, make sure he doesn't have any weapons or a knife, and tie him up good to the posts." He looked at the big logger. "Don't be too gentle about it either," he said, knowing the brute enjoyed beating other men.

"I'd be glad to do that for you, boss," smiled Mickey. "Are you leaving him alive?"

"Yeah, I am," answered Colter. "That's why I want him tied good and tight. No one will find him out here, and if the cold nights and no water don't get him, the animals will. He deserves a slow death!"

"Yes Sir!" The big logger grinned. "And I'll let you know when we find Booker."

"Do that!" said Hal, letting the tent flap fall shut again in dismissal. *This might be easier than he thought.*

Chapter 44

Luke led the group, riding only slightly ahead of Clay and Jeremiah so they would not eat his dust. The sense of urgency roiled in his stomach and he wished his horse could grow wings, even though Pepper flew across the ground. He knew she was feeling his anxiety. He did not try to slow her down, and was relieved that the younger mounts of his friends were able to keep up. Clay had some good racing stock on his ranch, and Luke was grateful both men knew how to ride. As he rode, he prayed that they also knew how to shoot.

Luke's eyes scanned the horizon constantly, trusting Pepper to watch for holes or rocks. He wasn't sure what he was looking for; anything unusual would give him a hint of why he felt so driven to race to his ranch. Yet, he saw no dust plumes or smoke clouds. That should have been reassuring, but it was not.

As much as he hated to do so, the horses needed water and he swung to his right towards the stream that ran parallel to the trail. All three men dismounted and led their horses to the water. They also took on some water from the stream, having not taken the time to fill canteens before they started the run to the ranch.

"I've never been to your ranch, Luke," said Clay, lifting his hat and wiping the sweat from his brow. "How much further is it?"

"Well, Pepper is in good shape and a trained runner," answered Luke, "so it would take her about another two and a half to three hours to get there." He hesitated, looking at the other two men and appraising their horses. "But I don't want to kill anyone's horse getting to the ranch."

161

"Thanks for the thoughtfulness, Luke, but these are young, Arabian racers, bred for endurance and speed. I brought them out here to build a horse ranch with top notch mounts." He hesitated, shifting his gaze from Luke to Jeremiah, then back again. "Frankly, I was holding my mount back a little to let you lead with Pepper."

"What!" Luke looked at Jeremiah, who grinned sheepishly. "Well, I'll be a filleted buzzworm!" he laughed. "Those are some excellent horses you are sitting on," he said, running his eyes over the steeds with even more appreciation. "But still," he said, becoming serious again. "These horses have covered good ground for two hours now. At this rate, we'll get there in three and a half hours instead of four, but I think we need to slow a bit for another hour, take a quick break to water them, then we can run them for the last half hour or so."

"I see the point," agreed Clay, "especially since we don't know exactly what we are riding into." He let the words hang, waiting for Luke to give a little more detail.

"Do we need to slow down as we get closer?" asked Jeremiah. "Are we expecting an ambush?" The big man in black did not ask out of fear, but obviously out of experience. His eyes and his hands were steady.

"Fair questions," answered Luke. "When I was at the ranch, before I went looking for Ruth and little Thomas, there had been an attack and one of my men was badly wounded. My ranch hand, Paul, stayed with him, but there was another man there too. Jed had ridden with the gang that attacked my ranch, but when they rode up, he refused to go back with them."

"I've seen that a time or two," nodded Clay, "men who find themselves with a group they can't stomach. They see a chance to stand for good again, and they take it."

"That's my take on Jed as well," said Luke, "but what is gnawing at me is what he told us. He said they would be back. That's what is eating at me; I can't shake the feeling they are comin' soon."

"Then we best be lightin' a shuck," said Jeremiah, snapping his hat lower on his head.

"It's not your fight," said Luke, "I can't ask you to risk your lives for me and my men," he protested again.

"You didn't ask, and we aren't backing down now," said Clay firmly, getting a nod of agreement from Jeremiah. "We aren't yellow bellies, and the West is our home too! Now stop jawin' and let's ride!" He smiled grimly at the other young rancher, turning his horse as he did so.

Clay nudged his mount in the sides and the horse took off running. Jeremiah set his jaw and did the same, leaving Lucas eating their dust until he urged Pepper forward. He was proud of these men; they were true western men, determined to carve out a good life for themselves and their families. They knew the price that could be required, and they faced it square on.

Pepper caught up with the other horses and they ran like there was a fire behind them. They all knew they would need to stop in the next hour to rest the horses a bit, but for now, they were three tough men riding hard towards a probable showdown, and determined to make it count.

Lucas Randall was smart to listen to his gut feeling. At that very moment, Hal Colter sat his horse, overlooking the Rocking R Ranch. On either side of him were six experienced, armed men with rifles. They were killers, every single one of them.

Chapter 45

Paul watched the men on the top of the hill, staying well out of the window. He counted ten men, but had a feeling there were a few he could not see. He and Jed had been taking the watches, telling Rusty he could do his turn when he got better.

"We need your expert shooting, Sir," said Jed, "so please stay in bed and recover. We can take turns watching, but you are the best shooter we have and we are going to need you."

Rusty locked eyes with the young doctor for several seconds, then nodded, lay back down, and closed his eyes to sleep. Paul could swear the older man's eyes were misty before he nodded off. Getting shot had taken a lot out of McMath, especially since he was not treated right away, and he still tired easily.

Paul was in awe of the way Jed could get Rusty to do something while making him feel respected. Now, he was hoping the extra days of rest were going to be enough. Without taking his eyes off the outlaws, Paul spoke softly, hoping not to wake Rusty.

"Jed." Instantly, the young doctor was at the window, standing across from Paul, rifle in hand. He quickly assessed the scene before them, rubbed his chin, then met Paul's eyes.

"I sure am glad Luke stocked up on ammo. Looks like we are going to need it," he said.

"Do you think they will try to surround us?" asked Paul.

"Yeah, I do," answered Jed. "Do you want to take the front or the back?"

"In this room?"

"Yes," nodded Jed, "but be prepared to run to any window." He chewed his lip. "That's some heavy fire power. I just hope they don't riddle us with bullets so badly the wood just gives out." He turned his head to Paul and was surprised to see him grinning. "What in blue blazes are you smiling about?" he asked irritably.

"The wood might get a bit holy, even though it is oak, some of the hardest wood the good Lord gave us. But Luke was smart when he built this house. He framed the walls on the outside with a couple inches of space between them and the inside walls. In the inches between the hard wood, he put rocks."

"Rocks?" asked Jed, a puzzled look on his face.

"Yep, rocks. Hard, igneous rock. It is all around us here in the mountains and high desert, but Luke is the only man I have ever known that thought to put rocks inside the walls. These walls are all filled with rocks, chest high on a man." He smiled at the look on Jed's face as the impact dawned.

"Bullets would have a hard time getting through two layers of hardwood with rock in between them!" Jed laughed. "Lucas Randall is one smart man!"

"He sure is! It's why most of the windows are a little higher than normal too!"

"This sure evens up the odds a bit!" said Jed. He stepped to the cupboard and stuffed several boxes of ammunition in his pockets, then brought a handful to Paul, who did the same. He turned to see Rusty at the cupboard, filling his pockets as well.

"I'll take this spot," said McMath, stepping to the window on the other side of the room from Paul. It gives me a good shot at anything moving towards the side of the house or the barn, as well as from the front." He leaned against a sideboard, and Jed noticed he could actually sit on the top of it if he got tired of standing.

"Do you think they will try to burn us out?" asked Paul.

"No," answered Jed, "no, I don't think so. They want to loot the house, and take the stock before they burn it all down. So, unless we give them too much trouble, burning us out is the last thing they will do." He looked at Paul. "Besides, the rock inside the walls will make it tougher to do!"

"Here they come!" growled Rusty. "At least two are trying to get around behind us!" He snapped off a shot, then chuckled. "Well, at least one is still trying."

Paul sprinted for the back room while Jed took up the spot that could fire from the corner of the kitchen. The outlaws were spreading out now and creeping forward under cover, but they were also laying down heavy fire. Even with the strengthened walls, bullets were flying through the windows fast enough to make it hard to get off well placed shots.

They were significantly outnumbered, and all three of them had to wonder if they would live through this battle.

Chapter 46

Cyrus groaned. He tried to move, but something was sitting on his chest. He forced his eyes open and saw little earthworms dangling in front of his face.

"Get away!" he swatted at them, trying to push them out of his face. "I ain't dead yet, you rotten little fish bait!" They were tickling his nose, and felt cold, but not...wet?

"Okay, partner! Welcome back," laughed Jim, swinging off Cyrus and standing to his feet.

"What the heck were you doing, sitting on my chest!" snapped Cy, realizing the dangling earthworms were really the fringe hanging down from the front of Jim's buckskin shirt. He tried to sit up, but a sharp pain in his right leg stopped him.

"I was sitting on you to keep you from moving," grinned Jim. "You have a nasty gash on that leg of yours," he said, pointing to Cy's right leg. "But when you got thrown, you hit the side of your face too. I thought you were totally out, but when I started checking your leg, you bellowed in pain and were fighting me to get to your feet. Crazy thing was, your eyes weren't open while you were fighting me!" He looked over when Jasper whimpered. The dog was sitting between the two men, like he wasn't quite sure what he should do.

"Come here, boy," said Cy to the dog, and Jasper came and lay down against him. "What happened?" exclaimed Cy, shaking his head, partly in disbelief, and partially to try to clear his mind. He stared at his bloody pants leg. "So, my leg isn't broken? It sure hurts like blazes!"

167

"The answer to the first question is, that buzz worm over there struck out at your horse," said Jim, gesturing to a rattle snake, blasted in half and laying in a heap, on the other side of the clearing in which they sat. "As far as your leg goes, if you will hold still and stop trying to punch a fist into my face, I'll check it."

"Sorry about that," grinned Cy sheepishly. "I'll mind my manners." He pushed himself up into a sitting position and looked down at his leg. He watched while Jim drew his Bowie knife and sliced through the blood soaked leg of his jeans. The knife was so sharp, it was like putting a hot knife into butter, and the cloth easily fell away from the wound.

Cy felt both relieved and sick. There was no bone sticking out, but there was an awful lot of blood still oozing out of an ugly slash that ran from just below his knee to his calf. Booker's one bullet had passed through his leg at a downward angle, causing more damage than usual. He looked at Jim. If he lost too much more blood, he might pass out and they would be too late getting to the Rocking R to be of any help.

Jim whistled and sprinted to his horse, coming back with a brown paper bundle in one hand and a small flask of whiskey in the other. He handed the flask to Cy as he started to unwrap the bundle, revealing clean bandages.

"Take a couple of good pulls on that, my friend, then hand it back." Cy did as he was told, then thrust the little metal container at Jim. The mountain man handed Cy a stick. "It's soft pine. Bite down on it and brace yourself. This is gonna hurt."

Jim poured whiskey up and down the wound and Cy howled through the stick in his teeth. Lights and stars flashed in a red heat in front of his eyes as the man fell back prone on the ground. Jim got up abruptly and walked to a bush, cutting off some leaves, which he rinsed quickly with water from his canteen. Still moist, he applied the leaves to the wound, then bound it tightly with the fresh bandages.

"Comfrey leaves," he explained to Cy. "They are good for stopping bleeding and healing. I don't think the rattler got you though!" He was pulling the bandages tight. When he was done, he took some piggin strips from his saddlebags and poking makeshift holes up and down the denim, roughly laced the leg of Cy's jeans back together.

"How long have we been here?" asked Cy, suddenly aware that the sun was getting lower.

"I'd say about an hour and a half," answered Jim, looking up at the sky himself.

"An hour and a half! Then quit your sewin' old woman, and help me get on my horse! We have to get to the ranch!"

"We need to keep that leg protected a bit, but I'm done with my lacing anyway." He walked to his horse, put the supplies back in his saddle bags, then led his horse over to Cy.

"Where's my horse?" asked Cy, putting his fingers to his lips and letting out a whistle. There was no response. "He must have run farther away than usual," said Cy, concern shading his features.

"Actually, he didn't run too far," said Jim soberly, "but he ain't comin' back. Rattler got him good. He's just over there in the bushes, where he fell."

"Well, I'll swallow a horn toad backwards!" Cy proclaimed, letting out a few more words that would have gotten him a whuppin' from his mother.

"It ain't gonna do no good to sit there and cuss," said Jim mildly. "Come on," he said, getting behind Cy and placing his hands under the armpits of the other man. "Shift all your weight to your left side, and when I count to three, push up with your arms and stand on your good leg."

Jim lifted more than Cy helped, but they got Cy to his feet and Jim switched to his side, acting as his crutch on the right. They got him to the horse and leaning almost completely on Jim, Cy put a hand on the saddle horn, one on the back of the saddle, and his left foot in the stirrup.

"Just stand in the stirrup on one foot," directed Jim, steadying Cy from behind as he boosted himself up and bent slightly forward over the saddle. Jim hopped up on a stump right next to the horse, and grasping Cy's right arm at the elbow, he lifted Cy's leg over the saddle.

A cry escaped Cy's lips, and gritting his teeth, he slumped forward over the saddle horn for a minute, eyes scrunched tightly shut, and sweat pouring down his face from the exertion. When he sat upright and opened his eyes, Jim was standing beside the horse with a canteen in his hand.

"Take some water. You've lost a lot of blood and it won't do anyone any good if you fall out of that saddle." Cy took a couple of good swallows, and hung it back over the saddle horn. "Hang on," Jim directed, as he took the reins and walked the horse in the direction of Cy's dead animal. Jim ground hitched his horse and stepped into the bushes, coming back with the other cowboy's rifle and ammunition, which he handed to Cy.

"You want me to ride in the back or do you want to hop up behind me?" asked Cy, stuffing the shells into his pockets, and resting the rifle across his lap.

"Neither," answered the mountain man, reaching up and removing his rifle from the scabbard. "Put your rifle in there until you need it. You might need both hands to hold on to the saddle horn until we get within shootin' distance." He walked to the other side of the horse so he would not be on the side where Cy would need to draw his rifle. He picked up the reins from the ground and handed them to the cowboy astride the horse."How much further do you figure it is to the ranch?" he asked. Cy twisted in the saddle, resetting his bearings. He pointed to the ridge that looked to be another eight to ten miles away.

"Just over that ridge yonder," he pointed. Jim followed his arm, nodded and then turned back to Cy.

"Holler if I get too far ahead of you," grinned the tall man. With that, he turned and started off in a loping, easy run towards the ridge.

Chapter 47

Hal Colter sat on the top of the ridge, watching his men below circle the ranch. They had ridden down the back of the ridge on which he sat, then split to come at the ranch from two different sides. They did not know how many men were still inside the main house.

The outlaw boss watched as three of his men fired through the windows of the bunkhouse, laying down scathing rifle fire meant to kill anyone inside the building. Then they charged into the bunkhouse, guns blazing, but the firing quickly halted. The men came out of the door, and one looked up the hill and shook his head. There was no one in the outer building. This was both good and bad. That meant all their forces were inside the one building. They had been smart not to split them, but Hal took that to mean they did not have many men.

"Looks like they have all their men inside the main house, boss," said the man sitting beside him.

"Yeah," snapped Colter, a little irritated that the cowboy beside him would not give him credit for figuring that out himself. He watched the fire pattern for a few more minutes from his vantage point. He saw one of his men get picked off as he tried to race between two boulders to get closer. His men laid down a volley in response and Colter noted that the return fire came from only three locations. "They only have three men," he said, pointing, "in the front, the back, and at that end," he said, gesturing to the area that was the kitchen in the ranch house.

"How can you be sure they don't have more men waiting to give them relief?"

171

"Because..." Hal Colter turned to berate the young cowboy beside him, but stopped as he saw the earnest expression on the face of the rider. *He really wants to know!* Hal had chosen this man to stay with him, because he was known as a fast, accurate gun hand. But now, Colter studied him a minute, then realizing he had a chance to groom this young man to be a real asset, decided to answer. "They are greatly out gunned, and trapped. If they had more men, they would have them all firing at once, trying not to lose any vantage point, and not to let any of us get too close. If we get too close, we might be able to fire heavy volleys into the windows or breech the door." The rider nodded, his eyes logging all that was going on below.

"Their best shooter is at the window at the east end of the house," remarked the gunman. "If we could take him out, it would really help. The rifleman in the back is the least effective."

"You're right!" said Hal, with new respect for the man beside him. "Do you have any ideas on how to make that happen?" He kept his eyes on the other rider's face, finding it interesting to actually see the thinking process going on as it showed on his visage. He might not be good at poker, but he appeared to be very sharp at warfare

"If I could get down to that barn, I might be able to get a shot from the hay loft into that window," nodded the younger man.

"You any good with a rifle?" questioned Hal. He fixed his eyes on the prospective scene and came to the conclusion that a good rifleman just might make that shot.

"Yes Sir. I learned in the war."He met Colter's eyes with a solemn hardness.

"The war!!! You mean the War Between the States?" asked Hal in disbelief.

"I surely do," replied the young man. He sat stoically, staring at the ranch.

"But you're just a kid!" exclaimed the bossman.

"No Sir. I was just a kid when I first picked up a gun to fight the soldiers that came for my family. I was twelve then. It made me a man real fast." He said nothing more, and neither did Hal. Choosing to be a hardened outlaw was one thing, but having to fight for the lives of your family at twelve...that was another.

"What's your name, son?" asked Hal, a slight softness creeping into his voice in spite of himself.

"Wade," he replied simply.

"Got a last name?"

"Just Wade will do," said the young shooter with finality. In the west, a lot of men went only by their first names. Many a grave had been marked with only a given name; the surname remaining unknown to those laying the person in their final resting place.

For the first time, Hal realized this young man was not in the least afraid of him, and it sent a cold shiver down his spine. A round of rapid rifle fire drew their attention back to the scene below. Hal cursed as he saw two of his men fall under the fire of the man at the east window. His riflemen retreated, hopefully to regroup and attack again, but it was hard to hire men with sand these days, and they might just cut and run.

"You sure you know what to do with that rifle?" He was simmering and in a foul mood now.

"I learned from the best." Wade shucked his Yellow Boy and checked it, then dug extra shells out of his saddlebags and put them in his front pocket.

"Who was it?" Colter could not explain it, but he found himself curious.

"I doubt you would know him," replied Wade, a cold smile playing across his lips.

"Just wondered if he was anyone I have met along the trails," said Hal, finding himself a little defensive. "I guess you owe him a debt of gratitude."

"I owe him all right," said Wade grimly, "I owe him a bullet. He killed my brother. I plan to return the favor if I ever find him again."

"He taught you to shoot, then killed your brother?" asked Hal incredulously. "Why?"

"No need for you to know," said Wade coolly, ending the subject of conversation abruptly.

Hal felt the heat rise along his neck and considered drawing and shooting this insolent pup out of the saddle. He was known for his quick draw too! But he tamped down his anger just as quick as it started. He would use this kid for his own purposes, then maybe…

"Do me this favor here, and kill that man in the window," soothed Colter. "Then I'd be happy to ask around for you. I know a lot of people outside the law."

"I'd be obliged," said Wade. "We'lltalk more when this is over." Wade did not smile, just stared briefly at Hal with icy eyes, then turned his horse and walked it carefully down the shale on the hillside, and began to circle around, using the trees for cover to get to the barn.

Hal looked down at his men and began to get angry again. They were sitting behind rocks, drinking from canteens, and chewing on jerky! He watched them taking their time and thought about pulling his own rifle out and burning a few shots in the ground around them. *Where is that good for nothing Sly Booker?* He hired him to boss these men around for him, and then he takes a powder just when he needs him to do his job! He studied the ranch house and saw no movement at the windows. That could mean they were getting a break, and he did not want that! He wanted them to be constantly hammered with gunfire, unable to rest or even eat. He wanted them exhausted; tired men made mistakes, and that's when they would kill them all.

Movement in the corner of his eye caused him to turn his head. Wade was already at the back of the barn, ground hitching his horse! He would need the men in the house to be firing to be able to pinpoint their sharpshooter. He glared at the lounging men below, willing them to get up and fight, but they sat in the shade with the hot sun beating down on them, not at all worried about the men they had pinned down. He just might have to go down there himself, and then there would be the devil to pay!

Chapter 48

Rusty shrank further into the corner away from the window and looked around the room. Several of Ruth's dishes lay strewn about, shattered by bullets and Rusty wished they had found time to move them before the fighting began. Jed still stood at the window, rifle at the ready, but there was a thin line of blood running down his cheek.

"You okay?" asked Rusty, sinking into the chair Paul had moved over for him before going into the back room.

"Yeah, just grazed my cheek," Jed answered, pulling a handkerchief out of his vest pocket and dabbing at the red line that started just above his right ear.

"Paul?" called Rusty softly, not wanting to be heard from the outside.

"Here!" he replied quietly. "I'm still holding my own."

"Do you think they pulled back to lick their wounds?" chuckled Rusty.

"Well, we sure gave them reason!" He glanced at the older man. "You are something fierce with that rifle! I'm mighty grateful you're on our side!" Jed smiled briefly at Rusty, then turned back to watch intently for any sign they were renewing the attack. "How are you feeling? You look a mite pale."

"Now don't you go puttin' on your doctor hat in the middle of a fight!" growled Rusty. "We ain't got time for that! I'm fine! That's just gunpowder dust making my face look pale!"

"Gunpowder is black, old soul!" Jed was only half teasing. He was a little worried that the sharpshooter had spent his energy reserves already.

175

"Pshaw! You think I don't know that, you young pup?" Rusty tried to sound indignant, but did not quite pull it off. "The black powder makes the rest of my face look like it ain't seen the light of the sun for days! Come to think of it, it hasn't! I've been cooped up in here with the likes of you two acting like fawnin' old women for nigh a week now! Pale!" He stormed and mumbled and Jed grinned.

"At least you still got your good natured disposition!" He chided, feeling slightly reassured his patient was not going to fall face first onto the floor.

"Yeah, well a cup of that coffee would help!" He started to get up and Jed put his own rifle down. As he rose to his feet, Jed stepped to the coffee pot.

"You stay right there, lean on that table there. We need our best shot at the window." He was only half kidding.

Jed rapidly poured three cups of hot, black coffee, and keeping low, took a cup of the strong black liquid to the red haired cowboy, and handed him a biscuit and a piece of jerky too. Rusty nodded thanks, and took a swig of the coffee, breathing a sigh of pleasure as he swallowed. The doctor crept cautiously to Paul next, carrying another cup of coffee and meager, but nourishing food.

"How's Rusty holding up?" asked Paul, sipping the coffee.

"Cranky!" Jed smiled wide and Paul laughed softly.

"That might be a good thing in a fight!" Paul smiled too, but then turned serious, his mouth drawn into a thin line. "How many of them do you think are still out there?"

"Could be as many as ten still, and one of those we got was only wounded, so might still be able to shoot." The young doctor sipped his own coffee and took a bite of his jerky.

"Whew," whistled Paul. He shook his head. "I sure wish we had a few more men." He was silent a moment, peering out the window, and started to raise his rifle, then lowered it again. "Just a rabbit," he grinned sheepishly.

"Do you think Luke will come back?" asked Jed. He did not know the rancher like Paul, who had worked for him for a couple of years.

"Yeah," said Paul, nodding, "I'd stake my life on it." He laughed nervously. "In fact, I guess I'm already doing that! I sure hope he hurries!"

"Me too," said Jed. "In the meantime, come late afternoon, we need to start taking turns sleeping. I'm thinking Rusty first for about three hours, then you, then Rusty again, then me. He'll fight it, but he isn't strong enough yet, and we really do need his shooting skills. We don't dare let down our guard. They might try to rush us if we don't get help before dark." Jed left Paul still chewing on his biscuit and crouching as he moved, returned to his place at the window.

Rusty nodded at him. Jed noted he had laid his rifle on the table within easy reach and was resting his head on his hand while he chewed the last of his lunch. A few minutes later when Jed looked over, the wounded man had his head on his arm on the table and was asleep.

"Thanks for not arguing with me about taking a nap," chuckled Jed to himself. He kept his eyes roving over the yard and buildings in his line of sight. He said a little silent prayer for help too. They were going to need it.

Chapter 49

The three riders rode rapidly towards the ranch. As edgy as they all were, they had to admit the wisdom of stopping to rest the horses and themselves in a small clump of aspens near a pool of water. They had prepared coffee while they waited, Clay having planned a little better for food, just in case. Or rather, his wife had, he chuckled as he explained the presence of coffee, a pot, cups, and some very welcome sandwiches. The slabs of homemade bread with a chunk of beef between them eased the gnawing hunger of the men who had not taken time for breakfast.

"What is this yellow coating on the bread?" asked Luke, pleasantly surprised at the added moisture and flavor in the sandwich.

"It's my wife's recipe," answered Clay. "Her grandmother was French, and I guess this recipe has been in her family for generations. Got it from a monastery in France, way back. Do you like it?" He took a bite while he waited for Luke's answer.

"Yes, I really do!" Luke took another bite and chewed thoughtfully. "What's it called?"

"It's called mustard," grinned Clay. "It uses mustard seeds, so we have the plants in a little fenced garden right now. The plants are okay for the cattle, but not for horses, so we are going to have to keep them contained."

"Would your wife be willing to share the recipe?" asked Jeremiah, licking a finger that had saved a small glob of mustard from falling on the ground.

"I'm sure she would," nodded Clay. "It is nice to have a little extra taste on a sandwich or a piece of meat from time to time."

"I think Ruth and Hannah would enjoy getting together with your wife to make it the first time," said Luke.

"That sounds like a great idea," said Clay. "I know my wife gets lonely for the company of other women, so maybe we could give them a day to enjoy each others company and make some mustard. Maybe Faith and Susan would like to join in, if you are still here," suggested Clay to Jeremiah.

"I think we could wait a few days longer, so Ruth is stronger," said Jeremiah. "That is, if your hospitality will extend itself that long."

"I will talk to Gabrielle when we get back, but it would be a good way to get to know more of our neighbors."

The men finished their sandwiches and coffee, cleaned up the camp, and doused the fire with dirt. They had given the horses nearly an hour to rest, and all of them were anxious to get back on the road. They saddled the horses, checking their hooves for stones, and their legs for any cuts, then, satisfied, they swung into the saddle again and urged the horses into a canter, then a hard ride. They were still an hour from the ranch, and Luke wanted to close that distance as fast as was wise. Each was silent, saving all their energy for the ride, and thinking of the impending danger ahead. They swiveled their heads frequently, looking for any sign of trouble – the glint of sun off a rifle barrel, smoke, a lone rider on a ridge. They did not want to ride into an ambush themselves.

They were roughly two miles from the ranch when the air exploded with the sudden, thundering report of multiple rifles being fired simultaneously and rapidly repeating. The three men reined their horses in; Clay and Jeremiah looking to Luke for direction. The young rancher listened for only seconds, then turned to the riders beside him.

"The ranch house is there," he said, pointing to the south, "on the other side of that hill. The attack is likely to be coming from the front, or at least mostly. I think we should go in carefully, stay under cover, but not too far apart. If we can get into the barn, it will give us some good cover, and we can shoot down at them from the hayloft."

"May the Lord bring us through this," said Clay, and the other two nodded in agreement.

"I can't thank you enough," said Luke. "Be careful, my friends."

Three determined men shucked their rifles, checked their guns again, and rode into the fray, knowing not exactly what they faced, but wearing the mantle of courage shown by western men fighting for their very lives.

Chapter 50

Hal Colter watched as Wade went through the back door of the barn. He waited, and saw the hay loft door creak open a mite, and a rifle muzzle peek out, then get pulled back in. The door was opened another several feet, and then the rifle reappeared. Colter knew Wade was looking for the right angle. He also knew he needed to get a bead on the shooter by watching the fire from that window. He looked down at his men again and spat, then let loose with a string of curses that would make a bordello madam blush. They were still sitting in the shade of the rocks, taking their time over their lunch. Angry, he turned his horse and rode down the back side of the mountain. He jumped off his horse and strode to the nearest cowboy, jerked him up by his shirt front and bellowed in his face.

"I ain't paying you to sit in the shade and have a tea party! Git your sorry butt out there and take that house now!" He threw the man backwards, sprawling him face first in the dirt. The rest of the men froze, staring at him in surprise.

"Boss, we were just getting something to drink and eat," explained one man, rising carefully to his feet. "We have them pinned inside." The well meaning cowboy quickly regretted speaking, as Hal stepped forward, drew back his arm, and back handed him across the face, knocking him off balance and into another man.

"I can see that, you petticoat wearing, lead-footed, fiddle head! You planning to let them have their dinner too before you get this job done? " His face was red, and some would have sworn his eyes became red glowing coals in his head, so much did he look like a raging demon at that moment.

The men jumped to their feet almost as one, some spilling their canteen contents into the dust, not taking the time to put the cap back on. They picked up their rifles and began firing in a fury at the house, riddling it with bullets, more afraid of the man behind them than the rifles they faced. A few moved out to other cover, trying to get away from Hal. One of the unlucky chaps fell under Rusty's rifle, not living long enough to regret his hasty decision.

Hal looked to the barn and was rewarded with a muzzle flash. He shifted his eyes to the window in question and fired his own weapon in that direction. There was no return fire from the vantage point inside the house! Could Wade have been lucky enough or good enough to take out their sharpshooter on his first attempt? Hal watched the window as the firing continued. Several minutes went by, then the firing started again, but it was different somehow. Riveted, he watched, and suddenly realized shots were alternating between the two windows!

One person was moving between the two windows. He was sure of it. He laughed. Maybe Wade could take out this guy too. Wouldn't that be sweet?

"Move up!" He shouted at his men, some of whom glowered back at him, while others frantically looked for cover to scramble forward. He kicked the nearest man in the leg, and the scared young cowboy bolted towards a boulder a little closer to the ranch house. It cost him.

A shot rang out immediately, and the young man jerked rigid, then fell in a heap. Colter was not sure if he was dead, but he was definitely out of the fight. He cursed again and swung his head towards the barn. The smile spread across his face as he saw Wade stand and level his rifle again. He fired, then worked the lever to fire again. Hal turned with glee to the house and saw the shot rip through the window frame, throwing splinters of wood inside and out of the window.

"That has got to at least sting!" he chortled gleefully. He was enjoying himself; he took pleasure from seeing pain inflicted on others.

Suddenly, shots came from the side and slightly behind them! He crouched, narrowing his eyes, and saw a sight he could not believe! Just before he ducked behind a couple of bales of hay, Hal Colter was sure he saw Lucas Randall running up and firing at his men! He seethed at being blindsided, not owning that he had done the same to the people inside the house.

Three rifles were now firing at his men from the side, and he retreated even more, into the safety of the boulders. Who was with Randall? Fuming, he looked towards the barn again, but Wade had withdrawn inside. Was he turning yellow bellied too? The bile rose in Hal's throat and he roiled at the idea that he could lose!

But as he watched, Wade stepped again into the opening. *Why is he pointing the rifle down?* Following the barrel of the gun, he looked beneath Wade and in shock, he realized he just might win this battle after all. Lucas Randall, unaware of the rifleman above him, had moved up closer, behind a wagon in front of the barn. That put him in easy range of the man in the hay loft. Wade raised the rifle and smiled as he set his sights on Luke.

At that point, there was a lull in the shooting. A rifle shot rang out, and the body fell.

Chapter 51

Ruth paced in the kitchen and listened to Hannah talk to customers in the store as she watched the children play together. Thomas was still a little pale, but he was giggling with Adele and her heart warmed at the sound. She was frustrated at her arm still being in a sling, but the doc had told her to get used it, with a stony stare that said he would brook no nonsense. Her ribs still ached, and it was painful when she tried to lift her son, so she usually sat and coaxed him to crawl into her lap, or up on the bed beside her.

But she was restless, and she was worried about her husband! First Cy and Jim had gone tracking the man who stole food from the general store. They were expected back at least by the next morning, but had not returned. Then Luke had gone to the ranch without her!

"I can't believe my husband would go off to our home without taking me and the baby!" She had railed and cried while Hannah tried to soothe her.

"My friend, you know he loves you! He wants to make sure it is safe to take you and your son back to the ranch," said Hannah.

"I don't mean to hurt your feelings; you are my best friend and I love you and your family," began Ruth, "but there is just something about being in your own home." She bit her lip. "Besides, I am worried about Rusty. I couldn't forgive myself if he ...," She didn't finish the sentence, but a tear escaped her eye and slid down her cheek.

"That is probably one of the reasons Luke went back to check on him and Paul. He said there was another man there, a man who was a doctor in the War Between the States." She put her hands on the shoulders of her friend and looked her in the eyes. "Rusty will be alright and Luke will come back for you when he is sure it is safe."

"He could have ridden right into an ambush!" Ruth hiccupped a sob.

"Axel said he saw Luke ride off with Clay and Jeremiah, so there are two other men with him." Hannah tucked a strand of hair behind Ruth's ear and smiled. "I think you are tired, my friend. You do not usually cry so easily."

"You are right," sighed Ruth.

"Why don't you take a little nap. You are still recovering; it would do you good."

"Hannah," said Axel, stepping into the kitchen, "do you have any more of your jam to sell? There is a man here from Virginia City that is getting some supplies to take back with him."

"He is from Virginia City?" she asked, a frown creasing her forehead. "How odd that he would be here to buy supplies, instead of getting them in Carson City."

"I wondered about that myself, but then a sale is a sale!" Axel grinned at her. "And you were just talking about how you need to use the fruit off our peach tree and make more jam before the fruit goes bad." He laughed and kissed her on her cheek. "Oops! Here comes Mark to pick up his order. Do you need help getting the jam? He wants six jars, if we have it to spare."

"I can help her," replied Ruth, "I still have one good arm!" She laughed, without much merriment, but it was a start.

The friends gathered the jars of jam out of the back storeroom by the kitchen, with Hannah carrying four of the jars in a basket, and Ruth carrying two that would not fit in the container Hannah was using. The women took them out to the front of the store and placed them on the counter, where Axel was finishing up the man's order. The man paid and walked out with two big, flour sacks, each half full of jams, dry goods, and a few other things he said were not easy to get right now in Virginia City.

"Now," smiled Axel at his friend Mark, "anything else to add to your order?"

Mark acted as if he did not hear the store keeper; he was staring after the man who had just left the store. Now he walked to the window and peered out as the man rode slowly out of town. Axel

185

watched his friend, puzzled at his odd behavior. Finally, the hotel keeper turned and faced the store keeper.

"What is John Roberts doing in Bridgeport?" asked Mark.

"Who?" asked Axel, confusion on his face.

"John Roberts," repeated Mark, "the man who just left."

"I don't know who that is – should I?" asked the big German, shaking his head.

"He is a cattle and lumber buyer from Virginia City," answered Mark.

"Are you sure?" asked Axel.

"Yeah, I'm positive. I don't think he recognized me without my beard and mustache, but I remember him!"

"You had a beard and mustache?" laughed the bigger man. "That would have been a sight to see!"

"Okay, have your fun! I had the face hair before you got here – helped keep my face warm in the winter. But then I started doing more of the cooking at the hotel, and it was too hot under all that hair! I decided I liked being clean shaven." Both men chuckled.

"So, if that man is a cattle and lumber buyer, how did you come to know him?" asked Axel, his curiosity rising.

"He sold me a few head of cattle when I first opened my restaurant. I just had a tent operation; it was before I built the hotel and a real kitchen. One day I was low on food and John Roberts came through with a small herd of cattle. I talked him into selling me a couple head."

"Sounds like he did you a favor," said Axel. He was perplexed. Something was off with his friend.

"Huh!" snorted the hotel keeper. "A favor my old jackass! He almost got me hung!"

"I don't understand." The big German shook his head in concern.

"He sold me cattle he didn't own! He never paid the man who owned those cattle, he just drove them off. It's how he got started in his business."

"How did that almost get you hung?"

"The real buyer came riding up and Roberts told them it was me stole the cattle and he was bringing them back." His jaw set and his eyes hardened. "They had the rope out when some boys from the Hunnewill Ranch spoke up for me. Roberts laughed and told them it

186

was all just a mistake, but I will never forget he almost got me hung."

"If I had known all that, I would not have sold him anything!" spat the store keeper. "What do you think he is doing in this area? It's quite a ways to Virginia City from here."

"I don't know, Axel, but that man is a crook, and whatever he is doing here, it isn't good." Mark's face was grim as he collected his order and headed back to his hotel and restaurant.

Axel watched his friend trudge back to his business, as he thought about what Mark had just told him. After several minutes, he sighed and turned back towards the kitchen. Ruth was standing in the doorway, her face pale as a full winter moon.

"Ruth! Are you alright? You are so pale! Sit down," he said, taking her by the good arm and setting her down on a chair by the pot bellied stove. "Are you in pain?"

Ruth was transfixed, her eyes going from the door to the face of her friend. Her hand was shaking as she reached out and clenched his forearm.

"Axel, I am scared," she whispered. "That man. I heard you say his name is John Roberts."

"What is it, Ruth?"

"I heard what our friend Mark from the hotel said about him. I heard it all! He sounds like a very bad man!"

"You don't need to worry, Ruth," he said softly, "he is gone and we wouldn't let him hurt you anyway. You are with friends. No one is going to do you harm." He felt sorry for her. Usually a very strong woman, she was obviously fatigued and overwrought by her ordeal.

"No! No, Axel, you don't understand! John Roberts is the name of the man that Luke went to meet in Virginia City. He went to sell him our cattle. Why would he be here now, after Luke came back? Where is he?" Her lip quivered and she was breathing rapidly. "What if he did something to Luke to get his money back?"

Chapter 52

Rusty McMath stood looking down at Wade, as he lay in the dirt, a crumpled and bloody heap. Jim and Luke stood beside him. Cyrus rode up and dismounted with the help of Jed and Paul, who had come out of the house. Jeremiah and Clay were checking the bodies lying about to see if any were still alive.

"You say you knew this young man?" asked Luke, looking at Rusty.

"Yes. I sure did," replied Rusty. "What a sad case." He stared at the body for a few moments without speaking. "I taught him how to shoot, you know," he said, almost absently, as if his mind had flashed onto something else.

"What brought him here?" asked Luke, studying the face of one of his top hands.

"Durned if I know," Rusty murmured, shrugging his shoulders. "He swore he would kill me one day, but I have no idea how he would have known I was here." Sad eyes rose to meet those of his boss. Rusty sighed. "He was a young un when he first picked up that rifle. Just twelve years old, but he had the eye of an eagle and a natural talent with a gun. I took him under my wing and taught him how to hunt. We used to have shooting contests, and by golly, sometimes he would win," he said wistfully.

"Sounds like you were pretty close," said Jim quietly. He almost winced at the pain that flitted across Rusty's face when he spoke those words.

"Yeah. We sure were. Then the War Between the States came and Wade's younger brother ran off to fight. We looked everywhere and couldn't find him. Wade and I got forced into the

188

mess and we were some of the best shooters the Union Army had."
He ran a hand over his face, rubbing it hard.

"The war wasn't your fault," began Luke. "What he saw
wasn't on you," he said gently.

"Yes it was!" Rusty raised his voice as he answered Luke,
and those standing near stopped to stare . This was not like Rusty, in
fact, Luke could not remember him ever raising his voice in anger at
any time the whole year he had been on the ranch. "What he saw, no
boy should have to see!"

They were surprised at the twisted agony on the face of their
friend. The men stood silently as a few sobs escaped the older man.
They gave him time, and after several minutes, Rusty gathered
himself and continued.

"It was the day we were at Shiloh and the Confederate Army
was fighting us something fierce. That's when it all changed." His
voice softened to barely above a whisper. "I was…killing men as
fast as I could; didn't even focus on their faces. I couldn't, you see."
He raised his eyes and ran them over the faces of the men who stood
around him, seeking understanding.

Luke and Jed exchanged a look, then stared at the dirt a
minute before they met Rusty with misted eyes. They knew that
nightmare. Luke gently clapped McMath on the shoulder, nodded
once, his own lips a thin line, then withdrew his hand. Everyone
knew there was more to the story and they did not rush him. Rusty
swallowed hard and looked to the sky, closing his eyes as if he was
saying a sudden, short, silent prayer, then down again.

"A young boy came running at us. I heard Wade yell
something, but I fired anyway; there was no time to think. I heard
Wade scream in agony and I turned, thinking he had been hit, but he
was running towards the boy I just killed. He fell to his knees and
picked up the body, rocking and holding it, screaming and sobbing.
The Rebs started to retreat, and I went to Wade." The older man's
voice broke and he stopped talking to sob, covering his mouth as he
did so. His shoulders shook and he rocked back and forth as he
stood.

Jed took a small flask out of his pocket and held it out to
Rusty. The older man looked at it, took it, and gulped several large
swallows before he handed it back. Western men did not talk about
their past much. Something unusual was happening here, and no one

wanted to break the spell. They respected the rare moment too much, waiting patiently until McMath was ready to continue..

"Was the boy Wade's brother?" asked Jim. He had put the pieces together for them all.

"Yes," was all Rusty could say.

"Have you seen him since that day?" asked Luke softly.

"No." Rusty shook his head sadly. "I tried. He wouldn't come with me. He wouldn't leave the body. He looked at me with such hatred in his eyes, such accusation..." Rusty shook his head again. "He swore he would kill me someday. He told me to get away from his brother, that he hated me." He cleared his throat. "I walked off to give him some time, but when I came back a couple hours later, he was gone and so was the body of his brother. I never saw him again. I looked, but I couldn't find him. Not until now."

"I had to shoot him," said Jim gently. "He was going to kill Luke."

"I know it," agreed Rusty, bobbing his head slightly. "He was the one shooting at me from the loft. He creased my head and it knocked me silly for a few minutes or he might have killed me too." He touched the hasty bandage Jed had put around his head to stop the blood from getting in his eyes.

"Do you think he knew it was you?" asked Luke.

"I have no idea," replied Rusty. "I'd like to think he didn't know." He pondered that statement for a moment. "What a shame, though," he said wistfully. "He would be just seventeen now." He shook his head with a heaviness that was so much more than physical weariness.

"You know a lot about him," began Luke, his eyes sharpening. "Do you know how to reach his next of kin?"

"Yeah, I do." he nodded. "And you already have," said Rusty sadly. "He was my nephew." Rusty turned and walked away. No one stopped him.

Chapter 53

Hal Colter rode hard and fast towards Virginia City. His plan had not played out, and he lost a lot of the men he had hired. He was fuming over the turn of events at the ranch. His men were not the seasoned fighters he thought they were! With no regard for the fact they lost their lives, he cussed and cursed them for failing him. Then he turned his attention to those who had foiled the murder of the men in the ranch house.

"Damn meddlers," he fussed, thinking of the unexpected support that had shown up for Luke. It was bad enough that two men from the town had ridden out with him to help, but where in blue blazes did that mountain man come from?

He had turned gleefully to watch Wade kill Lucas Randall, but instead saw the young boy jerk back, then fall like a sack of lead from the hay loft to the ground. In disbelief, he swung his head in the direction the shot must have come from, and saw a tall, slender man clad in buckskin and standing at an unbelievable distance, just bringing his rifle down from his shoulder. Colter thought about shooting him, but he knew his pistol would not do any damage at that distance, and the stranger was gone behind cover faster than Hal could blink.

Colter looked around quickly and it did not look good for his boys. There was another man on horseback shooting too! Eight, fast shooting men were too many for his crowd to handle. Hal had eased himself back in the rocks until he reached his horse. He led the horse around a cluster of boulders to make sure he was out of the line of sight, then mounted and trotted the horse until he was sure he could run without his dust drawing attention. He did not want anyone following him; the rest of the plan was still to be executed!

"Well, at least I won't have to pay those dead men back there!" He chuckled as he talked out loud to himself. "That makes up for what I would have taken from that flea bitten ranch! They already did all that logging work for me, and now I don't have to give them any money!" He laughed out loud as he rode, slowing to a canter.

He directed his thoughts to the lumber mill and the wagons. They had a two day head start from him, and he had arranged for teams to trade out the horses along the way. They should be making around thirty miles a day even with the heavy loads, with the fresh horses being changed in. That should have them arriving by tomorrow night to the small sawmill outside of Virginia City. He had promised Mickey a bonus if he got the teams and wagons to the agreed upon point by tomorrow evening, and the big logger had agreed.

Colter did not like the way the logger had insolently sized him up, as if considering the offer and the likelihood of being paid. He also didn't like the way the man had rested his hand on his belt, inches from the revolver on his hip.

"Bah! You're beginning to sound like a scared old woman, Colter!" he chastised himself, out loud again, then laughed like a hyena. "Get yourself together, man. You are still one of the meanest, fastest outlaws in the west!" He turned his focus to riding, wondering where that no good Sly Booker was loafing!

He thought about John Roberts and his face hardened. What a weak excuse for a man! He wondered how much money Roberts actually had. And then he made plans to relieve him of every penny. He would be gone before anyone came looking for their payday.

Chapter 54

"Hey Luke!" called Clay. "We have a live one over here!" He was kneeling beside a young cowboy sitting on the ground, holding his head. Jeremiah stood beside them, his gun leveled at the outlaw.

Luke gave quick instructions to Jim and Paul to lay Rusty's nephew on a tarp and cover him. He would be given a Christian burial later. He and Jed broke away from the group that had been listening to Rusty, and strode quickly to the trio of men. Jed knelt beside the injured man and began to check for wounds.

"He has a nasty wound in his shoulder," said Jed, "and a bump on his head. Looks like he got shot in the shoulder, then stumbled and fell, hitting his head on this old tree stump. Let's get him inside and clean him up."

Clay and Jeremiah each put a hand under the arms of the outlaw and lifted him to his feet. They guided him up the steps behind Luke and Jed, and sat him in a chair inside the house. Jed started working on him immediately, and was dabbing at the cut on his head when the man spoke.

"Is that you, Jed?" asked the man, who looked as much boy as man.

"It sure is, Ralph." He kept working, without speaking.

"What are they gonna do with me, Jed," asked the young man, whispering as if he thought they might not hear him. He looked scared now. The rider for Colter was tall and skinny, wearing worn jeans, down at the heel boots, and a faded red checkered shirt that didn't look like it had been washed in weeks. It didn't smell like it either; it reeked of body odor and smoke.

"That depends," said Luke, with steel in his voice.

193

"On...on what, mister?" Ralph raised his eyes to Luke now, and saw nothing that made him feel at ease. Randall stood, hands on his hips, with an icy glare fixed on the rider. Suddenly, Ralph tore his eyes from Luke's face and shot a panicked look at Jed. He jerked upright, his face draining of all color. "You ain't gonna hang me, are you? Please don't hang me, mister! Jed! Please don't let them hang me, Jed!" He grabbed the doctor's hand and, bloody cloth and all, clasped it between both of his hands. "Jed! We rode together! I never killed anyone before! I was just tryin' to eat! I didn't even fire my gun but once, and it wasn't at the house here! I think I hit that cherry tree out in the side yard – you can go look!"

Jed stood and stepped back. He looked at Luke for a moment, then stepped over to the sink to wash his hands. Ralph was sobbing now. He fell on his knees before Luke and clasping his hands together, looked up at the rancher that towered over him.

"Please, mister, as God is my witness, I never killed anyone. I was just hungry and no one else was offering a job."

"You use God's name lightly, son, and I don't take kindly to that," answered Luke coldly.

"Oh, no Sir! My mama raised me to be God fearin'!"

"What about your father? Why didn't he teach you to be a better man?" Luke was harsh, and he knew it.

"My daddy was killed by a bear when I was nine years old. My mama and me tried to scratch out a livin' on our little patch of land, but one morning I woke up and...well...she didn't. I finally left the little shack when I couldn't get anything to grow. I was so hungry, there was nothin' to eat at all and I couldn't catch anything either!"

"How old were you when your mama died?" asked Luke.

"I was...let me think now, ...I was eleven, Sir."

"Eleven! How old are you now then?" Luke was startled.

"Well Sir, I think it has been two years, so I guess I am thirteen now."

Luke assessed the boy in front of him. His height had made him seem older, and the dirt on his face hid his youth. Boys grew into men fast in the west, but in his mind, Luke could not help but see a boy in front of him.

194

"How did you get here? And where did you come from?"
Luke needed to know more. He glanced at Jed, who only shrugged
his shoulders.

"I walked most of the way. I came from Oregon; it was good
farm land in places, but none of it was mine. I worked a little here
and there, but heard there was gold in California, so I just kept
coming this way."

"How did you get hooked up with Hal Colter's outfit?"
demanded Luke.

"Who?" The boy looked genuinely at a loss.

"The boss of the outlaw gang you...we both rode for, at least
for a time." Jed answered the question, shot a quick look at Luke,
then looked away.

"I never knew his name. He was just the boss to me and most
of the other boys. And he fed us." Ralph licked his lips and stared at
the floor.

"I'll ask you again – how did you come to work for Colter!"
snapped Luke.

"I was around the mines in Virginia City, but couldn't get any
work. I didn't have any tools or any kind of an outfit. So I was
sitting, thinking my stomach was going to start eating itself pretty
soon, and this man comes up and asks me if I wanted to have a piece
of jerky. I sure enough took it and thanked him!" He shook his head.
"Then he asked me if I wanted a job." Ralph sighed. "He said it
would be driving some cattle or doing ranch work. He had a horse I
could ride and he gave me a gun. I was eating good and didn't have
to work much, so it seemed all right." He let his eyes travel over the
circle of men slowly. "He never said anything about killing anyone."
He slumped back on his haunches and hung his head.

Luke looked over the boy at Jed, then at Paul and Cy. He
took his hat off and ran his hands through his hair, then set the hat
back on his head.

"Sit back in the chair, Ralph," instructed Luke. Obviously, it
caused Ralph some pain to move, but he did as he was told. "What
was Colter's plan here?" asked Luke.

"He said we were to ride over here and talk to the men here.
He said they had killed one of our men for no reason, and we had to
make that right."

"Did he tell you they were going to kill everyone here?"

"No Sir! At least not all of us knew that until we got here. I heard some of the other men talking about how they hoped there was some good stuff here to take, and I thought that was odd. But it wasn't until we got here that the boss told us we had to kill the men in the house. He said it was the right thing to do since they killed Joe."

"So you just started shooting at us?" demanded Paul. "You didn't even know who we were?" He stood, hands on hips, lips pressed into a thin line, glaring at the young man.

"No! I mean, I wasn't shooting! But then the boss kicked me and told me to get up and charge the house and start shooting or he was going to shoot me! I jumped up and started towards you because I didn't know what else to do! I shot at that cherry tree over yonder and then I got shot and I don't know what happened after that," he said miserably.

"Joe got shot over a week ago," said Jed suddenly, standing up straight. "What were you all doing for the past week? Why didn't you come sooner?" His eyes were narrowed on Ralph, and Luke looked from him to the boy.

"Well, we were cutting down the trees," he answered. "We had to finish that job first."

"The trees?" Luke stepped to stand right in front of Ralph. "What trees?"

"The ones back there," he said, hooking a thumb over his shoulder. "Back in those hills a ways there were a whole bunch of trees."

"How many did you cut?" demanded Luke.

"I can answer that, boss," said Cyrus, who had come in and was standing quietly to the side. "Jim and I tracked Sly Booker after he stole a bunch of goods from the general store. He took the supplies to Colter's camp."

"He was camped on my land?" gasped Randall.

"Sure was," interjected Jim. "He had about twenty loggers and cowboys, and another eight with rifles standing guard when we found them."

"Twenty loggers?" Luke was dumbfounded. "How many trees did they take?"

"Pretty near all of them, Luke," said Cyrus. "Looked like a big, well planned job too. We saw wagons being loaded." He paused

196

and shook his head. "We were on our way to the ranch to tell you when we ran into Sly Booker. We thought you might already be here."

"Booker!" growled Jed. "I want him!"

"I'm afraid you're too late, partner," replied Jim. The men exchanged a meaningful look and then Jed nodded in understanding.

"What were they doing with the trees?" Luke was coldly quiet when he asked Ralph the question. He towered over the boy, arms crossed over his chest now, legs planted wide, and a scowl on his face.

"All I know is that they were taking them to a man in Virginia City," said the hapless Ralph, twisting his hands in his lap. He almost looked pathetic with blood on his shirt and a bloodied bandage around his tow head.

"They are going to sell my lumber!" said Luke angrily. All the men were in the ranch house now, all looking towards him for direction. The young rancher paced back and forth rapidly for several minutes. When he stopped, he looked around the room.

"Whatever you need, Luke," offered Clay solemnly. Every man nodded and grunted agreement, and Luke ran eyes filled with gratitude over all of their faces. They knew what they were buying into, and they did so willingly.

"Rusty, I need you and Cy to stay here. You are both good shots, but wounded so you can't travel fast. Can you watch things here?"

"You bet," nodded Cy. "We can tend to each other's wounds," he quipped. The two hands smiled at each other, clearly disappointed to be left out of the chase, but realistic enough to know Luke was doing the right thing. They would be of more use guarding the ranch and tending the stock as best they could.

"Anyone who wants to go back home, I understand – no hard feelings." He noted Jed was putting some supplies in a flour sack, but no one else spoke. They all checked their guns, then fixed Luke with steady eyes and waited.

"Sir?" It was Ralph, speaking timidly. Worry covered his face. "I'm sure sorry. I'd ride with you, if'n you'd let me. You know, to try to make right what I did." Luke hesitated a moment, studying the young lad's eyes.

"No," Luke said, shaking his head. "You are too young to be in this. You stay here and do the running for Cy and Rusty. If he gives you any trouble, whup him," he said to Cy, a twinkle in his eye. "There is a strap in the woodhouse out back, but make him bring it to you, or make him cut a switch off a tree, if it's easier. That's what my daddy used to do."

"Oh, I won't be any trouble, Sir! I've learned my lesson, I promise!"

"See that you keep that promise!" Luke said sternly.

He turned to the other men, who had been quickly gathering ammunition, with Cy at the cupboard, handing out what they needed. Rusty was helping Jed in putting together grub, and filling canteens as Luke spoke to Ralph. They did not know how long they would be gone, but they were all savvy enough to be prepared for the worst.

"I guess if he tries to get away, I'm a good enough shot I could just take off one toe or a finger," said Rusty, walking over, keeping a poker face.

"Now that's a right good idea!" Cyrus chimed in. "He could still work, just couldn't run fast and get away. Of course, we could always send Jasper here after him too. A bite would heal faster than a gunshot wound." Jasper obligated by baring his teeth and growling at Ralph. Cyrus knew the dog would never hurt the boy unless he commanded him to do so, or unless Ralph tried to hurt Cy or Rusty. But Ralph did not know that yet, and it was a sweet hole card.

Both men stared at Ralph and Luke smiled behind the boy's back. They were playing with him now, teaching him a lesson without actually hurting him. What the boy had done was serious, and other men might kill him for it, but they all knew he had a rough time of it growing up and might just come around with a little discipline and hard work. .

"I think we are ready," said Jed, coming up beside Luke.

"Then let's ride!" said Randall, seeing agreement on the men's faces.

Six tough, seasoned men, determined to keep law and order in their part of the country rode out after Hal Colter's gang of outlaws. Luke prayed it was enough.

Chapter 55

John Roberts had ridden by the encampment of loggers and cowboys that comprised Hal Colter's gang. He saw their dust long before he caught up with them, and being no stranger to the frontier, had made his way to the top of a hill and peered down at the group as they pulled hard to make good time. Clearly, the big burly Irish logger, Mickey, was in charge. He had hesitated to recommend him to Colter, as he had a reputation for working for whom ever paid the highest price. Well, maybe he would offer him more than Colter!

Where were Snake and Booker? They must be with Colter, he thought. Roberts considered all of this; wondering if he could make a lesser deal with Mickey and cut the three outlaws out altogether. But, he quickly discounted the idea, knowing he would either have to leave Virginia City or die trying. Killing all three of the outlaws would be impossible, especially if Mickey sided with them too.

Roberts had carefully woven his way back around the hill, staying off the main trail. The wagons would have to stay on the road, but he could make better time riding through the wooded areas. His horse was not pulling a heavy load, so he could ride later into the night and start earlier in the morning. He would get back to Virginia City and be ready for Colter with some back up of his own. He knew a few tough miners that could be paid to do just about anything. That would be cheaper than paying for the lumber!

He really needed to think this all through. He swung back and forth between cheating Colter and just paying him and making his profit off the sale of the lumber. The trouble was, he concluded, he didn't like Colter one bit, and he sure as heck didn't trust him. He

199

regretted ever entering into this deal; he should have just been patient and taken what Randall was going to bring him. But greed got the better of him...again. He sighed, and was glad he would have another day on the trail to work out his plan.

John Roberts rode ahead of the wagons a good fifteen miles before he stopped for the night. He lit a carefully concealed fire at the base of the roots of a huge fallen tree, so the light would not be seen unless someone was very close. He used dry wood so there would be no smoke. He made coffee and some pan biscuits, then opened a jar of the jam Hannah had made.

He stuck a spoon in the jar and ate a bite straight from the container, without mixing the taste with anything else yet. He was so surprised at the delicious taste of the peach jam, he ate another bite, then dumped the whole jar on top of the biscuits and ate them all.

"Almost like eating a fresh peach pie," he said to his horse, "mighty tasty! I'm glad I bought six jars!" He allowed himself to enjoy one last cup of coffee after he put the fire out, gazing up at the indigo blue sky of the Sierra Nevada, offering crystal clear bright white stars to be seen with the naked eye.

When he finished, he threw the dregs from the coffee pot into the fire pit, and curled up in his blanket, using his saddle for a pillow. He fell asleep, still gazing at the stars, and slept with his gun at his side under the blanket. He had lived too long in the west to underestimate the possibility of danger, whether it was the two legged or four legged kind, or a snake that ventured too close for comfort.

He slept soundly, unaware that he was being watched from the trees on the hill above him.

Chapter 56

Mickey O'Riley was a brute of a man in every way possible. He was big and strong, and he used that ferocious strength to intimidate, bully, and sometimes physically abuse men of smaller size or lesser fighting ability. Few knew he had also left a few broken lasses along his path, liking it too much when they had spirit and he decided to beat it out of them and teach them a lesson.

One unfortunate girl, for she was barely fourteen, had cried at his brutality after her uncle had sold her to the man who ran the red light district. She was an innocent, and he had paid more for that. But she had screamed, and fought, and raked her nails along his face, drawing blood. She had a small dagger from her long dead father, and she had plunged it as best she could into his massive shoulder. He laughed at her, and driven by his pain and rage at being defied, he had used her hard, punching her face as he enjoyed himself. By the time he was done, she was dead. The law came looking for him, but he was gone before the runner even got to the Marshall's office.

Now, he was restless, and roamed the camp looking for trouble. Most of the men avoided him; they just did their job and stayed out of his way, but one unlucky cowboy came around a corner and ran right into the massive bulk of Mickey's body.

"Oh! I'm sorry, Mickey, I didn't see you there." Rudy was tall, and well built, but years of riding the range and roping cows had left him with a few old injuries. The gray haired man looked into Mickey's eyes and knew he had a bull by the horns.

"Sorry! You ran into me on purpose, you good for nothin' piece of a buffalo chip!" Mickey had a good four inches and sixty pounds on the cowboy, and he was confident he could hurt this man with little repercussions to himself.

"No Sir, I did not see you," repeated Rudy, standing his ground, but knowing he would likely pay for it. Still, the man had sand.

"You calling me a liar, you petticoat wearing four-flusher?" Mickey was roaring now, and the whole camp became quiet. He was throwing every insult he could think of at Rudy, hoping he would take the first swing.

"Never said any such thing," said Rudy, "I said I didn't see you, and that's the honest truth."

Mickey could see Rudy's mouth was twitching and his face was getting red. He just needed to push a little more, make Rudy do something stupid, and Mickey would beat the living tar out of the man, probably cripple him, and then say Rudy started it.

"Hey Mickey, would you like my pie?" asked Jonas. "He was the youngest one in the crowd, and while he stood five foot eleven inches tall, he had not filled out much yet. Everyone knew what Jonas was trying to do. He knew Mickey really liked cherry pie, and Jonas was hoping to diffuse the situation by offering Mickey his pie. The kid held out his plate with the pie in it. Mickey looked from the pie to the young face of Jonas and smiled. He stepped forward, took the plate, and shoved the pie and plate into the face of the young man, pushing so hard, Jonas flew back into the fire.

Jonas screamed in pain as his shirt caught on fire, and several men scrambled to pull him out of the fire and put him on the ground, throwing a blanket over him to smother the flames. It was a mean, cruel thing to do to the boy, and half the men in camp wished they were brave enough to take on Mickey O'Riley.

"You had no call to do that to the boy," said Rudy evenly. "It was a yellow bellied, low down, rotten thing to do and you are nothing more than a big bully!" He set himself, knowing the blow was coming, but he could not call himself a man if he did not speak up.

"I'll break you in two for that," said Mickey, "no one calls me a yellow belly and lives!" An ugly smile spread across his face and he took a step towards Rudy, drawing back his ham sized fist as he did so. "I'm gonna kill you with my bare hands!"

He threw a punch and Rudy dodged just in time. He scooted around behind Mickey and braced himself to move again. Rudy backed up several steps, making Mickey work for it. Unfortunately, he backed up against a wagon and had nowhere to go with all the men crowded around. Mickey set himself to ram into Rudy, knowing he would probably break the other man's ribs when he hit him.

"Now, I'm going to kill you," grinned Mickey. The look on his face was so evil, Rudy silently made his peace with his maker right then and there.

"Hold it right there, Mickey!" The racking of the rifle gave Bean a stature his small body never could.

"Stay out of this, Bean," growled Mickey, "it ain't none of your business!" He shot the cook an irritated and menacing look.

"I'm makin' it my business! snapped Bean, "and me and Henry here are ready to open the ball any time you're ready. "

"You wouldn't dare! Colter put me in charge, and…"

"I don't know nothin' about that," interrupted Bean. "All I know is, you had no call to do that to this here boy. You were lookin' for trouble and you took it out on this kid! Now, git to your bed roll and stay there, or git outta camp and light a shuck for some other part of this country. I don't much care which!" He pointed the rifle directly at Mickey's chest, and held it steady. His eyes were like steel and they did not break under Mickey's ugly glare.

"Why you…" Mickey turned towards the cook, swearing a blue streak as he took a step towards Bean.

The wiry old cook shot Mickey's ear off, then levered the gun again, holding it steady. The big bully screamed and grabbed the side of his head where his ear had been. Frantically, he looked in the dirt for his missing appendage, but all he found was a bloody clump of gristle like flesh.

"You shot me, you crazy old man!" He was furious, and roaring with pain. "I'll kill you!" He shouted and took another step towards Bean.

"You take one more step and I'll cut you in half. This ole Henry rifle and I have put more than one big pole cat below the snakes." There was no give to his voice, and not a quiver to his hand could be seen. "Now git!"

203

Mickey slunk away, blubbering about his ear, walking by silent men who would not meet his eyes. Bean had broken his hold over the men, and everyone knew it.

"Take that boy over to my wagon," said Bean to Rudy. "We need to get those burns fixed up so he don't get them infected."

Rudy and another man gently helped Jonas to his feet. The lad cried softly as they guided him to the cook's wagon, where Bean opened his shirt up and carefully bathed the wounds with cool water.

"What can I do to help?" asked Rudy. He wished Mickey had beaten him instead. The blisters on the young boy's back were hard to see.

"Climb on up inside my wagon. Against the back is a cupboard of sorts. Behind the door in the center, there is a packet wrapped in brown paper. Bring it to me."

Rudy did as he was told, and was then instructed to put a pan of water on to boil. An hour later, they had the boy's back covered in comfrey poultices. Whether it was from the pain or the whiskey Bean had gotten him to take, he was sound asleep.

"I think we best be posting a guard or two tonight," Bean said to Rudy. "I might have taken him down a peg or two, but that Mickey is a mean one and I don't trust him."

"Let me go get my rifle and I'll be right back," agreed Rudy. He was good as his word, and came back shortly with four men, all armed. They settled down to keep watch, two at a time, while the others slept until it was their turn to stand.

Chapter 57

Hal Colter rode into the camp at the sawmill around supper time the next day. The men were unhitching the teams and brushing down their horses while Bean started serving up food. The wagons were still laden with the logs, and exhausted men sat or tended to chores all around him as he rode through. He dismounted at the cook's wagon and walked up to Bean.

"Evening, Mr. Colter," said Bean, handing him a mug of hot coffee while not missing a beat as he served up beans with chunks of beef, and a hunk of cornbread to the men, who stood hungrily, but patiently, in line. Bean ran a tight ship, and more than one cowpoke had gone to bed hungry in the past by demanding special treatment.

"Looks like you made good time," commented Hal.

"Yes Sir!" agreed Bean. He kept feeding the line as Colter stood beside him, looking over his workers.

"Where's Mickey? I thought he would be about, especially since I asked him to sort of keep an eye on the operations."

"That was a mistake," scoffed the cook.

"What?" Hal was surprised at the remark. There were not many men who could criticize or challenge Colter and not get a scathing reply or action in return. But he knew Bean's past, and he was respected all over the west as a good man who had sand, as well as someone who could work culinary miracles with very little supplies. If Bean took a stand, he had good reason and he would not back down. Colter knew enough to be careful around a man like that.

"I had to take your bully boy down a peg last night, and I ain't seen him since." Bean leveled steel blue eyes at Hal Colter. "You should choose your ramrod's more carefully, Mr. Colter." He served another cowboy, then a logger behind him before Hal spoke again.

"I guess you are probably right," he said grudgingly. First Snake, then Sly, and now O'Riley had all been huge disappointments and left him wanting when he needed their help most. "What happened?" It never even crossed his mind to be harsh with his cook.

"Mickey was ridin' the boys something fierce, and he was mean about it. They were workin' as hard and fast as they could without anybody getting' hurt. He kicked one, back handed another, and would curse at them like he was clearin' his lungs." The last man came through the line and Bean filled another plate, handing it to Hal, then one for himself. He began to eat while Hal took a few bites, chewing over more than the food before he spoke.

"Nobody stood up to him?" he asked.

"Not until last night," answered Bean. "He was on the prod and everyone knew it. He tried picking a fight with Rudy, but while he didn't back down, he wouldn't swing first either. Mickey always tries to get them to give the first punch so he can beat them to a bloody pulp and he can say they started it."

"I could see that," nodded Colter.

"Rudy was holding steady until Jonas tried to take Mickey's mind off fighting by offering him his pie." As if on cue, a moan came from the back of the wagon and Hal turned.

"Who's there!" he jerked around, hand going to his gun.

"It's just Jonas." Cook jumped up and slipped behind the curtain, returning a few minutes later. "I gave him some more laudanum to help with the pain."

"What is going on? Did he get hurt?" Colter showed more frustration than concern, a fact not missed by Bean.

"Mickey knocked him into the fire and he has some burns on his back and arms." He faced Colter, hands on his hips and feet spread wide. "And I shot Mickey's ear off because of what he did, and we ain't seen him since."

"Then who has been runnin' the crew?" asked Colter, studying Bean's face carefully.

"Rudy. And doin' a durned good job of it too. The men respect him."

"Well, as long as the job is getting done," he shrugged. He showed no empathy for the injured boy, and Bean noticed that as well. "Too bad about the boy. We'll drop him off somewhere in Virginia City. If he can't work we can't use him."

"He goes wherever I go," said Bean softly, but there was steel in the voice and fire in the eyes, and for one of the rare times in his life, Hal Colter broke eye contact first. Bean did not speak, but also did not take his stare off Colter.

"I'm gonna go talk to the man who owns the sawmill and see how early we can start," Hal said, wanting to be anywhere but at the chuck wagon at that particular moment. He walked away without looking back. He could feel Bean's eyes still boring into his back, and he did not want to look in those eyes again.

Chapter 58

Lucas Randall rode with a grim look on his face. He had five good men with him, two others who were family men, and they were all willing to risk their lives to save his family's finances. The lumber would mean plenty of cushion for the Randall family and the people who counted on them for food and shelter. Was he foolish to put all of these lives on the line for more comfort and security for his wife and son?

But he knew it was more than that. Every man who rode beside him was thinking of how they had to stop the lawlessness if their own families were ever to be safe. Between what Jed and Ralph had told them, these outlaws, led by Hal Colter, were vicious. They were bad men, who killed innocent people; men, women, and children, often after they had abused the women. They looted and burned, and had used the Civil War as an excuse initially, but now proved themselves to be black hearted and capable of real evil.

Colter's men had a two day head start, but they had to deal with the laborious plodding of heavy laden wagons. They could clearly see the trail the wagon ruts left, but they didn't need to stay on the trail, they could cut across country, which they did. Jim proved to be a valuable addition to the party; he knew of a trail that cut out several miles.

It was well past dinner time when the group of weary men and horses decided it would be smart to stop and get some rest. They found a secluded bunch of pines that provided cover, up against a granite face and with a stream not too far down the slope. They dismounted and brushed their horses down, hobbling them so they could not wander away during the few remaining hours of the night.

Luke tended quickly to Pepper, then gathered the makings for a small fire, close to the rock face. He filled the pot with water at the stream, then put it on the fire, throwing in a couple handfuls of coffee. It would be very strong, but that is what they needed. Jim walked up as the coffee was boiling and Luke poured cups for each of them. The other men came slowly to get some of the warm liquid, although the others only took a little and listened, planning to bed down as soon as they knew the plan.

"I looked around, and we seem to be alone," began Jim, "but I still think we should take turns standing watch."

"I agree," said Luke, and the others nodded assent. "I'm thinking two men, for two hours at a time – sound good?"

"Sure. I can do the first watch," offered Jim.

"I'll stand it with him, then we will wake Paul and Jed, then Jeremiah and Clay." Those not on sentry duty nodded and quickly disappeared into bedrolls. Jim and Luke refilled their cups, then made sure the coffee had plenty of water in the pot before they walked to opposite sides of the camp.

Standing away from the fire, Luke realized just how bone weary he was. It had been more than three weeks that he had been on the trail. When he headed out to take his own herd to market in Virginia City, his wife and son were healthy and happy at home on their ranch, with his trusted hand Rusty to help out. Their future looked good, with crops coming in and the sale of their first herd.

Then everything had changed, and it was because of greedy outlaws like Hal Colter and Sly Booker! Now his wife and son were pale, recovering from injuries caused by these bad men, and they were not even in their own home. He missed his family; longed to hold his son in his lap and read him a story before bed. He wanted to kiss his wife and sit on their porch together, making plans for their life ahead.

Two of his riders had been shot, and several men had died, and all because Hal Colter wanted what belonged to others. He felt his anger rise. They were right to be out here, chasing these bad men to hold them accountable for their wrong doings. They would attempt to bring them back to stand trial, but either way, those men would pay or these good men would die trying. He prayed it would not be the latter.

Chapter 59

John Roberts unlocked the door to his office and looked around before he entered. In Virginia City, he was known as a respected businessman, but one could never be too careful about who might be watching. Once inside, he locked the door from the inside, then stood to the side of a window, in the corner and in shadow, to survey the bustling town around his office. Satisfied that no one was watching him, he slipped through a door into an inner office that held a desk, and drew the curtains on the single window. They were only café style curtains, but they would block what he was doing well enough, while still giving him the light he needed to work.

Roberts knelt and opened the small safe inside the cabinet on the floor behind his desk. He removed several stacks of bills and counted them, then replaced two of the stacks inside the safe. Next, he took out a small sack of twenty dollar gold coins and counted those as well. He put three hundred dollars worth of the coins back in the safe, in stacks, and kept three hundred dollars in the sack. He closed the door to the safe and spun the knob to lock the safe again, then shut the door to the cabinet.

Standing, he walked to the inner door again and peered into the outer office. He knew he had locked the door, but he was still edgy. He shut the second office door too, and locked it, then walked to the wall across from his desk. He removed a framed picture of a map of Virginia City and set it on the ground to the side. He opened his second safe, and placed the extra stacks of bills and bag of coins inside. Closing and making sure the safe was locked, he hung the framed map over the recessed opening of the safe.

Congratulating himself on being so clever, he unlocked the inner door and stepped into the outer office, where he opened the drawer in the single desk and took out a bottle of whiskey. He poured himself a couple of fingers, corked the bottle, and replaced it. He pulled a chair to the corner where he had stood earlier, and sat, observing the town while he sipped from his glass.

He knew he would have to ride out to the lumber mill outside of town and meet Colter. He made a face. Distasteful scoundrel! He would not put it past the outlaw to force him to ride back into town to get the money for the lumber.

But Roberts was pleased with himself. He suspected Colter might try to rob him and run off with all the money he had. He chuckled. That's why he split the money. He would pretend to be angry or scared, maybe both. He would protest, but in the end, Colter would get just a hundred or so over their agreed upon price. Then he would leave, and Roberts would still have most of his money plus the lumber, on which he could turn a tidy profit!

For a moment he considered the danger of trying to deceive the outlaw, but quickly dismissed the idea. Virginia City was busy, and most people saw Roberts as a businessman to be respected. Colter would not want to draw attention to himself here.

He would be the sly one, and Colter would leave, none the wiser. He laughed out loud, then finished his drink and rose to his feet, stretching. It was time for him to ride out to the camp. John Roberts started for the door, pleased that he was so clever. It never crossed his mind that Colter might dare to kill him.

Chapter 60

Luke and Jim lay on their stomachs, surveying the camp below them. It was busy, and there were a lot of men down there! They each counted, then compared what they saw.

"I count fourteen men down there with rifles, not counting the ones at the sawmill," said Jim. He shook his head. "That's a lot of rifles to face."

"I wish we knew if the men at the sawmill were in this or not," said Luke. "There are six of them, and that would really up the ante."

"I don't think any of them have seen me anywhere," said Jim.

"What are you getting at?" Luke turned to the mountain man.

"Well, I could ride around the mountain and come in from the other side, right up to the saw mill. I could kind of get the lay of the land." Jim grinned. "Scout it out, so we know what we are up against."

"That's too dangerous," began Luke, "I couldn't let you..."

"In case you haven't noticed, partner, I'm a volunteer in this here posse, and I'm going to go scout around for us. I'm the most reasonable choice." He fixed Luke with a stubborn stare. "And it's no more dangerous than six men riding in against fourteen to twenty."

"I suppose it would help," sighed the rancher. "Just be careful." He watched Jim head down the hill to his horse, then start out and around to come in from the other side.

"What's happening?" asked Paul, coming up beside his boss. "We all saw Jim ride off. Where is he going?" Luke explained the plan.

"That's a really good idea! Nobody knows him; heck, he's even new in Bridgeport!" He nodded his head in approval. "I'll go tell everyone else what is going on."

"Okay," said Luke, "but I'm going to stay here and watch. Tell everyone to stay ready to ride in case Jim gets into trouble."

Randall watched for several more minutes before Jim rode slowly into the yard by the saw mill. He swung down and started to talk to some of the men there. At first, they hesitated to speak to him, which was not surprising. Luke couldn't see their faces, but from their dress, he guessed they were Chinese. Many Chinese people had come to the west to work on the railroads. They were not generally treated well, and some of them decided to stop and establish small settlements and businesses of their own in or outside of towns along the way. Luke had heard they put up a couple of saw mills in the general Northern Nevada area, but he did not know there was one this close.

"How does it look?" asked Jed, who had climbed the small hill to hunker down beside Luke. His eyes scanned the group of men below. Suddenly he tensed. "That's Colter, right there!"   He pointed and Luke followed the direction of his finger. Luke looked and recognized the man who had been lounging outside the general store in Virginia City.

"Wait! What is he doing?" He didn't like what he was seeing.

Colter had caught sight of Jim, talking to the Chinese working, and he immediately went into a crouch, putting his hand on the butt of his gun! At the same moment, Jim caught the movement and turned his horse to be between him and the outlaw. Jim pretended to want to see the inside of the sawmill, and the accommodating worker, walked him to the end of the building.

Colter hurried after them, knowing he could not start shooting with all his men and the workers in the line of fire. But Jim was too smart! Once he got around the corner, he thanked the man and leaping on his horse, hunkered down and galloped off into a stand of trees.

Colter started shouting and gesturing, but by the time the men understood he wanted a horse and several mounted men as well, Jim had a good head start. Hal's men reached the stand of trees at least ten minutes behind the mountain man. Luke and Jed watched them ride back and forth, and finally come out of the trees shaking their heads. Even from that distance, the two men watching from the hill could see Colter was livid.

"Guess Jim is too smart for them," grinned Luke. Looks like he covered his trail, and did it jack rabbit fast!"

"Yeah," laughed Jed. "But one thing is stuck in my head," he said, turning serious.

"What's that?" asked Luke.

"The only way Colter could recognize Jim is if the old skunk was at your ranch when they were shooting at us." He looked at Luke with serious eyes.

"You're right!" exclaimed Luke. "Jim is new to town, and he sure doesn't strike me as someone who would ride the owl hoot trail!"

"I can sure tell you he wasn't with the gang when I was in it, and I agree, I don't peg him as an outlaw." Jed's eyes narrowed. "All the more reason I want Colter! He directed that attack on the ranch and tried to kill all of us!"

Chapter 61

John Roberts mounted his horse and rode out to the sawmill. He knew Colter would come looking for him if he didn't show pretty soon, and he didn't want to take a chance that someone in town would recognize the outlaw and make the connection to him. He had a good reputation, and until he was ready to leave Virginia City on his own terms, he wanted to keep it that way.

Before Roberts paid Hal any of the money, he wanted an agreement with the owners of the business that the cut lumber could be transported to Virginia City. John congratulated himself on his forethought; he had brought enough money with him to pay Colter an advance; basically half, so he could pay his men. He knew they would likely come to Virginia City to let off steam after they were paid, but if they came in separately from Colter, no one would suspect he knew the outlaw.

Suddenly, there was a cloud of dust coming towards him at a rapid speed! He rode off the trail and into the trees on the side. He was carrying a fair amount of cash, and highwaymen were not uncommon in this area. As he watched, he was surprised to see Hal Colter ride by in a fury of dust, with four men close at his heels. They were riding towards town!

Roberts let loose with a stream of profanity, ruing the day he decided to enter into business with the likes of that scallywag! He had to get back to town quickly; in the state Colter was in, he would be raging about, loudly searching for him. This could ruin everything!

There was a little used shortcut behind him that he had discovered one day when he was out exploring. He had always found it useful to know the less used trails in the area where he was working. Many a time, they had saved his life as he ran from angry townspeople after he cheated them. He spurred his horse towards it, and arrived just after Colter, who was at the door of his office, pounding and shouting.

"Stop all that noise!" commanded Roberts as he dismounted, looking around to see who might have noticed the commotion. "You're making a scene!"

"We need to finish our business now!" shouted Hal, shoving into Roberts, glaring into his face.

"Tell your men to go get a drink and be quiet about what they are doing here," hissed John. "You want the Marshall to come see what all the fuss is about?" His eyes glittered with anger, and for once, Colter respected the businessman. He pushed open the door he had just unlocked, and flipped a twenty dollar gold piece to one of the burly loggers standing in front of his business. "Go get a drink, and don't talk to anyone!"

The logger looked at Colter, who nodded permission to his men, then turned and walked through the open door. He turned as soon as he got inside enough that John could follow. Agitated, he faced the businessman.

"We need to finish this right now!" he snarled.

"Calm down," said John harshly, "who lit your tail on fire?"

"One of the men from the Randall ranch was at the saw mill just now!" barked Hal.

"What do you mean?" probed Roberts. "Did Randall follow you?" He felt his stomach twist. If Colter brought Roberts into this, he was done in this town; he might even be arrested and hung!

"All I know is one of the men shooting at us at the ranch Randall owns, was just at the saw mill! I want my money, and I want it all, right now," growled Colter, menace heavy in his words.

"Why should I give you the money," hissed John, "I don't have my lumber yet!"

"Get the men at the mill to bring it in for you, I don't care! Just give me my money and do it now!"

"I'm not giving you anything!" Roberts reached for his gun, but Colter was faster, and had his six gun leveled at John's stomach before Roberts even cleared leather.

"I'd think about that if I were you," sneered Hal, "now get me that money and be quick about it or I'll kill you!"

"How do I know you won't kill me anyway?" scoffed John.

"Because I don't want that marshal of yours to come running when he hears the shots, you donkey brain!"

John Roberts eyes him briefly and realized he was not bluffing. But maybe he could get him to leave for less money, and still get the lumber. Slowly, he turned and walked into his inner office.

"Keep them hands where I can see them!" barked Hal, and the man in front of him, raised his hands out to his sides.

Inside, he knelt at the safe, with Colter leaning over him. He stalled for time, hoping maybe Luke had really followed him and would show up. He could deny he knew the lumber was stolen. He could say he didn't know it came from Luke's land. Maybe he would believe him. Maybe he would kill the outlaw before he had to explain. Colter nudged him in the back with the barrel of the gun, causing him to jump and miss the number on the combination lock.

"Now look what you made me do! I missed the number when you poked me and I jumped!" Roberts speared Colter with an angry glare.

"Well, start over and be quick about it!" He kept the gun on the other man, but stepped to peer through the door, and out through the window in the front of the building. He didn't see anything to worry about, and he turned back to Roberts just in time to hear the lock click and see Roberts pull the safe open. Colter pushed him to the floor and looked into the safe.

"What'd you do that for?" protested John.

"Making sure you didn't have a gun in there with the money! Now take that satchel and fill it up." He pointed to a bag lying on the floor against the wall. Put it all in there!"

"But there is more in here than we agreed on!" lied Roberts. He was hoping Colter wouldn't count it, thinking he was getting more.

"I said, put it all in there!" grinned Colter.

Roberts filled the satchel as he emptied his safe. He turned and rose to set it on the desk, hoping he could get the drop on Hal as he took the bag. Instead, he froze as he heard the hammer of the gun being drawn back. He looked up in fear as the wolfish grin spread over Hal's face.

"I can't leave any witnesses to send the posse after me," he hissed, his eyes dancing with evil intent.

The shots were loud in the small room. Roberts stood, his eyes closed, waiting for the pain to rip through him. But he felt nothing. Slowly he opened his eyes, and saw Hal Colter, for all appearances, dead on the floor. He swung his eyes up from the body to see a tall man with yellowish eyes staring at him, holding a smoking gun. He had bruises on his face, and one eye was blackened, but there was no mistaking he meant business.

"I guess I get the last laugh after all, you rotten skunk!" He spat on the dead body of his former boss. The rope burns on his wrist were still red as he smiled at Roberts. "I'll take that money now," said Snake. Roberts gestured at the bag on the desk and stepped back, hands up.

"It's yours," he said, "just don't kill me."

"I want it all!" Snake chuckled, and it made the hair on the back of Robert's neck stand on end. "While you was sleepin' last night, I rode in here and searched your office. I know about the safe on the wall behind that picture! Now open it and give me all the money!" He waved the gun at the businessman. "Be quick about it, or I will shoot you and take what I can get! If the law dogs come, you are a dead man!"

Chapter 62

Luke and his friends waited until the men in the camp were in line for the noon meal. Carefully, they had worked themselves down and around the camp, the majority still maintaining vantage points above the camp, but easily within rifle range. The men in the camp had no reason to think they would be under attack, and most left their rifles sitting by bedrolls as they meandered over for food.

Once the men were centered in the camp, Luke and Clay casually rode up to the chuck wagon. Paul had argued he should be the one to sit beside his boss, but Luke looked grimly at Paul and denied his request to flank him.

"I can go with you, Luke," offered Jed.

"Jed, it is likely someone in that camp will remember you from your time with them before. We can't take that chance; I need you to have my back." Luke looked the seasoned hand in the eyes and clapped him on the arm with a wry smile.

"I suppose that could be true," sighed Jed. Grudgingly, he took a step back and checked his guns again.

"Paul, I know you want to stand by my side, and there is no one I would rather have right there with me, but the truth is…" Luke's voice trailed off and he chewed on his lip as he caught the expectant and confused gaze of the man who was both his top hand and his friend. "The truth is," he repeated, "if something happens to me, I am counting on you to take charge."

"I…" began Paul, startled at the gravity of what Luke had just said, "of course, boss," he finished, and nodding his head, mounted his horse. He swiped at his eyes, which were suddenly a bit misty at the magnitude of the words he had just heard. He was proud and deeply sad at the same time.

"Sounds like you and I are up," grinned Clay, mounting his horse and waiting expectantly for Luke. A few minutes later, they reached the edge of the encampment.

Now all eyes turned to the two men riding casually into the camp. Luke and Clay did not miss that reaction; it was perfect. The eyes were all on them, and not on Luke's men as they slipped into their vantage points. Bean set down his ladle and exchanged a glance with Rudy, who stepped forward to greet them.

"Howdy, gents," began Rudy. There was no need to be confrontational; it was not uncommon for western men to approach a camp for a cup of coffee, a meal, or even just information. "Step on down and have a cup of coffee," he invited, smiling.

"We might see our way clear to do just that," grinned Luke, easing the tension with his easy manner. But he did not move to dismount. "I do have a question for you, though, if you don't mind," he said congenially.

"What would that be?" asked Rudy, noting that Clay's eyes continued to play over the group of men.

"Who owns all this timber?" asked Luke, sweeping his left hand around at the wagons, and including the stacks at the saw mill as well.

"That would be our boss, but it is already sold, if that is where you are headed." Rudy answered.

"Would he be around?" asked Luke. "I'd really like to talk to him. One businessman to another," he smiled. He took note of the fact the man in front of him did not call Colter by name.

"No, he just rode into town," offered Bean, scratching his chin. "He lit a shuck after some man that was nosin' around the saw mill."

"Where did you get all this lumber?' asked Luke.

"Up in the hills around Bridgeport," said Rudy, "but I already told you it has been sold, and there isn't any more where this came from. Now, if there is nothing else, you are welcome to join us, but I'm hungry and plan to eat." He was beginning to get the sense that something was not quite right here.

"Well, sir, I can understand that," began Luke calmly. "But I need to tell you this lumber does not belong to Mr. Colter. It was cut off my land."

The words hit Bean and Rudy like a pail of cold water, but once the shock wore off, they bristled. Rudy's hand moved closer to the six gun on his hip and Bean started to reach for his trusted Henry. The racking of multiple rifles cracked in the noon day sun like a thousand pound bull stepping on a sheet of ice. Everyone froze.

"You planning to rob us, mister?" asked Bean, his eyes burning into Luke.

"No sir, I am the one who has been robbed." Luke stood in his stirrups and raised his voice so it could be heard by all. "Those are my men holding those rifles and every man jack of you is covered, so nobody move and no one gets hurt."

"You can't take us all," began one big logger, who started to bring his rifle up. Immediately, the rifle stock was shattered, along with his hand. He screamed and dropped the weapon, falling to his knees in the dirt as he clutched a bloody mass of mangled flesh where his hand had been.

"Listen to me!" shouted Luke. "I am Lucas Randall, and I own the Rocking R Ranch outside of Bridgeport. Hal Colter brought you in to cut my land clear of trees. He stole my lumber and I want it back!"

"Can you prove that, mister?" asked Rudy, uncertainty creeping into his voice.

"Yes, I can," answered Luke. "But right now, my fight is with Hal Colter."

"We didn't know the trees weren't his to cut," said Rudy, looking at the cowboys around him. "At least some of us didn't know we were signing up to be outlaws." He eyed a few of the loggers and hard case cowboys who were backing up little by little.

Suddenly, a shot rang out, followed by several others, and Mickey O'Riley was charging into the fray with guns blazing. Luke and Clay dove off their horses for cover, and men scattered to shelter as Luke's men began to fire at the charging group of loggers Mickey had gathered to him.

Bean jumped into the back of the chuck wagon and positioned himself to protect Joshua, who raised his head for a moment and was promptly pushed back into a pillow. But Bean did not fire. He was not sure whose side he was on, but he knew one thing for sure. He was too darned old to become an outlaw now!

Rudy and several men ran behind the stacks of logs and held their guns ready, but did not fire. They watched through the chinks in the wood as Mickey and his men fired like mad men at Luke and Clay. Suddenly, Bean saw the mountain man reappear beside the chuck wagon and he made a decision. He nodded at Jim, and they were in the mix, shooting at the rogue loggers. Jed and Paul rode in and caught the vicious logger and his men in a murderous crossfire.

"Luke! Look out!" The warning came from Jim as he reloaded his rifle.

Luke swung his gaze in time to see Mickey O'Riley leveling his gun at the young rancher. An evil grin spread across the logger's face as Luke fought to swing his own weapon around in time.

Suddenly, the huge logger faltered and his weapon jerked to the side, the shot catching Luke in his right side instead of the middle of his chest. Mickey turned his head and cast a venomous glare at Rudy, who stood, working the lever of his rifle again. The distraction cost the outlaw. Simultaneously, Rudy and Luke fired into the huge logger at the same time, and the man fell as a tree would, face first and hard onto the ground. Luke caught Rudy's eye and nodded. The other man nodded back, but holding his rifle now by the barrel, put his hands up and backed behind the logs again, clearly signaling he was out of the fight.

"Drop your guns and put your hands up!" bellowed Jeremiah, looking like the angel of retribution himself as he stood, black hair and coat flying behind him, black hat on his head, and a face running red with blood against his pale skin. He could have been a banshee for all the Irish loggers knew, and hands rose as guns dropped.

Bean stepped out and stood on the back of the chuck wagon, his Henry at his feet. Jim and Jeremiah ushered Rudy and his group of cowboys around the logs, until all the Colter forces were standing in a circle, under the guns of Luke's posse.

Quickly, Luke's men separated the belligerent, sullen, and violent loggers and cowboys from the few that seemed somewhat bewildered and confused. Once they had the troublemakers bound together and sitting under guard, Luke turned to the others.

He noticed shrugging shoulders and forlorn faces. He also noticed Rudy and Bean were helping Jed as he went from wounded man to man, patching up a flesh wound on Clay's arm, a gash on Jeremiah's head, and was surprised when they stopped in front of him.

"Sit down, Luke," said Jed simply as he led him to a log and gently shoved him down to a sitting position.

"What are you doing," he protested. "I need to get to the bottom of all this!" Suddenly he was very tired. He wanted to be done so he could close his eyes for a few minutes.

"Not until I stop that bleeding," commanded Jed, cutting Luke's shirt away from his side.

Surprised, Luke looked down and saw his right side and pants were soaked with blood. He vaguely remembered Mickey firing at him, but had not allowed himself to think about being wounded. Jed went to work while Clay and Paul grabbed their rifles and walked about the groups of men. They came back with Rudy and Bean just as Jed finished the bandage.

"Luke, these two want to have a word with you," said Paul simply.

"Mr. Randall, I want to apologize for any harm we may have done to you," began Rudy, literally standing hat in hand. "Some of these men are real hard cases, and I guess that makes sense if what you say is true."

"It is," growled Luke, irritable from the pain and the frustration of not capturing Hal Colter.

"I'm not sayin' it isn't true, mister, I'm not sayin that at all," said Rudy, holding both palms up and out. He looked at Bean for help.

"What he is trying to say," spoke Bean, "is that some of us thought we were day riders just doing a job. By the time it started to feel wrong, we were almost done. Frankly, we didn't have any proof that Colter was doing anything illegal, we just had a gut feeling. Even so, the boss made it clear that no one left the outfit until it was all over, unless you left carrying some lead in your gut. "

"We just wanted to get paid and move on," offered Rudy. We never signed on to kill people or steal from an honest man."

Silence hung in the gun powder flavored air as Luke weighed each man before him. His men stood patiently, deferring to the judgment of a man they respected, despite his young age. The rancher's gaze swept over the other men, gathered in two distinctly separate groups.

Bringing his eyes back to the wizened and wiry Bean, nearly bald on top of his head, except for a wisp of hair that stood almost straight up before he folded to one side, Luke nearly smiled. There was an unabashed frankness in the spirited cook that tugged at Luke.

In sharp contrast, Rudy was lean and muscular, but every inch a real cowboy, from his calloused hands to his weathered face, right down to his down at the heel boots. His holster was well worn, but there were no notches on the handle of his gun.

Luke studied the two men who stood in front of him, and decided he liked what he saw. They appeared to be truly repentant and sorry for their part in the injustice done to the Rocking R Ranch and its friends. They had owned their part in the operation, but they did not whimper or grovel.

"Who was Colter selling the lumber to?" asked Luke. The two riders for Hal looked at each other quizzically and rubbed hands over their chins.

"I only saw him once," said Rudy. "He is a tall, slender man, with collar length dark hair." He rubbed his hand over his face and seemed to be thinking, searching for any other details.

"Do you know his name?" asked Luke, leaning forward, but grimacing as he did so. Jed placed a hand on his shoulder and gave him a warning look that was almost fatherly.

"No, I don't," said Rudy apologetically. "I wasn't privy to those conversations, I'm afraid."

"You know, he came by the chuck wagon once for a cup of coffee," mused Bean. "I think he said his name was John, but he didn't give a last name."

Luke exchanged a grim glance with Paul. "Get your horse," he said to Paul. "I think we have business in Virginia City."

"You aren't going anywhere without your doctor," declared Jed.

"I think I'll just come along too," said Jim. "I ain't seen Virginia City yet."

"I can't leave all these men with just Clay and Jeremiah," protested Luke.

"Beggin' your pardon, Mr. Randall, but we don't much like being roped into robbin' and killin,'" said Rudy firmly. "If you could see your way clear to trust us, sir, we would sure like the chance to make up for our transgressions by helping your men."

"We would turn over our guns if it would make you feel better," offered Rudy. "We know we haven't earned your trust back yet, but we can use our fists if those rotten buzz worms get out of line."

"Actually, it's up to Clay here," said Luke slowly, "I'm leaving him in charge. But I did see you shoot that big logger just before he got me." Luke met Rudy's eyes as he spoke. "If you hadn't shot him when you did, I would probably be under the snakes by now."

"It was the right thing to do, mister," answered Rudy solemnly.

"I'd welcome the help," said Clay, grinning. "Maybe I'll find myself a few new day riders before this is over."

"Alright then," said Luke, "let's get to Virginia City and see what Mr. Roberts has to say for himself!"

Jed just shook his head. Why were all his patients so dang stubborn? He sighed and raised his eyes to the heavens. It sure seemed like the good Lord had plans for him that he did not think were ever in his cards again.

Chapter 63

Ruth sat on the bench under the apple tree in the small yard behind the general store, tapping her foot impatiently. Hannah brought her some fresh lemonade and sat beside her on the carefully hewn seat Axel had made for their little yard.

"He is looking better every day," said the gentle German woman as she watched Adele sing to little Thomas, who sat mesmerized by the attention from the older child.

"Yes," agreed Ruth, "he still looks a little pale and still tires easily, but the doctor says he will be alright." As if on cue, Thomas turned sparkling eyes on his mother and smiled, then giggled as he turned back to Adele.

"She loves playing the little mama," laughed Hannah, "he is much more fun than her doll!" The two women laughed and sipped their lemonade, watching the children and feeling a sense of simple pleasure.

"I want to go home," said Ruth suddenly. She turned to her friend and grasped her hand. "I need to see my home, to be there when my husband returns," she pleaded.

"I was wondering when you were going to ask," smiled Hannah.

"I am so grateful for all you have done," stammered Ruth, "but I want my own clothes," she touched the skirt of the pretty green dress she was wearing.

"It looks really good on you," said Hannah, chuckling, "but I know what you mean."

"I think Thomas will get better faster in his own home too," she said hopefully, "and I think we both miss Rusty. I need to know he is really alright."

"I understand. You have been through so much, but there is no place like your own home. Tomorrow is Sunday. Let's make some food to take to the ranch with you and after church, we can all take the wagon out to the ranch."

"Mama, eat!" said Thomas, pushing himself to his feet. He tottered over to her and grabbed her knees, drooling a wet laugh.

"I'm hungry," chimed in Adele, getting to her feet with more grace than the small boy, but smiling expectantly at her mother just the same.

"I think our talk of making food has made them think of lunch," laughed Hannah. "We might as well go in and plan what we will make for tomorrow while we make some food to eat now."

Ruth stood and took Thomas' small hand in one of hers, carrying her lemonade in the other. Hannah picked up the blanket the children had been playing on and shook it out, folding it into a square before she picked up her drink and followed them into the house through the back door.

They found Axel just setting a package down on the table in the kitchen. Adele ran to him, and he scooped her up for a hug before setting her down again. Next, he swung Thomas up in the air and they all laughed at the giggles spilling from the small boy.

"Clay's wife was just in town and brought you a jar of something she calls mustard. She brought a jar for us, too," he said, looking at his wife.

"Smells interesting," said Hannah, removing the top of the jar and sniffing.

"She said it is good on sandwiches or as a spice on meat." The storekeeper was pleased at the idea; as much because it was a gesture of friendship by new people in town, as it was the prospect of trying something new.

They enjoyed a lunch of slabs of meat on fresh bread, with a little of the mustard spread. They agreed it was tasty, although the children were not as impressed. Axel thought the idea of a ride to the ranch tomorrow sounded pleasant, and the women began to discuss what they would take.

"I will take my tools," said Axel. "Mark rode out yesterday and said Cyrus and Rusty are both recovering from wounds. They have a young man named Ralph that Mark said they kept running," he laughed. "But still, I think they could use the help of another man too."

It was a pleasant afternoon filled with happy thoughts. None of them had any idea that danger was still lurking around the ranch, watching, waiting for the chance to settle a score.

Chapter 64

The four men rode abreast towards Virginia City, watchful in case Hal Colter and his men decided to head back to the saw mill. Jed kept shooting his eyes towards Luke, who had lost more blood than the rancher realized. Jed would have preferred to have Luke resting in a bed, but he knew the degree of stubborn with which he was dealing and thought it best to just get it over with.

Two hours later, they rode into the outskirts of Virginia City. There was no trouble on the way in, but every man of them stopped outside the town and checked their weapons. If John Roberts was in cahoots with Hal Colter, they could be riding into some real trouble. Roberts was a respected man in Virginia City, and Colter was unknown in these parts. It would be their word against Roberts, and it was a gamble as to which way the hand would be played.

Cautiously, they rounded the corner onto the main street through the town. Halfway down the street was the office of John Roberts. There was a crowd gathered outside in the street, and men and women on the other side were standing on the walk, and on the balconies, watching the proceedings.

Sunlight glinted off a badge on the chest of a tall, middle aged, slender man. He wore a round brimmed black hat, white shirt, black frock coat, and black pants. His black boots and black gun belt all seemed to fit the man who peered at the riders as they approached. He stepped to the side, away from the gathering of people, and rested his hands on his belt, handy to his guns.

"Something I can do for you gents?" he challenged. He was not unfriendly, but he clearly read them as no ordinary cowboys coming to town.

"Howdy Marshal," greeted Luke. "I am Lucas Randall, owner of the Rocking R Ranch near Bridgeport. These are my men," he said, gesturing to take all of them in.

"Looks like you've already had some trouble," said the Marshal, his eyes flicking ever so quickly to the dried blood on Luke's right side, then back up to Luke's face. He skimmed his eyes over the group, assessing the level of danger.

"Yes sir, we did run into a group of outlaws." Luke watched the man now, taking his turn at evaluating the measure of the lawman.

"Outlaws you say?" asked the Marshal, narrowing his eyes. "Where are they?"

"About two hours south of here," answered Luke, "but they are under the control of the rest of my men right now."

"Why are you in town?" the Marshal asked, with steel in his voice. Something was off here, and he didn't like it one bit.

"We actually came to look for the rest of the gang," said Luke. "We believe their leader is here, and...," he paused, scanning the crowd, "that he might have come in to see John Roberts."

Something moved in the Marshal's dark eyes and he stood rock still for a few moments, pinning each man in turn with his cold stare. The silence was unnerving and Luke started to speak, but was stopped by Jim.

"Luke," he said simply, turning his head to Luke, causing the rancher to turn his head towards Jim. The mountain man shifted just his eyes behind them and back again. In his peripheral vision, Luke saw two deputies with shotguns fencing them in. The Marshal had distracted them while his men moved into place.

"I think you four better get down slow and easy and come inside," said the Marshal.

"We aren't looking for any trouble with the law, Marshal," Luke assured him. He nodded to his friends, and they all slipped carefully out of their saddles, hitched their horses to the rail, and stepped up onto the porch.

The Marshal ducked quickly inside, and was facing them when they walked in, no doubt to see the reaction they had to the scene before them. Luke and his men entered and stood in the dim light of the outer office. The deputies crowded into the room, and they all stood, looking to the Marshal for direction. The smell of gunpowder still hung in the room, along with the smoke from the guns that had been fired in the small space.

"Mr. Randall, follow me please," he walked through the door to the inner office and was waiting when Luke stepped inside.

"That's John Roberts!" Luke, knelt by the prone form of John Roberts, running his eyes over the man."He's dead!" He looked at the Marshal, who said nothing. "And that's Hal Colter!" Luke pointed to the man closest to the safe, lying in a pool of blood on the floor.

"Colter!" exclaimed the Marshal, his head snapping up to look at Luke. "Are you sure? What would he be doing here?"

"Pretty sure it's Colter, but I have a man with me who could definitely identify him."

"Get him in here, then!" snapped the lawman.

"Jed! Come on in here please," said Luke.

The young doctor stepped slowly into the room, took one look at the bodies and strode to Roberts first, kneeling, and placing his fingers on the man's neck. Without speaking, he did the same to the leader of the outlaws. He stood, looking first at Luke, then at the Marshal.

"They are both dead," he said, his brow knit in puzzlement. Clearly, they did not need him to tell them these men were dead.

"I could see that," drawled the Marshal sarcastically, "but you had to check. The only one I've ever seen do that was a doctor."

"Jed is a doctor," said Luke, "he's my doctor; he works for me," the rancher declared possessively.

"That right?" probed the Marshal.

"Yes Sir. I'm a doctor." Luke caught the slight catch in Jed's voice, but did not believe the Marshal noticed.

"I thought you said you had someone could identify Hal Colter," began the Marshal, irritation infusing his words.

"I can identify Hal Colter," replied Jed, no give in his words. "That body right there is the outlaw leader, Hal Colter." Jed pointed to the man near the safe.

"How do you come to know that?" asked the Marshal suspiciously.

"Even outlaws need doctors from time to time," said Jed, without missing a beat, "and they aren't real good at treating them well." He did not offer more information and the Marshal stared at him, but got nothing further.

"What happened here, Marshal?" asked Luke. "Colter was shot in the back. Roberts was shot in the chest, but his own blood would not have sprayed all over the front of his shirt. From the blood spatter on the front of John Roberts, he had to have been standing in front of Colter when he was shot from behind."

"Looks that way to me too," sighed the Marshal. "But who shot Roberts then?"

All three men looked at the body of John Roberts, who lay crumpled on the floor in front of a safe he obviously thought was hidden in the wall behind a painting.

"Who would have known he had two safes?" murmured Luke.

"And why kill Roberts too? Nobody would have cared that someone killed Colter, in fact, there is a reward for him, dead or alive," said the Marshal. "You asked about John Roberts," said the Marshal suddenly. "What do you know about this?"

"I had a business agreement with John Roberts to deliver three wagon loads of trees for lumber," said Luke.

"What does that have to do with Colter?" The Marshal was exasperated.

"Colter wanted to steal the timber from Mr. Randall's ranch," said Jed, "and as near as we can figure, John Roberts made two deals." He paused to make sure the Marshal had time to digest what he had said. "Roberts made one deal with Mr. Randall here, and apparently, another deal with Hal Colter."

"He made a deal with me to deliver three wagon loads of felled trees," Luke explained patiently, "but then it appears he entered into a deal with Colter to deliver everything he could cut off my land."

The Marshal paced between the two bodies, then stopped and rubbed his hands over his face. Finally, he turned and looked at both men.

"Then who killed these men, and where is the money from the safes?" The Marshal peered into each of their faces, but none of them had an answer.

Chapter 65

Ruth scoured the ranch with her eyes as their wagon approached. It looked like some of the work had been done, and the cow was not mooing, so maybe she was getting milked regularly. She hoped the silence did not mean the cow was dead, but she quickly pushed that thought out of her head. They could get another cow. That was the least of her worries right now.

Suddenly, the door to the bunk house opened and Cyrus and Rusty both walked out on the porch. She noticed Cyrus was limping and her heart gave a tug as she noted they were thinner and both walked a little slower than usual. The big grins they wore on their faces caused a mist over her eyes. She dabbed at the tears with her apron and laughed as Thomas giggled and pointed at the men, excitedly babbling as Adele held him and helped him wave a greeting.

"Mrs. Randall! You are sure a sight for sore eyes!" said Cyrus. He helped Ruth down from the wagon, then reached up to assist Hannah and Adele down while Axel set the brake and held the wagon steady.

"Come here, little man," said Rusty, reaching out to take a squirming Thomas from Adele as the toddler struggled to reach the old man, arms outstretched. He took the boy into his arms and both man and child cried tears of happiness, Rusty swaying back and forth as he hugged the boy. "It surely is good to see you laughing and jabbering again," he said, gently touching the small scar that still remained on the boy's head.

233

"Ow," nodded the child solemnly, brushing his own head with his finger tips. Grinning, he forgot all about the injury and threw his small arms around Rusty's neck.

A tall, gangly young boy appeared out of the barn, toting a pail of fresh milk. Ruth breathed a sigh of relief; they still had a cow and that meant fresh milk for Thomas. The boy walked with his head down until he was about ten feet away from the group.

"Ralph," said Cyrus. The boy raised his head and suddenly realized there was a group of people watching him. "Meet Mrs. Randall, the other owner of this ranch.

"Hello Ralph," said Ruth, extending her hand. Secretly, she swelled with pride at the title Cyrus had given her.

"Is that fresh milk you are carrying?" interjected Hannah.

"Yes, Ma'am," stuttered the boy.

"Well come on, everyone, let's get out of the hot sun and go inside the house," Hannah directed, taking charge. "Axel, grab the basket please, and Cyrus, take this peach pie inside." Ruth picked up a basket of bread, butter, and a jar of Hannah's homemade specialty, apple butter.

For the first time in nearly three weeks, Ruth walked into her home. She stopped inside the door and took in everything; her sink, family dinner table, handmade chairs by the fireplace, and her dishes stacked, neat and clean, on the sideboard. The bed they had dragged into the living area had been returned to its place in the bedroom, and the floor had been swept clean.

But as she ran her eyes over her home, she noted some of the dishes were missing, and so were some of the glass window panes. There were a few bullet holes freshly patched in the walls and one of the curtains had been torn.

"What happened here while I was away?" She turned to Rusty, who had come in behind her. Hannah was supervising the spreading of the food on the table and the dishes were set, ready to eat the meal they had prepared, but she glanced with concern at her friend.

"The ranch was attacked, ma'am," answered Rusty softly. "After you left with Thomas, the men did come back. I am so glad you were not here."

The young rancher's wife stared at Rusty, then moved her gaze to Cyrus, who stood, eyes sad as he examined her reaction.

Suddenly, she stepped to Rusty and surprised them all by giving him a hug. Next, she pulled away and put her hand on Cyrus' arm, saying nothing, just looking at him with an expression that tugged at his heart.

"You are our family," said Ruth, her voice breaking. "I am so grateful for you, and so very sorry this has happened here at our home. I don't know what I would have done if anything had happened to you! Either of you!" She split her tearful smile for both men, who shifted uncomfortably at the sudden and unexpected display of affection.

"We are all blessed to be here together," said Hannah, breaking the awkward silence. "Please, everyone, let us sit and enjoy a meal together." Axel set Adele in a chair at the head of the table, then moved the chair from the foot of the wooden surface. He then picked up Thomas, setting him next to the other child.

They all settled on the benches on the sides, pulling up the two chairs from in front of the fireplace as well. Ralph was urged to the table, and being a young man, his stomach growled at the fine meal spread before them. Fried chicken, corn on the cob, fried potatoes, and fresh bread with butter and apple butter made for a feast such as the young man had never seen in his life.

So engaged was he in eating and listening to the talk of the friends around the table, he completely forgot to mention what he had seen out in the barn. No one on the ranch smoked, so when Ralph saw the fresh stub of a rolled cigarette in the dirt outside the back door of the barn, he meant to mention it to Cyrus and Rusty. It was out of place, and he should have told them what he saw. But he didn't. And that mistake would cost him dearly.

Chapter 66

Luke Randall sat his horse with all the stubbornness he could muster. His side throbbed and his head pounded from the loss of blood. He fought down slight nausea, determined to get back to his men at the camp. There were now seven of them riding towards the camp, which made him feel better if they did encounter any trouble.

The Marshal had finally agreed they had nothing to do with the killings and, after considerable discussion, decided they were on the same side of the law.

Once that had been settled, they discussed the matter of the lumber that sat at the saw mill. More interested in helping to build a town than a silver mining industry, the Marshal had sent a deputy to get a couple members of the town council. They listened to Luke's story with interest and a little excitement.

"I don't mean to accuse you of anything mister," said council member Raleigh," but you can prove you own that timber, right?"

"It's a tough town right now, Mr. Randall," interjected the other council member. "We need the silver mines, but we also need houses and buildings for people to set up a business. We just built a church last year, and we sure would like to build a school. But...we have to be sure..." He didn't finish the sentence and he looked uncomfortable posing the question.

"Marshal, if you can send a wire to Sheriff Zachary Tinkum in Bridgeport, he can vouch for me," offered Luke.

"I know Sheriff Tinkum," said the Marshal, "but getting a wire to him could be tricky. How about if I ride out to this camp with you and see what we can sort out?"

"We can ride along as well," said Raleigh. "If that lumber is really yours to sell, I think we can speak for the whole council. If it is a fair price, we will buy it all!"

Jed and Paul rode on either side of Luke, half expecting him to topple from his saddle. They were riding at a canter, and that had to be hard on the wound in his side. In fact, Jed was sure he was seeing fresh blood seeping through the bandage wrapped around Luke's waist. He was relieved when they rode up to the camp, and all seemed to be under control.

"Luke, let me help you down," offered Jed, springing from his saddle first. Clay and Jeremiah looked at the young rancher with concern. Bean took one look, and turned to walk to the fire, where he put on water to boil and jumped up in the wagon for fresh bandages and comfrey compresses.

"I'm fine!" snapped Luke with irritation. "We have business to complete!" He swung his leg over the cantle and dismounted. Paul did not miss the knees buckling slightly as his boss landed on the ground. Luke clung to the saddle, his head against the horse for just a moment before he shook himself and walked to a barrel, where he perched against a wagon. He glared at Jed and Paul before he turned his attention to the Marshal.

"Marshal McCleery, this is Clay Matthews," said Luke, introducing the two men. "He owns a ranch outside of Bridgeport as well. He came along to help get my property back." The two men shook hands.

"I'm over from Gold Hill to stand for Police Chief Downey while he is chasing down some outlaws, but I know the name Colter. I would surely like to get to the bottom of this, so if any of you have something to say, let's hear it." He swung his eyes over the small group gathered at the chuck wagon, which seemed to be the center of camp.

"Well, Marshal, I guess I can shed some light on what happened here. I'm the cook – go by the name of Bean, and Mr. Colter hired me to feed this crew."

"Do you have another name?" asked the Marshal.

"Just Bean will do," said the wiry old man. It was not uncommon in the west for a man to go by a nickname, and often died with no one knowing his given name at all.

"Mr. Colter said he had a logging job, but I thought that was a little curious since most of the men working for him looked more like wranglers to me." He rubbed his hand over his whiskered chin. "We waited at a camp for several days, and he finally showed up with a bad man I knew from another trail drive. Sly Booker did not remember me, but I shore would never forget him!" Bean spat in the dirt and scowled as he finished his story.

"Marshal, my name is Rudy Jenkins," he said, continuing the story, "and I can swear to what Bean here is saying. Some of us are just day riders and were looking for work when Mr. Colter sent in a man to recruit riders over in Carson City. Only he told us it would be some cattle wrangling."

"Why did you stay when you found out it was logging and not riding herd?" asked the Marshal.

"Well, sir, most of us were hungry, and we didn't know what we was doing was stealing," said Rudy. To his credit, he looked properly ashamed.

"By the time any of us realized something was off, he had brought in wagons, rifle men, and a bunch of big loggers," explained Bean. "That's them, over there." He pointed to the sour looking bunch of men still under the watchful eyes of Jeremiah and some of the honest wranglers.

"It was pretty clear that if we left at that point," stated Rudy, "we would go out full of lead."

"Maybe that would have been better than to stay and become thieves!" growled McCleery. The lawman scowled at the tight bunch of almost thieves.

"Marshal, I will vouch for these men," spoke Luke, waving a hand to include Bean, Rudy, and the men guarding the trouble makers. "They were caught in a bad spot. None of these men are among those who attacked my ranch. They jumped in and helped us when Mickey O'Riley and his bunch tried to kill us before we went into town. In fact," he looked at Rudy, "that man saved my life. This wound would have been in the middle of my chest and I would not be here if Rudy had not shot the leader of this bunch of thieves." He paused. "It is, after all, my ranch that the thieves hit, and I do not want these men charged. Please."

"I will speak for Bean as well," said Clay, "he picked up that scattergun and used it to help us when O'Riley surprised our posse."

238

No one spoke for several minutes. The Marshal stared into the souls of the men gathered about, until he finally leveled his eyes on the group of prisoners.

"Many a man in the west has made a mistake," he said. "What matters is what he does when he realizes he is walking on the wrong path." He took a step closer to Luke and extended his hand. "Mr. Randall, as far as I'm concerned, Rudy, Bean, and their men are in your hands. I think the council members here would like to talk business. When they are done, they can help my deputies haul these sorry skunks back to town and jail."

"How about some coffee and something to eat, Marshal?" grinned Bean.

"Why that suits me just fine! Got enough for my deputies?"

"Shore do!" Bean turned and walked back to the chuck wagon and began to pour coffee.

"We will watch them while you eat," offered Jeremiah, nodding to the lawmen.

Twenty minutes later, a deal was struck for the lumber and the council men and deputies secured the ropes on the prisoners and put them in the back of one of the empty wagons to start back to town.

"Begging your pardon, Mr. Randall, but you don't look like you could make another ride to town right now," said Mr. Raleigh. "Why don't you stay here and rest and we will be back by nightfall with a contract and a bank draft."

"I'm fine!" growled Lucas Randall, as he shook the hand of the town council members to seal the deal in a gentleman's old west style agreement.

He would have fallen on his face in the dirt if Jim and Mr. Raleigh had not caught him as he folded.

Chapter 67

Ruth was glad to be in her own home. The Schmidt family had loaded up the empty dishes after insisting she keep any of the food that was left for her and Thomas to eat tomorrow. They waved and drove off amid smiles and lots of calls of thanks. Ruth felt peace in knowing her friends would be home before dark, and she now had time to appreciate the solitary time on her own homestead.

Cyrus and Rusty had allowed her to fuss over their healing wounds, and Ralph had timidly shared some of his past with her as he fetched fresh bandages and clean water for her to treat the two hands. In spite of her own injuries, she managed pretty well, enlisting Ralph's help at times. The two hands brought her up to date with the state of the ranch, apologizing for not getting more done.

"Don't you dare apologize for being hurt!" she admonished! "Both of you were wounded while defending my family and home. It is I that should be telling you I am sorry!" Combined with her own injuries, her time away from home, and her affection for these two men, it was almost too much and tears slipped down her face.

"Now look what you did!" sniped Rusty. "You made her cry!" He stood, hands on his hips, glaring at Cyrus.

"Me?" growled Cyrus. "Why you crusty old coot! You had her worrying all about you after you made her leave you here to take Thomas for help!" He thrust his chin out as he leaned forward, putting his face within inches of the sharp shooter.

"Gentlemen!" Ralph spoke with such authority, the two cowpokes both stared at him with open mouths. "Mrs. Randall has had a long day," he said, sounding surprisingly grown up. "Maybe we should leave her to some peace and quiet. If you are feeling better, I wouldn't mind some help with the chores tonight." His confidence was short lived and Ralph wilted under the stares from the two men, who stood, not speaking, just boring their eyes into what he felt was his very soul. He stepped back and swallowed hard. "I...I just meant..." he murmured, flustered now as he shifted from one foot to the other.

"Well I'll be a frog on a hot rock!" declared Rusty. Both men burst into laughter.

"Look who went and grew up on us all of a sudden!" Cyrus was looking at the boy with new respect.

"You are absolutely right, there Ralph! Come on boy, let's go get those chores done and then we'll play some cards." Rusty clapped him on the back good naturedly and Cyrus shook his hand.The three men retreated to finish the evening chores, then lounge in the bunkhouse for the rest of the Sunday evening.

After straightening up the house, Ruth put Thomas to sleep in his own little, handmade bed, and for the first time in over a week, pulled up the quilt she had made for him and tucked it around his small, but smiling form. She leaned over and kissed the little boy on his cheek, watching him sleep for several minutes, just so grateful he seemed to be all right now.

Ruth walked out on her porch, leaving the door to the house ajar in case Thomas called out, letting the fresh, cool air of evening waft into the house. She sat in one of the rockers on the porch and breathed a sigh of relief.

Her eyes took in the beautiful low mountains that surrounded the ranch buildings, and the pine trees that stood majestically on the slopes, filling the air with their fresh, crisp smell. The sun setting behind them made their dark silhouettes stand in stark contrast to the orange, yellow, and pink of the sky, blending in to the clear blue of the night.

Her gaze took in the apple and cherry trees they had planted, and beyond them, the little garden she had nurtured herself. The light was too dim for her to see if the garden had been watered or weeded recently, and she vowed to give it some attention tomorrow. Maybe there would even be some fresh vegetables for dinner.

"Lucas, where are you, my love?" She spoke the words softly into the night. It felt like months since her little family had all been home and happy together. She longed to have her husband sitting in the other rocker on the porch beside her, sharing their dreams and hopes for the future. She said a silent prayer for his safety, and hoped he would be back in her arms by tomorrow night.

Ruth took one more deep breath of the pine scented, cool evening air before she went into bed herself. She stopped as she stood. There was something different in the air. It took her a moment to identify the smell. Cigarette smoke. Cyrus and Rusty did not smoke. It had to be Ralph! It came from around the corner of the house. She started over to speak to him; he should not be smoking, and certainly not near the house!

She was almost to the end of the porch when she heard Thomas cry out in his sleep. The poor babe had some bad dreams since the shooting. Ruth turned back and went in to comfort her son, closing the door to the house as she went inside. She would talk to Ralph tomorrow. She hesitated, looking at the closed door. Something made her slip the bolt over the door.

The sound was not lost on the man standing in the shadows just around the corner of the house. He ground out the cigarette and smiled to himself as he walked into the night. Soon. It would be soon, he told himself.

Chapter 68

Luke heard a soothing, deep, sing song melody drifting through his sleep, lulling him into a sense of floating along a soft, warm river of feathers. Sweet odors of cinnamon and sugar mingled with the smell of freshly cut Christmas pine trees and brought pleasant memories of holidays from his childhood; days at home with his mother, father, brother, and sister talking quietly by the fire after a fine meal, enjoying a home baked treat with coffee or fresh milk. His stomach growled and he asked his mother for another piece please.

The song of soft, low murmuring stopped abruptly and the cinnamon and sugar smells now faded into the odor of leather, wood smoke, and trail dust.

"Luke?" said a voice through the haze still covering his mind. "Are you awake?"

Slowly, he realized this was not his mother talking to him. The voice was familiar, but it was not his brother or father either. It was a man speaking to him. He forced his eyes open and stared at a brown expanse in front of them. It wasn't dirt, and he wasn't laying on the ground. Leather. He was staring at a leather vest. His eyes moved upward and concerned blue eyes in a face ringed with sandy blond hair met his gaze.

"Luke? Are you feeling better?" asked Paul.

"Where are we?" said Luke, noticing his throat was dry and his voice scratchy.

"Here, take a sip of water," said Paul, helping Luke lift his head. He waited until Luke stopped drinking, then answered. "We are still outside of Virginia City. You are in the back of a wagon."

"Why?" asked Luke, still pulling out of the grogginess that enveloped his mind.

"You dropped like a sack of grain falling off a wagon. Jed said with the constant running of the past three weeks, and losing a lot of blood, you just went out."

"How long have we been here?" Luke asked, urgency to his voice.

"You have been asleep since yesterday afternoon, Jed answered, swinging up into the wagon."You nearly slept the sun around." He put a hand on Luke's forehead, and opened his shirt to look at his side. He nodded with satisfaction. "You stopped bleeding, now that you were laying still," he chided gently.

"Ruth! The lumber!" he exclaimed, trying to sit up too fast and gasping as he fell backwards.

"Take it easy!" commanded Jed. He looked at Paul, who moved so they could both get an arm under one of Luke's and slowly raised the rancher to a sitting position.

Luke found he was breathing hard and felt droplets of sweat run down his face. He looked at Jed and Paul in surprise. He felt so weak! Just then, his stomach growled again and the two men beside him chuckled.

"Paul, why don't you slip out and see if Bean has some of that broth ready," suggested Jed. Paul got up and jumped off the end of the wagon.

"Broth!" grumbled Luke, "I'm hungry enough to eat a couple of steaks!"

"We got to talking after you collapsed and decided you hadn't eaten in almost two days. Then you got shot, and that didn't help. We'll start with broth, and then if you behave, you can have some steak and potatoes, and maybe even a piece of that apple pie Bean is baking."

Luke realized that was the cinnamon sugar smell that had brought him out of his dream. The men outside had resumed talking in a low, melodious tone of riders sitting easy around a fire, and Luke knew that was what he had heard, not a song.

"I'll eat what..." he started, but stopped when Jed shot him a warning look.

"I don't work for you, Mr. Randall," said the young doctor, "and right about now, every man in this camp will do what I say, so you best calm down and listen to the doctor's orders."

Luke was not used to men telling him what to do, and the two stubborn young men glared at each other for several moments before Luke finally laughed. The effort cost him, and he bent forward slightly with a twinge of pain.

"Okay, okay, you got me, doc," he smiled. He was surprised at his own weakness, and he sure did not want to pass out again!

"Let's get you sitting up before Paul gets back," said Jed. "Put your hands out to steady yourself," he directed, as he took Luke's legs and helped swing them around to rest on the floor of the wagon. The makeshift bed, which Luke realized was blankets on top of boxes, was set against the side of the wagon, and he leaned back gratefully.

"Hey Jed, here's that broth," interrupted Paul, sticking his head in the wagon and extending an arm holding a cup. He stayed at the opening, looking into the cramped space.

Jed took the cup from Paul and held it out to Luke, but kept one hand on the mug. Luke put a hand on the other side and sipped the hot broth slowly. Part of him wanted to gulp the tasty liquid, but his stomach, while protesting it's hunger, was still a little out of practice. It actually took him several minutes to consume the broth, and when he was done, he leaned back against the side of the wagon.

"I need to know what is going on," asked Luke. "What happened with the lumber? I need to get back to Ruth soon! She will be worried!"

"Hold on," said Paul. "First, Police Chief Downey came back to town and he and his deputies assisted Marshal McCleery and they took the outlaws back to the jail in Virginia City last night, with the help of the town council men. The council men will be back tomorrow morning to talk about buying the lumber, and they will bring the money and the police with them, for safety."

"Tomorrow!" exclaimed Luke, "Ruth…"

"Hold on," smiled Jed, "be patient a minute longer. With the outlaws gone, Clay and Jeremiah rode back to the Rocking R to let the hands know what is going on, and then tell Ruth on their way through town. Unless she is a lot like you, and already back at the ranch." He chuckled at the thought. "Then they will go on to Clay's ranch and their own families."

"Oh." Luke suddenly felt tired. It was like he had the important questions answered and did not need to rush to get anything done. His eyelids seemed abnormally heavy.

"Okay, swing your feet up again and lay down until dinner is ready," said Jed, helping Luke so he would not break open the wound again. The young rancher was asleep almost as soon as he closed his eyes. Paul draped a blanket over his boss and the two men left him to sleep.

Chapter 69

Luke ate dinner that evening, and did it a fair justice. Bean eyed the young rancher critically, then motioned Jed aside. The doctor followed the cook around the side of the wagon until they were out of hearing from most of the men.

"Mr. Randall is looking better," began Bean.

"Yes," agreed Jed, glancing back towards the fire. "He sure is determined to head for home tomorrow, but I am still a little worried about his strength."

"Well, I was thinking about that my own self," nodded Bean, "and I have something that may help." He reached into his pocket and withdrew a small vial. "I got this out, just in case," he said, offering the small glass bottle to Jed.

"What is it?" asked the young doctor, squinting in the dark at the label on the container.

"I keep some laudanum on hand for when the boys get injured," smiled Bean. "We don't usually have an actual doctor with our drives, so I do the best I can. I was thinking if Mr. Randall took a little of this, it would surely help him sleep better. That might make him a sight more able to ride home without passing out again."

"This would definitely help," smiled Jed, "if I can get that stubborn cuss to take it!"

"Well, that part is up to you," grinned Bean. "I put a cup with a couple inches of warm water in it on the chuck wagon gate. I also poured in about an inch of honey. Put one drop of this stuff in that water and honey and he might drink it."

"That might cut the bitterness enough to work," agreed Jed, nodding his head as he thought about the challenge before him.

"Just bring it back when you are done so I am ready for the next broke cowpoke," said the wiry old cook.

"I'm going to give it my best!" Jed put the vial in his pocket and went looking for that cup of water and honey, which he set inside the wagon by the side.

"What's that?" asked Luke suspiciously as Jed climbed in with him when he was getting ready to lay down. Jed was holding the cup and had just pulled a small bottle out of his pocket.

"Something to help you sleep well and relieve some of the pain so you can work on healing faster," said the young doctor, setting the cup down. He opened the bottle and carefully put one drop into the water in the cup. He swirled the liquid around slightly, then held it out towards Luke.

"I'm fine," said Luke, which was not true. His side was throbbing slightly, but at least it was no longer bleeding.

"Do you want to go home tomorrow?" asked Jed. He stared at Luke with an unwavering expression of determination.

"Stop treating me like an old woman!" he grumbled, but he took the cup and drained the liquid, then thrust it back at Jed. "Arghh! That tastes awful!"

"Well, if you behave, I won't make you take it again," laughed Jed, smiling even more as he noticed Luke slumping over, eye lids drooping. He guided the man to his sleeping position to avoid sudden movement that would undo the stitches in his side.

"Do you think he will be ready to ride tomorrow?" asked Rudy as Jed jumped down from the wagon.

"He's young, strong, and pig-headed enough for all of us, so I expect that will be the case."

"I'll let the men know to be up and ready in the morning," Rudy looked at Jed seriously.. "Whatever Mr. Randall decides, we all need to be getting on our way."

Chapter 70

Cyrus was uneasy. He couldn't put his finger on it, but something was off and it worried him. He had crossed behind the main house to water the fruit trees on the other side and his eye caught something out of place. It was at the edge of a small rock, but it was clearly a cigarette butt. That coupled with the boot print he had noticed two days ago behind the barn had him on edge. He hadn't mentioned it to either Rusty or Ruth because he had nothing other than a hunch to go on, although many a western man was alive because he listened to his hunches.

It was at the far edge of the barn; not a place they usually walked or worked. The impression was slight and he probably would have missed it completely except they had a light drizzle of rain the night before; just a smattering, really. But it had puddled in the shallow depression made by a bigger boot than any of them wore.

It worried him that they really knew little about Ralph's past. They had trusted their instincts and taken him in, even coming to like the gangly youngster. But now, Cyrus wondered about the boy. The cigarette butt could have been just boyish experimentation, and he was going to talk to him about keeping that away from the house, as well as fire danger. He hoped he could get him to give it up; he knew young boys sometimes smoked – he did at that age.

But the boot print was something else. Could Ralph be meeting with the old gang members and setting them up to be raided? He hated to be so suspicious, but the nagging worry would not quit. He reminded himself that even though Ralph looked and seemed young and innocent for the most part, looks could be deceiving. He knew that John Wesley Hardin was only fifteen when he killed his first man.

Where was that boy, anyway? He had sent him out to check fences this morning and it was already getting close to supper time. It was not like Ralph to miss a meal; he really enjoyed Ruth's cooking. He had also warmed to them and his eyes held a dancing good humor now when they shared stories around the supper table. He had filled out a little too, now that he was eating regularly. He had changed from a nervous and sometimes sullen teen into a helpful young man, willing, even eager at times, to learn from him and Rusty. Cyrus walked to the corral where Rusty was checking the shoes on all the horses, trimming nails and prying a rock out of the hoof of one.

"Have you seen Ralph?" asked Cyrus, continuing to scan the hills and open fields around the ranch.

"No, I can't say that I have," answered Rusty thoughtfully, dropping the leg of the horse he had just finished. "Didn't you send him over to the south pasture this morning to check the fences?"

"Yeah," said Cyrus, rubbing his chin, "but he should have come back by now."

"He's probably napping under a shade tree," chuckled Rusty. "I wouldn't worry too much. He won't miss a meal."

"Just the same, he could have been thrown or something," replied Cy, walking towards the barn. "I'm going to saddle up and go take a look."

"You taking Jasper?" asked Rusty.

"Not this time," he smiled. "I'm not sure which one wore the other out, but I looked for him a few minutes ago and he and Thomas were curled up together taking a nap.

"Alright," said McMath, "I'll feed the stock while you are gone. Ruth is making a fine smelling stew tonight and she cooked a big pot so there would be plenty! She harvested some onions and carrots today, so it should be right tasty! Don't tarry, or I might eat it all myself!" He laughed and Cyrus grinned as the younger man saddled his horse.

"Save us some dinner, old man, or we'll have to listen to that youngster complain about an empty belly all night!"

Cyrus urged his mount into a gallop towards the south pasture. He didn't want to miss that dinner either, but he would not enjoy it until he knew Ralph was alright and enjoying the meal beside him.

The range rider found the fence line and followed it, scanning the landscape as he rode slowly, searching for some sign of the young man. The fence had been repaired, and Cy felt a sense of pride at the quality of the work. Ralph was really growing on all of them. He was sure Luke would let him stay on; after all, they could use another hand the way the ranch was growing.

He caught movement at the top of the rise and squinted at the shape. The horse's head came up and nickered at his mount as Cy breathed out in relief. As he neared, he smiled. Ralph was indeed stretched out under the shade tree nearby, his legs splayed out towards the setting sun on the far side of the tree. He swung down from his horse and walked towards the tree, smiling.

"Ralph! Are you so tuckered out you plan to sleep through dinner?" Cy started to laugh, but it died in his throat as he stepped around the tree. He knelt quickly and took stock of the boy's wounds and pulse.

Someone had stabbed this young man several times, first in the gut, it seemed, then several times in the chest. The boy was dead. Cy rocked back on his heels, great sadness sweeping over him like a dark rain, pelting him with sharp pangs of grief. He ran both hands over his face, tears escaping his eyes as he gazed at the innocent face of this young man, who did not yet even have beard stubble on his soft cheeks. Ralph was just a boy. *Who would do such a thing? Why would anyone want him dead?*

Suddenly he stood, his anguish replaced with a burning red rage at the virtual slaughter of his young friend. Ralph was not armed. His only weapon was his rifle, and it was still in the scabbard on his horse. Was he caught off guard and away from his horse? Did he know the man who did this; was that how he got close enough to stab the youngster?

Cyrus bent and picked up Ralph's hands. There were calluses from the hard work he had been doing, but no wounds. There were no signs he tried to defend himself; no cuts on his hands or arms as if he were trying to fend off the attack. Was Ralph just so trusting that he would let a stranger walk right up to him, or did he know his killer?

251

Cyrus walked around the area, not wanting to move the boy just yet. His stomach turned as he thought about bringing him in at the ranch. Mrs. Randall had come to look at him like a younger brother, and Rusty had taken to him like a son. Even little Thomas had tried to say his name as he gurgled a smile.

He searched the ground for footprints, horse shoe prints, anything that should not be there. The ground was hard here, so he found no prints in the dirt. But he did find a cigarette butt. It was off to the side, behind a small boulder. Whoever had killed Ralph had waited here for him, probably watching him work his way up the hill. But where had the killer left his horse? Cyrus loosened the thong on his six gun and walked towards a small grouping of tall bushes. The murderer had used a knife, but that did not mean he didn't have a gun.

Cautiously, he edged around the bushes to the other side. The bad man's horse had been ground hitched here and nibbled at the grass. This was no heat of the moment killing, it was murder. But why?

He stood and stared off over the valley for several moments. None of this made sense, unless one of the gang he had been with decided to come back and kill him for some reason. He shook his head. What would Ralph have known? They already knew about Colter and Booker, and Jed knew more than Ralph.

Cyrus James walked with heavy steps back to where the boy lay. For efficiency, he crossed Ralph's arms over his chest and then crossed his legs at the ankles. He took Ralph's bedroll blanket from behind his saddle and laid it out on the ground next to the body. For the first time in years, he felt tears rolling down his cheeks.

Cyrus reached across Ralph's body, grabbed a handful of the shirt material and another of the jeans, and rolled him onto the blanket. The seasoned cowboy could not help being gentle, even though logically, he knew it made no difference. Retrieving rope from Ralph's horse, he secured the blanket around the body.

Cyrus was used to lifting heavy ranch gear, but Ralph was one of the heaviest burdens he had ever carried. Gently, he laid the boy over the saddle, then carefully tied his hands and feet under the horse so he would not fall off .

It was nearly dark when he walked the horses into the ranch yard. Rusty heard him coming and came out of the bunkhouse. His smile faded as he saw the second horse. He met Cy's eyes and did not ask any questions, but instead started for the steps to try to spare Ruth and Thomas the heart wrenching sight. No one was very hungry at supper that night.

Chapter 71

Lucas Randall was tired and sore, but those conditions were both overridden by his feelings of satisfaction. He had negotiated a fair deal for the lumber stolen from his property. He had paid all the loggers and cowboys that had stood down once they found out they were stealing the lumber and that Colter had no right to cut the trees. Most of those men humbly thanked him and rode on their way, happy to have a few dollars in their pockets instead of a rope around their necks. They rode away vowing to make sure their future employment was honest.

The few loggers that had fired at his men and sided with Colter or Mickey, were either dead or headed to jail with the Virginia City Chief of Police, George Downey, and his able officers Ben, Higbee, and Charles Morrow. The Chief had assured Luke that the City Jailer, Eugene Blair, was more than ready to hold the outlaws tightly in his well built jail with no frills until they stood trial. Luke thanked him for all his help and shook hands.

"Mr. Randall," said Rudy, riding up beside the young rancher, "I sure want to thank you again for not standing charges against me and some of the other boys."

"Rudy, you fell in with a bad crowd," said Luke turning his head to meet the other man's eyes. "But you and Bean stepped up and did the right thing once you saw what was really happening." It was not a new story in the west. Many men strayed and righted themselves, some in time to live long lives afterwards.

"Well sir, even though me and a few of the boys will be working for Clay now, if'n you ever need any help, you just call on us and we'll come a runnin'."

"Rudy, you are a good man," nodded Luke. "I will remember this. You are welcome on the Rocking R anytime; stop by and there will always be a meal and coffee for you."

"I just might do that," grinned Rudy," after all, I might miss Bean's cooking!"

"He will have plenty of apples for those pies he makes," laughed Luke, "we planted several apple trees before we even finished building the house."

"Then you can count on a visit from me for sure!" Rudy tipped his hat and turned his horse to ride back and join the cook as Bean drove his chuck wagon along.

"How are you doing?" asked Jed, riding up to take Rudy's spot.

"I'm fine! Stop fussing at me like I'm some old woman!" Luke knew he was edgy because he wanted to get home to his family. "I know you mean well, Jed," Luke sighed, shaking his head.

"Well, you're my only patient, so you get all my attention!" smiled Jed. The two men rode without talking for several miles, taking in the beauty of the rolling high desert, mostly lacking trees other than a scattered pine.

The smell of the desert sage was one of Luke's favorites. The honey scented aroma drifted through the air, providing a pleasant alternative to the dust that arose with the smart stepping of the horses as they kept up a canter. The Wyethia plants, commonly know as Mules Ears, dotted the landscape in clumps of soft, light green leaves and bright yellow flowers, intermingling with the lavender of the Lupine. With the sage, the effect was beautiful and peaceful to behold.

"Jed, you have been a good friend and likely saved my life and Rusty's with your doctoring," said Luke. "What are your plans, now that it looks like the trouble has been put to rest?"

"I haven't really given it much thought," answered the young doctor, chewing on his lip. "I certainly can't go back to my outlaw ways, seein' as how my boss there is dead." He kept his face straight when he said it and Luke looked hard at him, but the crinkle around his eyes gave him away.

"I could use another hand around the ranch, even part time," smiled Luke, "especially one with your medical skills. And I know

Doc in town would really like to be able to take a few days off now and then."

"I could give it some thought," nodded Jed slowly. His eyes traveled over the scenery, and he had to admit to himself, it was nice.

"Jed, I'm just going to lay it out straight. We need men like you here. We are trying to build a good town with more families like Clay coming in to settle. Doc needs help already, and I could use you at the ranch when you aren't working with him. You could do well here."

Jed was quiet and Luke let it lay. He had said his piece and now it was for Jed to mull it over and make his own decision. They rode without talking until they reached Eagle Station in Carson City. Luke turned to the men and told them he was springing for a hot meal for all, which brought smiles he had not seen much in the past week.

"Let's pitch a camp over in that clump of trees," suggested Paul.

"Looks good to me," nodded Luke. He signaled to Bean, who drew his wagon around and put it in a position so that the trees made one side of a triangle and his wagon made another. They could picket the horses between the two formations and build a fire at the top of the opening, with places for the men to sleep inside the triangle.

"I'll stand watch while you all eat the first round," offered Rudy, swinging down from his horse and leading him to the back of the camp.

"I will stay here with Rudy until you all get back," volunteered Paul.

The men all dismounted, led their horses to the slight opening at the end of the chuck wagon, and tended to their horses. Paul and Rudy took care of Bean's horses too while he put out a basin of water and some soap, along with a clean flour sack to wipe off excess water if they wanted. Eating at a chuck wagon with dirty hands and face was one thing, but they were going inside an actual restaurant, and there were different cowboy codes of conduct for that eventuality. It was a special occasion, and it made it feel more so by washing.

Paul and Rudy drew their long guns out of their scabbards and checked to see that all the horses were secure. The two men walked the perimeter of the camp from opposite directions to satisfy their cautious natures, then sat across from each other, but well back from the fire. Each appreciated the savvy training of the other; staring into the fire could temporarily blind you to what was outside the circle if they had to use their weapons. Likewise, sitting across from each other created a complete circle of vision around the area, with each able to detect any movement behind or to the side of the other. Neither was expecting trouble, but it was always wise in the west to be prepared.

Chapter 72

The next morning at the Rocking R Ranch dawned bright and
sunny, a complete contradiction to the spirits of those who lived on
the land. The three adults had a discussion the night before, after
Thomas was asleep.

"Where would you like us to bury the boy?" asked Cyrus
softly. Ruth stared at him with enormously sad eyes and said nothing
for several minutes. The two men waited patiently.

"We have not established a cemetery on the ranch," she said,
a catch in her voice. "The outlaws that were killed here were taken to
town and buried on boot hill."

"Ralph left the outlaw life," said Rusty, wanting to trust
Ruth, but not sure where she was going with her comment.

"Oh, Rusty, I know that!" She placed her hand on his arm
and a tear rolled down her cheek. "I only meant we haven't had to…"
her hand flew to her mouth as she repressed a sob.

"You haven't had to bury someone you loved here yet,"
finished Cyrus. Ruth met his eyes with gratefulness; he had said the
words she found so difficult.

They had buried Rusty's nephew in the town cemetery,
unsure if any other relatives were still alive who might object to the
young man being buried on the ranch where he was killed, especially
with Rusty living there. They all knew Rusty went to visit the grave
at times, but he did not want the grave to cause even more pain if
any of his family turned out to still be alive and came to see his
nephew's final resting place.

"Yes," she nodded, "that's exactly what I was trying to say."
She sighed deeply. "Do either of you have a place on the ranch that
you think would make a peaceful resting place?"
She got up and refilled all the coffee cups in the silence that
followed.

"There is a nice little knoll up behind the barn," said Rusty.
"It's on the way to the trail you took over the mountain, but it does
look down the valley. The view is pretty." He was miserable. The
deaths of two young men so close together brought back thoughts of
the carnage he saw in the Civil War.

"That would be a good place," nodded Cyrus. "We don't run
cattle there, and it isn't really good soil for farming."

"Then that is where we will lay Ralph to rest tomorrow," said
Ruth. "I don't think we can wait for Luke to get back." The weather
had taken a rise in temperature, and the only place they had to keep
the body away from the animals was in the barn. The smell of a dead
man would begin to bother the animals.

Cyrus and Rusty lit the lanterns in the barn and began to
gather up planks of wood left from building the house and
remodeling the bunkhouse. They had stored the planks near the tack
room for repairs, or for the day Luke's brother came and they would
use them to build him a house of his own. The two men shared an
unspoken thought; neither expected to use these boards for a coffin.

The next morning, Rusty and Cyrus loaded shovels and the
coffin with Ralph's body into the back of the wagon. The two ranch
hands dug the grave on the top of the small hill before the sun even
reached over the mountains. When the coffin was laid in the ground
and the grave filled in, Rusty went to the back of the wagon.

"I made this for him last night," he said, pounding a simple
wooden cross into the mound of dirt. "I didn't know what all to put
on it," he said sadly.

"You have his name carved on it, and that shows someone
cared." Cyrus clapped the older man on the shoulder. "We should go
down and get Mrs. Randall. She will want to say some words, and
I've got some riding to do." His jaw hardened and Rusty knew he
was going to track Ralph's killer.

Ruth was walking from the barn with a pail full of milk and a
basket of eggs when they came back. She stopped and waited until

they jumped down. "Wash up and come have some breakfast. Then we will all go up and read from the Bible over Ralph."

Breakfast was hearty, with bacon, biscuits, gravy, and eggs. Each of them drank several cups of strong, black coffee; Rusty and Ruth adding milk to their dark nectar.

Thomas knew something was different, but still chattered as small children do, sneaking bits of bacon to Jasper, then giggling when the dog licked his hand. Cyrus did not usually allow Jasper to be near the table when they ate, but the dog was smart, and he seemed to understand something troubling had happened. He had slept with Thomas last night, and Cyrus was glad the dog had become protective of the boy. He was wrestling with leaving the dog at the ranch for added protection instead of taking him with him for tracking.

Breakfast was over, and the group walked quietly to the wagon, Ruth carrying her Bible . The trek up the hill was short and silent, and Rusty helped Ruth down from the wagon while Cyrus lifted the boy. They all stood around the fresh grave as Ruth read from the Bible, then joined together to sing *Shall we Gather at the River*, a hymn Rusty and Cy had heard all too often during the war. Back at the bottom of the hill, they all walked into the house again.

"I'm leaving this morning to track Ralph's killer," said Cyrus, "and I'm thinking of leaving Jasper here while I am gone," he said, drinking more coffee.

Ruth turned from the sink where she was placing the dishes, fixing him with a piercing look. She walked back to the table with the coffee pot and refilled the cups before she took her seat again.

"You worried the killer will come here?" asked Rusty, mulling over his own question.

"Yes," answered Cyrus simply. "I don't know for sure he is working alone." Thomas giggled and all heads turned to him and Jasper as they played on the floor. Ruth smiled at the pair and Cyrus chuckled.

"No," Ruth finally answered, shaking her head. "I have Rusty and I can shoot too. Clay and Jeremiah said Luke was only a day or two behind them at most, and that was the evening before last night. He could be back at any time, but you will be out there alone. You take Jasper."

"But Ma'am," began Cyrus, "it isn't safe..."

"It is not open for discussion," said Ruth, her mouth set firmly. "Jasper goes with you, and that is final." Ruth rose and took more dishes to the sink. Cyrus looked at Rusty for support, but the older man threw up both his hands, palms out, and shook his head.

"Sorry, partner," he laughed, "I'll back your play in a fight to the death any day, but I didn't get to be this old goin' against a woman with her mind made up!"

"Maybe I should wait until Luke gets back," said Cyrus, rubbing his chin.

"You will do no such thing!" Ruth plunked a sack down on the table in front of him. "The trail is already a day old, and Luke will be back any day! These provisions should last you a couple days, at least. I imagine Luke will come looking for you or send Jim if you aren't back by then." The subject was closed, and she leaned down and gave him a sisterly peck on the cheek. "You come back now, you hear me, Cyrus James? Don't you take any chances. Losing Ralph is enough." She scooped up Thomas and took him into the next room.

Cyrus and Rusty stood and pushed in their chairs, then walked to the barn. Jasper seemed to know what he was supposed to do, and he trotted along behind Cyrus.

Chapter 73

Yellow, snake-like eyes watched from the loft as Rusty came out of the house and headed to the barn to unhitch the wagon and tend to the stock. He heard the old man open the barn door and bring the horses in to be fed in their stalls. The man in the loft waited quietly, listening and identifying each sound as Rusty moved about, mucking the stalls and combing the horses used in the wagon this morning. He turned them out in the pasture with the rest of the horses when they were done eating. It took about an hour before he finished the work in the barn and the yellow eyes watched as he went back in the house.

Snake had watched the ranch, trailing Cyrus through binoculars, lying on the crests of hills miles from his original tracks. He bedded down in the hills above the ranch and woke with the dawn. He watched them dig the grave, and when they all went up the hill to pay their last respects he had hobbled his horse behind some boulders and slunk down into the barn to wait.

The outlaw smiled as Cyrus rode away. There had been one tense moment when he drew his gun and waited as the dog turned to look right up at the loft as if he had seen Snake move. But Cyrus had called to him and started to ride away, and the four legged protector ran with him. It was working out perfectly. He had been watching the ranch for nearly a week, and knew the child took a morning nap. All he had to do now was wait for the old man. He shimmied down the ladder and hid in one of the recently emptied stalls. He listened as Ruth and Rusty stood on the porch talking.

"Take these scraps for the chickens, please," she said, handing Rusty a small pail. "Could you help me with the fruit trees after I put Thomas down for a nap? I think they need some pruning and there are some peaches I need to get down before the birds get them."

"Yes, Ma'am, I would be glad to help you with the fruit trees."

"It means a peach pie tonight," she smiled.

"You got yourself a deal! Let me feed the chickens now and set aside some harness to mend, then I'll come back," said Rusty.

Mrs. Randall went inside, leaving the door slightly ajar. McMath stood still, scanning the hills from the porch, and noting nothing amiss, walked towards the barn. He stopped again at the door and ran his eyes over the ranch yard and garden. He couldn't shake the feeling he was being watched. Rusty shrugged, deciding he was still missing the chatter Ralph kept going while he worked. He stepped into the darkness of the barn to finish the chores.

Rusty removed the cover on the bin of grain for the horses and set it against the barrel. He reached into the bin for the scoop to sprinkle a little grain on top of the table scraps he had in the pail. The chickens would need a little more than the scraps if they were going to continue to lay good eggs. He heard the step behind him too late. Searing pain and red sparks exploded in his head right before everything went black. He did not even feel himself falling, spilling the contents of the pail in the dirt.

Snake stood over him and snickered. The old man would not be a problem anymore! He got to work saddling a horse for Ruth, then led it out the back door of the barn and circled around the house. He ground hitched the horse on the side of the house and removed a lariat he had fashioned for the work he was about to do. Snake stepped quietly to the door. He could hear Ruth singing softly in another room. Licking his lips, he pushed the door open a little more and grimaced when it creaked. The singing stopped!

Swiftly, he tiptoed to the far side of the doorway to the rooms in back, and flattened himself as best he could against the wall. Light steps came down the short hall and Ruth stepped through the door. He dropped the lasso over her head and quickly pulled her to the ground, wrapping the rope around her arms, waist, and legs, tying it tightly at the ankles.

"Let me go," she hissed, hoping not to wake the toddler. She looked towards the door.

"The old man ain't coming," grinned Snake through tobacco stained teeth. He took a dirty handkerchief from his back pocket and tied it over her mouth. She writhed and twisted, trying to break free. "I got you good now, and no one will be coming to help you." He reached down and grabbed her arms, yanking her to her feet, slamming her hard against him. He nuzzled her hair as she tried hard to turn her head away.

Ruth was beside herself. She could not move, and the filthy handkerchief made her want to vomit. Where was Rusty? Thomas! What would he do to Thomas! She looked desperately around the room, but saw nothing that could help her.

"Nobody is going to save you now," he chortled. "I am going to enjoy taking you where that man of yours will never find you. He ruined all my plans, and now I am going to ruin his life! We are going to have some fun." He slung her over his shoulder and walked out the door, pausing only briefly to look outside.

He left the door open! Little Thomas could wander out or a mountain lion could get in! She prayed Luke would be back in time to save their child.

Snake threw her over the saddle and tied her hands and feet with a rope that went under the horse's belly. He picked up the reins and walked the horse around the house, towards the boulders where his own horse was hidden. Luke would never see Ruth again, and that made him a very happy man. He laughed, loudly this time.

"I don't think the lady wants to go with you." The voice rang out in the stillness of the open yard.

Snake dropped the reins and whirled, reaching for his gun as he did so. It was the last thing he ever did. The tall stranger drew and fired before Snake's gun even cleared leather. The outlaw fell face first into the dirt, two round holes in his left shirt pocket.

Ruth's horse panicked with the gunfire and the smell of blood, and took off in a full gallop, bouncing Ruth brutally on the saddle. She could not see anything in the dust being kicked up by the horse, and closed her eyes to protect them for now. How far would he run before he stopped? She fought with all she had to keep from sobbing. That would do no good. She had to remain as calm as possible if there was any hope she could get back to her child.

Suddenly, she felt the horse jerk and start to slow down. The jarring run and her tongue had managed to push the filthy gag out of her mouth, and she spit it to the ground. The horse stopped and she heard the crunch of boots on the dirt. A man was standing beside her on the other side of the horse. She could not see him, but she did not think she knew him, and he did not speak. *Was this another member of the gang?* Panic shot through her again as she heard a knife slide out of a scabbard. *He was going to kill her!* The tension on the ropes under the horse released and she started to push off the saddle. A strong arm pushed down on her back, pinning her to the horse. She writhed in an effort to break his hold.

"Easy there," laughed a stranger. "Let me get the rest of the ropes cut so you can stand." The knife easily slid through the rope binding her, setting her free. Ruth pushed off the horse now, intending to fight, but as soon as her feet hit the ground, her legs betrayed her and she slumped towards the dirt. The man scooped her up in his arms and walked her over to a tree.

"Let me go!" she struggled feebly, striking uselessly at his chest and trying to kick her feet, but she had been bound so tightly and bounced so hard, her limbs were useless.

"I'm just going to set you down under this tree for a minute. I'm not going to hurt you."

For the first time, she stopped struggling and looked into the man's face. He smiled at her, his eyes sparkling. Luke's eyes! How could that be?

"You must be Ruth," he grinned. He set her down gently and clicked his tongue. His horse came to him, and he stood to retrieve a canteen, which he opened and held to her lips. She drank, watching him over the rim of the canteen.

"Thank you. Now I need to get back to the ranch. Don't try to stop me!" she growled. He threw his head back and laughed!

"My brother told me he married a spit fire!" The tall, handsome man stood and offered her his hand to rise. She took it, staring at him.

"Your brother?" she gasped.

"I'm Thomas. Luke's brother," he said. His face suddenly grew serious. "Is my nephew back at the ranch alone?"

"Yes!"

"Can you ride?" He was already gathering the reins on her horse.

265

"Yes," she nodded. He swung her into the saddle, not waiting for her to step into the stirrup, mounted his own horse in a single leap, and they both urged their mounts into a dead run.

Chapter 74

Luke was two miles from the ranch when he heard the gun shots. Every one of his men kicked their horses into a run, except Jim.

"Rudy! You and the rest of your men stay with Bean and come in careful! We don't want the chuck wagon dumped," said Jim.

Rudy nodded and Jim turned his horse into a gallop, catching up to the other men quickly. Luke's horse, Pepper, was already outdistancing the others, but they were not far behind. When the ranch came into sight, they all drew their guns, ready to face whatever might be in front of them.

Luke jumped from his horse at the sight of Snake lying in the dirt and leapt onto the porch without even hitting the steps. He cautiously edged around the door, saw the signs of a struggle and heard his son crying softly. Quickly, he walked towards the sound, but did not holster his gun until he stepped into the room and saw Thomas was alone.

Paul jumped off his horse and approached Snake with gun drawn. He knelt and turned the man over carefully, not discounting a possible trap. He whistled as he saw the two closely spaced shots.

"That's some shootin," observed Jed, "but that isn't from a rifle. Where's Rusty?" He met Paul's eyes, then swung his eyes over the other buildings. "Spread out and check all the out buildings!" Two of the men that had been riding with Rudy and Bean had ridden up and dismounted, and they drew their guns and headed to the bunkhouse. Jed and Paul headed to the barn, but did not get more than a few steps when Jim called out.

"Riders comin' in hard!" He positioned himself beside the house, rifle ready.

"That's Ruth!" said Paul.

"Who is that chasing her?" asked Jed.

"I don't know him, but let's go easy until we know who he is." Paul stepped out in the yard, rifle up. "Do not shoot unless he draws his gun!"

"Luke! Thomas!" cried Ruth, pulling her horse to a stop and tumbling off. She staggered with her momentum and the rider behind her catapulted himself to her side, grabbing her arm.

"Let her go!" shouted Jim, showing himself. Ruth glanced at the Luke's brother as he nodded, and she jumped up the steps.

"Easy gents!" The stranger put both his hands up and smiled.

"Who are you and what are you doing with Ruth?" demanded Paul. He still had his rifle trained on the stranger.

"Thomas!" All eyes turned to Luke as he stood on the porch with Ruth and young Thomas. "Thomas!" Ruth took their son and Luke jumped off the porch and embraced the stranger. The two men laughed and clapped each other on the back. Luke turned to the men in the yard. "Put your guns away, everybody! This is my brother! Ruth! This is Thomas!" She stepped off the porch, laughing.

"We have already met," she said, "he saved my life. Thomas, meet your namesake, this is little Thomas!"

"You look just like your father at this age," he said. Little Thomas responded by gurgling and reaching his arms out to his new found uncle. Happily settled in his arms, Thomas jabbered at him while Uncle Thomas laughed.

Luke's men gathered round to shake hands and greet the recent arrival, relief showing on all their faces. It was Ruth that brought them all back to focus.

"Where's Rusty?" she asked, sudden concern etched on her features. The men spread out, resuming the search that had been interrupted by her arrival.

"He's here!" called Paul. "He's hurt!" Jed ran to his side and crouched beside the prone figure, checking for a pulse. "Is he alive?" asked Paul hoarsely.

"Yes, but barely. We need to get him where I can work on him."

The men carried him carefully into the house and put him on the table Ruth had cleared. She was already putting water on to boil. Jed threw off his coat and gun belt, then washed his hands. He worked swiftly without talking, Paul and Luke hovering to help as needed.

"I need a needle and thread," said Jed, without stopping what he was doing. Ruth silently left the room, returning a moment later with her sewing basket. She extracted three needles, which she lay on her open palm and extended it for Jed to view. He studied her hand for a few seconds, looked again at Rusty's head, and pointed. "That one, in the middle. Can you string it with a fine, but sturdy thread please?"

"Yes," Ruth said, taking the two he did not want and putting them back in her basket. She took a card of thread and pulled a string out so he could see the thickness. He nodded and she strung the needle, raising an eyebrow at a suggested length.

"That's a good length," he said. "String the needle, then dip the needle and as much of the thread as you can in the hot water, but don't burn yourself."

Ruth walked to the sink and took a clean fork, looping the thread over one of the tines, and immersing the entire thread and needle in the water. Jed smiled with approval.

"Smart!" he said with admiration. "That should be long enough; bring it here please." Ruth stepped over to him, still holding the needle and thread on the tines of the fork. He stepped back from Rusty, holding his hands up, arms bent at the elbow. He looked around the room at the expectant faces. "I could really use a shot of whiskey before I start this," he said.

"Okay," agreed Luke, and stepped to the sideboard by the table. He opened a cupboard and removed a bottle, twisted the cork out, and stood close to Jed, putting the bottle to the man's lips. Jed took a couple of swallows, then signaled with his eyes and a slight nod that he had enough.

The young doctor took the needle from Ruth's fork and taking a deep breath, bent over Rusty. Paul gasped slightly when Jed gently lifted a good sized flap of skin on the top of Rusty's head, towards the back.

"What is that thing that looks like someone drew a line on his head?" asked the young blond cowboy.

"It's a linear skull fracture," answered Jed. His face was somber as he looked at Paul.

"A skull fracture?" repeated Thomas, who was off to the side, holding the younger Thomas while Ruth kept the water hot. "How bad is it?"

"It's not good, but it could have been a lot worse. It appears Snake used something sharp and hard; likely a shovel, to hit Rusty. He essentially scalped part of his head," he indicated the flap of skin, "and cracked the skull. But, it is like a crack in the cranial bone. It did not shatter, and it is not bashed in."

"What are his chances of survival?" asked Luke.

"Actually, unless the brain is bruised more than I think it is, his odds are pretty good," he said, focused on stitching the flap of skin back in place.

"Will sewing his skin back on," began Paul, swallowing hard, "fix his head?"

"The skin will protect the crack and hopefully, let the brain heal. He may lose the hair on that part of his head, but I am hoping he will make it through okay."

Jed worked carefully for another twenty minutes, with Ruth helping when he needed extra hands. Paul and the older Thomas stepped out on the porch.

"I think I need some fresh air, Thomas," said Paul, looking a little pale.

"It's not easy to watch that kind of thing," agreed Thomas. "Call me Tom or TJ, if it is easier with the little guy around."

"What's the TJ stand for?"

"Thomas Jefferson, after my grandfather." He grinned. "Our grandfather loved to study how this country began," he said. "In the war, there was another Thomas in our unit, so I took to being called TJ."

"That would be less confusing around here," laughed Paul.

Luke and Jed stepped out on the porch and little Thomas reached out to his father. Jed sat down on the step and rubbed his hands over his face.

"You did a heck of a job on Rusty," said TJ.

"Thanks, but he isn't out of the woods yet," Jed sighed. He looked at Luke. "You sure if I stay on you won't need me to be a full time doctor? Working for you seems to be a pretty hard job!" He smiled. "And what if I get hurt?"

"Well, we'll get you a pretty nurse," grinned the older Thomas.

"Where are you going to find one of those?" laughed Jed.

"As a matter of fact, we will be picking one up from the stage tomorrow," smiled Thomas, enjoying the look of surprise on his brother's face.

"Anna? Is Anna coming in tomorrow?" Luke stared at his brother.

"Yes! In all the excitement, I haven't had time to tell you! She graduated nursing school and she and I decided we wanted to come west and all be together again!"

Ruth walked outside and hugged her husband. Luke had a sleeping little boy on his shoulder, his arm around his wife, and his brother and good friends standing in the yard with him. Finding out his sister, whom he had not seen since before the war, was coming in tomorrow was almost more happiness than he could absorb all at once. He felt like the luckiest man in the whole world!

"It looks like things have calmed down a bit," said Rudy, joining the group. "Bean sent me over to tell you he made enough to feed everyone. Jim and us boys took care of your stock for the night, and if it's alright with you, we'll bed down here for the night and go on to Clay's ranch tomorrow."

"That sounds good to me!" said Luke. "Let me put our little boy in his bed and I'll join you." The men walked over to the bunk house where the chuck wagon was set up, and Ruth and Luke put their little one to bed. They stopped at the door, and Luke took Ruth in his arms and kissed her. Yes, he was a lucky man.

To receive notification of new releases, special offers, or order a signed copy, contact jconnerbooks@gmail.com

Books by JoAnn Conner

Detective Frank Riley Series

Death Song, volume one
Coyote Man, volume two
Cold Dreams, volume three

Westerns

Heartwood
The Mountain
Blood on the Timber Trail

Children's Books
Sneaky Sneakers

About the Author

JoAnn Conner is a former English and history teacher who has always been fascinated with mysteries and the history of the Old West. She relies heavily on research and personal experience to bring her stories to life with intrigue and unexpected details.

JoAnn also recently published a children's book with her granddaughter, Eleanor, as the illustrator.

She spent nearly forty years in South Lake Tahoe before she moved to the Central Coast of California, where she currently spends most of her time.

She has been recognized by a prestigious Townsend Press Award and is honored to be an invited author in the Author's Booth at the California State Fair.

Visit her Author's page under J. Conner Books on Face Book or follow her through her website, Amazon Author page, Linked In profile, or Instagram for upcoming events and new arrivals.

Made in the USA
Columbia, SC
08 December 2022